MOMEN

The Misadventures of Living Other People's Moments

Craig Jonathan Reekie

Vegageist

Cover Illustration: Synaxis
Book Design: Vegageist
Book Formatting: Jaz Saleem

ISBN

Paperback - 978-1-7391765-1-8

Hardcover - 978-1-7391765-2-5

Ebook - 978-1-7391765-0-1

First published in October 2022
Hardcover published in January 2023
by Vegageist Ltd.
Glasgow, Scotland
www.vegageist.com

Content Warning

This novel is for a mature readership. It contains acts of illegal drug use and domestic abuse. The plot is driven by the theme of child abuse, although there are no direct scenes depicting this.

"Aren't you bored of seeing profound quotes by prestigious people at the beginning of things to set the tone?"

- A banned member of a book club

One: Accusations

4151 moments

The countdown ends. I blink into another client's consciousness. My surroundings, emotions, clothing, posture and body are switched in a blink. I go from sitting at my station to standing in a stranger's body, from turtleneck to sports team shirt, from calm to nervous.

"Why are you acting so weird? You're not Kevin, not the Kevin I know and love," A woman aiming both index fingers at me says.

She's right, I'm not Kevin, I'm inside Kevin's mind acting out this moment for him. The side notes in the corner of my vision read that the aims (what the client last instructs before leaving their consciousness) say to: Avoid accusations.

The notes fade out. I'm in a dining room, I move these limbs and stretch Kevin's neck. Imagine if you blinked and were instantly somewhere and someone else. You never get used to this abrupt perplexity.

"Are you a lizard person?" The woman yanks my hair.

I've got a Rouser. This is the name my company, Pritek, gives to individuals that suspect, or sometimes know that the client they are with is being piloted by an agent like myself. The knowledge arrives in this client's memory that his woman is named Sam.

"Sam, listen, how could I not be myself?" I say, in a voice lighter than my own.

I use my training to subdue Sam's correct accusations. This involves discussing the improbability, laughing at the correct keywords like 'imposter' and creating a calm by moving slowly.

Sam throws a pen but I catch it and remain calm. I pretend to cry (badly) because she thinks I'm not Kevin. Typical horrible gaslighting.

Ten minutes jerks by, Sam taps my shoulder, I turn. Her eyes mellow.

"Do you promise you've not let someone else into your mind again?" Sam says.

This is rare. You know those moments you zone out so deeply that it doesn't feel like you're inside your body? At Pritek we've, sorry, they've developed an advanced and classified technology that allows elite clients to voluntarily zone out of a moment to avoid living it. Instead, our agents will 'momenteer' by entering your consciousness and live out the experience for you. Yes, anything—no matter how boring, painful or awkward. Including funerals, giving presentations or your distant cousin's piano recital with no refreshments.

I shrug like a clueless fool and shake my head to follow the aim. A technique learned from training. Rouser training was the module that came naturally to me, unlike the quick lies or fake crying modules. Before my mother's death in the asylum, she often accused me of not being her *real* son. That's my job. If there was a title it would be a 'momenteer', think but mispronounce 'volunteer'. This awkward atmosphere makes us self-aware of our movements.

"We're not good together anymore," Sam says.

And here comes that drifty sensation. When the moment passes and moves to another. Who knows how Pritek calculate this, maybe the atmosphere in the room or emotions? My eyelids get heavy and drop. The blink turns psychedelic blue and wavy. It looks like I'm travelling backwards through outer space. A pressing urges me to open my eyes and within a couple of seconds, *voilà*—I'm back in my body, at my station, sitting in my suit and turtleneck. The headset tight around my skull.

2

If you're struggling to imagine what momenteering is like, turn your television on and flick through the channels, then suddenly stop and imagine being that person on screen and what they're doing in seven seconds.

In the top corner, my tally ticks up one to 4152 moments. Once I reach 5,000—I think I'll travel abroad. I'm not a top agent so I don't know why there are so many moments today. Before I have time to process the last moment, I blink into another.

"Why, I'm dizzy Daddy, am I dying?" This kid says.

It's unprofessional but when faded-skills kick in and I understand their kid's named after that puppet frog Kermit, I must bite my lip to avoid laughing. Faded-skills are the knowledge temporarily inherited while you're inside a client's consciousness. For example, last week I aced a Swedish language test and taught a yoga class, despite having no knowledge of these subjects myself. You're able to know what you know plus the client's skills and desires. It's weirdly empowering but when you're returned to your body, you lose their knowledge and feel like you're missing something.

The side notes fade, but I catch this moment's aims which instruct to: *Deflect accusations*. That's not too rare a job, but considering this moment's putting their tween son to bed... my expression crinkles this client's forehead.

"Our bodies are smart and we must listen to them when they're trying to tell us something," I say, stretching the client's arms to get a sense of being in their body. This body feels familiar but after thousands of jobs, I guess anybody's body would feel similar.

The blinds are half shut. Streaks of the setting sun cast shadow lines on the wall. The room's also brightened by a shifting glow from a small muted television. There's a map of the world on one wall and three different posters of flamingos scattered on the others.

From the few sentences I exchange with Kermit, you can sense this kid's a good soul. His connect-the-dot freckles aid his trustworthiness. He mumbles nonsense, "If you, was it, in sleep, dream I tonight."

What the what? I walk across and pull his cloud print sheets over his shoulders. Once Kermit falls asleep I'll return to my own body. Accusations dodged, another moment to my tally.

"Metally. You sure, are you? Cola. Taste likes metal," Kermit groans.

He points to the dresser and grunts before rolling over.

I peer around, another affluent household. High ceilings and large bay windows. Over I go to the bottle of cola on the dresser. What's that? Something's telling me to look in the top drawer. Beyond the socks, at the back. Uh oh, it's there: sedatives. I inspect the popped pill packet.

An ache pierces my chest. Ouch, this client I'm being is drugging their kid to go to sleep. This is wrong on so many levels, especially the child abuse levels. Over my shoulder, Kermit roars a yawn for what seems like medically too long. He leans back, his light floppy hair fighting for position on his forehead. His soft eyes reflect the glow of the television while my posture stiffens. He's too young for sedatives, faded-skills tell me he's 12.

Triggered, memories of my father drugging me and my brother so we'd sleep sedates me still to the mahogany floorboards. The client's eyelids flicker and I'm ashamed because one of my own tears sneaks down this client's cheek. My dad's actions must be why I can't remember much of my childhood, either that or I wore my cool light-up shoes too often that they outshined my other memories. There's no noise for a while. A floorboard creaks and I wipe my face. I forget where I am, who I'm being. Accusations don't come. Why haven't I returned to my own body?

4

I wince before flicking my head back. Oops, that's right. I better make sure this kid isn't going to die. I flick the light switch. Kermit confirms he's alive by screaming "No" again and again until I turn off the light. Going over I take his arm to check his pulse, could be fast but could be normal. Kermit snatches his arm and waves me away. This is messed up. Who drugs their kids so they fall asleep? My arms tense so tight my fists shake. Against policy, protocol, whatever rule, I decide to get a good look at this client's face. See what this monster looks like. There are no mirrors here and when I exit Kermit's bedroom I see a mirror in this hallway but it's not facing me. After a couple steps, I feel that familiar drifting sensation, legs wavy, vision too. I'm blinked out and return to my own body.

Back at my station, I undock, slam my palm on this titanium desk and press and press the inbuilt call button for a supervisor. During the extended wait, time mellows my rage as I stare at the shiny unidentifiable crystals contracting and expanding within the glowing purply-blue power cylinder. I can predict Pritek's excuses before I hear them, yet, I still want to hear what they've got to say.

Each moment varies from a minute to a maximum of two hours. Wait. Don't give up on the opening pages of this paperback. I understand. I was thinking and rolling my eyes exactly the same. Sounds like banal sci-fi gobbledygook, but with the right money, power and Illuminati-like connections—you'd already avoid telling anyone about it. If you could, you might have already momenteered out of reading these opening chapters and jumped to the action.

Wait, I hear steps echoing from the hall. Here comes a supervisor.

Two: Shrug

4152 moments

The supervisors are in charge but who knows who's supervising the supervisors. They march alone in Velcro-leathery bodysuits, all black with a futuristic type of fencing helmet. They wear gloves and boots, with no skin exposed. A red light brightens around their helmet's frame when they speak. Supervisors in visors all sound the same with distorted low-tone ransom voices. Each supervisor has a different body type and vocabulary so you can tell there are different supervisors. If I guess, I'd say I've met at least 14 different ones.

The door clicks, a beep signals it's opening. *Dah-doo-dum.* A supervisor approaches with a calm walk.

"What's wrong now Komo?" The supervisor says before locking the door behind them with a click on their tablet. Of course, it's the supervisor with thin shoulders that smells of peaches.

I explain the situation of child abuse but the best I receive is an understanding shrug. There's no one I can talk to other than a supervisor.

"This must be against your company rules or the law. How am I supposed to help this kid?" I say.

The red light from their visor interrupts the darkness and competes with the purply-blue glow of my station.

"Your job is to live out clients' moments, not to interfere with their lives. We are not and will never be, affiliated with law enforcement. What makes you believe we can provide evidence? We operate, not above, but outside the law."

My hands shake my skull in an attempt to align my thoughts with my emotions. The more I think about it the more it makes sense. If I can't convince the supervisors how can I get them to tell management—if there's even management.

"What If I report them myself?" I say with my chin propped high like theirs.

I can tell by their slow shaking head they believe I'm dumb. They lean into my ear.

"Gentle reminder, if you go rogue. Who would believe you? What proof do you have? Other than what's in your head."

They show me their tablet with meaningless random buttons. I do the beginning of a shrug and they reply with the exact same. My lips fumble words and they interrupt.

"You'd be looking at a future of a mental asylum, death or at best perpetual homelessness."

The mention of an asylum makes me wince because that's where my mother was stuck before her death. They're right. I have no proof and can't go rogue.

"Can't you report the client to the police? Have someone local check?"

The supervisor rubs the chin of their helmet. "How did you know the child was drugged? Did faded-skills inform you?"

"F.s told me where the sedatives were. When I picked up the pills, I felt the guilt and understood."

"Hmmm," The supervisor flicks their tablet. "The exit report details the moment didn't count towards your tally. What's this... you purposefully attempted to leave the room you were in. Please explain."

"It was warm. I wasn't looking for identification," my lying voice bends.

Supervisors can't see or know what happens in moments. They may only read the exit reports or any privacy violations. They rely on agents reporting most things. Before clients return to their consciousnesses, momenteers leave snapshots of events in the back of memories upon a mind's re-entry. These memories aren't

8

triggered unless their present moment requires it. It'll be like remembering a vague dream. You won't know how you know but will.

Their head tilts and they lean in, "Did you try to view your reflection?"

Caught between a urgh and an um. I give in and nod towards the cold marble flooring.

"You may have been upset and you've never done this before, so I'll let this one go. I'm sure you're aware this action is prohibited. Never do this. Not only does it risk our client's privacy, but it can cause severe psychological distress. You'll require an Identity Crisis Break that'll take you longer to complete this session."

Even though the clients are advised to avoid momenteering while facing mirrors they sometimes do. Plus, there's this one prankster client who does it on purpose. I've reported them to supervisors but despite them saying that it's noted it still happens. My nostrils and top lip rise as I remember working a few moments involving facing mirrors. It's insanely surreal looking at your reflection and seeing a complete stranger.

It's clear Pritek won't do anything. I deliver my own shrug which stalls mid-way.

The supervisor's posture arches like they're thinking of what to say but only shrugs again. Has a shrugging contest begun? We shrug and shrug at one another as the supervisor walks backwards and leaves. The door makes its locking beep. *Dah-ding-duh.* I'm left with my shoulders up and arms spread. No answers appear in my open palms.

My shift finishes when I reach the minimum of seven moments for the day. A couple of jobs involve waiting, one before boarding a plane, then another in a reception before I use faded-skills to deliver a University history lecture as a professor with a bad back.

I undock and set my status to leave by clicking on the session menu and down to exit. Minutes later, a supervisor comes and escorts me across the blackened hallway to the secret lift/elevator. This supervisor has broader shoulders than the one with understanding shrugs. Outside, as usual, there are skateboarders doing tricks by the fountain. A delicate breeze guides me over. "Step off fool. What you starin' at weirdo? Step off." A skater with puffy jeans and eyes says.

I dip my head back to readjust my focus and notice another skater with a *The Muppets* bag and in the group portrait is the celebrity none other than Kermit the Frog. A few other girl skaters join to tip the scales of this emerging standoff. They throw a drink can down and giggle like parrots when the sugary liquid sprays up my sock. I take this as my cue to "step off" and get to my car that's parked in the lot blending in with all the others. I drive home as fast as legally permitted.

At home, I'm glad not to bump into the man from my building that I avoid. The cleaners have been so my rooms smell nice. I order expensive artisan tacos with Merlot. I get tipsy and I think about Kermit and his similarities to my life. My parents too gave me a silly name—I'm named Komo after the Komodo dragon. Damn, I don't want to think of this let alone talk about it but let's rip the bandaid/plaster off. If you're going to help me, guess I better let you get to know me.

Don't judge, okay? Safe space? I sometimes imagine momenteering as my brother and committing suicide. Don't worry, I won't ever harm him. My useless father left home for another woman and my brother used dad's technique on me and stole my long-term girlfriend. Meaning my ex-girlfriend's now legally my sister-in-law. A fact that should be against the law. Their hippie attitude meant I was invited to their wedding then their gender reveal party for their child. I politely declined the latter invitation by hiring a plane to fly over their garden with a banner reading 'your ex-bro disaaproves'. Yes, proofreaders assemble! Due to a rush and awkward interaction with the slightly overweight pilot, a typo was painted on the banner yet I had to pay double somehow.

Let's keep my brother and ex nameless as they don't deserve names but I can mention my niece Emma. She'll be six years old soon. I have no reason to dislike her, right? Last summer I had to stop myself from sending her a birthday card I stupidly bought. Thankfully I sent that card to the shredder or the gruesome twosome would try and be friends with me again. No way. Those understanding hippies will never understand me.

It's fine, I'm not too lonely. For the last three years, I've been dating Donna off and on. She's nice, wouldn't help you carry anything heavy or smelly but nice enough. We're not in love but not out of it either. She's been saying she's 29 since we've been together, but I saw her ID once and she's born two years after me in 1991. Due to my job I need to keep Donna at a distance. Our love is stuck in trial mode, unsure if we have the connection to unlock love's full features.

While I'm brushing my teeth, some vitamin pills fall from the cabinet and into the sink. It reminds me of the sedatives and in the mirror, I see myself as the ten-year-old boy that had his father drugging him and his brother. An urge twinkles within to save Kermit. But how can I with Pritek's control, technology and power? Have you ever wanted to do something but didn't know how? It's frustrating. All I can do is powerless shrugs in the mirror. I knee the sink but hurt myself.

Sorry for the confusion but in this, you'll notice I'll use both Anglo and American English spellings and punctuation. This is for my protection, in case any of this doesn't go to plan and you

11

won't be able to locate me. You can't trust many people. Listen. I'm sworn to secrecy and if they catch you reading this, we both could be in serious trouble. We're talking the life-ruining kind. Maybe you can help? Can I trust you? Please, stop reading now if you can't be trusted.

Three: Slide

An Uninvited Time Skip Forward to 4804 moments

I know. I dislike non-linear narratives too, they're difficult to follow but you must know this before we progress.

Donna's tongue peeks between her lips and back in. Her expression twitches as if it's autocorrecting itself. Suspicious. She scratches her nose.

"I need to know what you've done to hurt me in order for us to progress."

I step back. "Progress? Didn't we break up? Again?"

"Err. Why? What did you do? Please elaborate and be specific."

"Huh? Are you serious?"

Puzzles appear attempted but incomplete on our faces. We look in the corners of the room from the corners of our eyes. Silence is fractured when Donna throws a dictionary from the shelf above the fridge at me, the sofa behind me catching. "Well, you must know why you did… why I'm upset," she says.

I duck from another hardback. She waves her index finger. "What happened? Tell me now, or I'll cry and you'll tell me later,"

Each second seems disjointed from reality. A growl in my guts informs me she's not herself. I step closer. My gaze dives into her pupils, instead of sensing Donna, a chill pinches my shoulders.

"What's wrong with you? Don't you remember what we *just* agreed on?" I say.

The atmosphere turns furrowed-eyebrow odd. I close my eyelids for an extended blink. My eyelids open to see Donna's arms shuffling, readjusting her earrings. Ha, a sharp laugh seeking reassurance escapes my mouth. This prompts her to throw a thesaurus at me, followed by a cookbook I forgot I owned, and then an atlas. I dodge and deflect, remaining clueless where any of this came from or is going to.

"We need to communicate Komodo. What you've done may be partly my fault," she says. "If you cheated on me, be honest. Should we fix this?"

Why did she use my full name? Weren't we both cheating together? I try something that'll either make her hit me and run away or confirm she's not in her own mind.

A sensation wildfires until it becomes my only thought: her words, they seem dubbed and misguided. Was it instinct? Was I accessing a nuanced understanding I didn't know I possessed? A feeling that's making my knees bend and shake urges me to ask, "Pritek? Are you from Pritek?" A risky and rogue move. Speaking the company's name out loud to a non-employee outside the office made everything feel fake. Similar to when you say a word so often it loses its meaning.

"Pritek?" I say, this time with less meaning. "Pritek, Pritek, Pritek," each mention makes Donna retreat until her calves graze my front door.

Donna rushes and grabs her ID from her bag and blinks her focus onto it. Jackpot—I'm a Rouser. Feels good to be on this side for change. I use this technique myself to escape moments, but she's not doing it well. When I approach, she looks flustered. Her face flutters, each facial muscle freestyle dancing independently before it stalls mannequin-still. I catch her swaying and lay her body over a reclined armchair. Her tongue slides out as her stiff legs slide off. This is what must happen when a client's consciousness is abandoned mid-job. My legs end up hopping remembering the times I emergency exited jobs this way. Mouth ajar, I sit beside her shaking my head in disbelief.

Whoever was piloting Donna's consciousness must have panicked while meeting a Rouser, had their aims distorted or

14

faded-skills corrupted. I've had all those happen. You don't know how to act, what to do or say. I feel my face to find I'm smiling in pride of noticing all of this. By the vagueness of Donna's questioning, I sensed novice Pritek training. This added to her ever so subtle face twitching only a Pritek agent could notice, made me suspect Donna was having her mind piloted. Her father's a well-connected socialite so I shouldn't be surprised. He's bought her a swanky townhouse and a hair salon with the money he made inventing a solar-powered microchip. I should've suspected but it's always surprising who has Pritek's implant.

We were taught and threatened as agents to never, under any circumstances, reveal information that'll expose the company or our roles. Although I've been feeling so disillusioned lately that I fail to care. Two momenteers from Pritek meeting within the exact same moment. At least it's only one piloting a client's consciousness and not both.

Lately, my job feels like I'm tangled in a bad dream. Considering how powerless I am to help Kermit depresses me.

With the back of my hand, I check Donna's nostrils are breathing. Still alive. Her pulse is calm. When clients zone out their consciousnesses, they enter a dreamlike state. I spread her eyelids, trying to see the implants which allow her to momenteer, but I can't see anything but her glazed irises—the implants must be within. I inspect the back of her head and find the expected miniature dot scar clients have under her perm (situated around the superior nuchal line). This situation is perplexing... knowing you weren't talking to your part-time lover but an unknown colleague inside their mind. Lately, my thoughts have been struggling to determine what's an authentic experience. Especially since I seem to be living other people's moments more than I'm having memorable moments of my own.

In one of this city's grandest buildings, a deluxe top-floor apartment/flat houses me. It's got a balcony and two bedrooms,

15

each with an ensuite. Pritek pays for every bill including an electric car with a private parking spot. Cleaners come on Mondays and Fridays to tidy up my unrestricted access to food deliveries. This comfort comes at a cost—Pritek's name's on my bank account and this property. It's an increasingly lonely job as I don't meet colleagues, oh true, technically I just met one as a Rouser inside Donna's mind but that doesn't count.

My gaze falls on Donna. My hand squeezes hers. I hope she isn't dead. Surely not. We just broke up but I hope she finds someone to belong with. I wait until the waiting becomes too long. She's warm. I zip the collar of her comfy tracksuit and splash water on her face. Nothing, maybe she's brain-dead?

Holding her hand, I remember how we met, at her hair salon, just under four years ago. The first time she cut my hair. The cut resembled the back of a dish sponge. We got to talking because she was wearing a faded Green Bread t-shirt but didn't know our music. Her hand twitches in mine and my whole body jolts. She groans the greatest groan I've heard. What a relief. We look at each other like we're separate species.

"Don't look at me like that. We're not getting back together," Donna says.

She's back, it's her, 100% authentic Donna. No one was in her mind for a couple minutes. I think about quizzing her on the implant but my words freeze as I don't want to be caught. A few moments pass and we reconfirm our situationship is over. We talk abstractly about love again to detach ourselves from it. When we speak I notice her eyes are wet but with no tears, she must be thinking about her high school girlfriend, the one she doesn't tell anyone about, the one that died when they were both 17.

Of course, this chapter ends as there's a thud at the door. Guess we'll return to this action later. Don't worry, I trust you to remember throughout this that Donna is a Pritek client.

Four: Me But Not Me

Shifting back to 4190 moments

My fav client to momenteer for is this type 1 diabetic that not only has warped vision like they wear the wrong spectacles but often momenteers out when they're experiencing low blood sugars (hypos). Maybe I shouldn't enjoy momenteering hypos but they're thrilling. The hypoglycemic sensation makes you feel alive as dizzy butterflies tickle the stomach, heartbeats pinball around the ribs and you sweat. It's inadvertently zen because the body only allows you to consider one thing in these moments: carbohydrates. I hope the diabetic's well, there's no way to know. The last time you momenteer for a client may in fact be the final time. Inside his body, there's a calm yet groggy fuzz. If only I could be his friend than be him. He indirectly made me switch to wearing diabetic socks, a looser fit with elastic that doesn't dig into your shins.

Here's the deal: once I work 5,000 moments, my first session will be complete and I will receive a two-and-a-half-year holiday/vacation. Followed by another session of 2,500 before another two and a half. The moments keep halving. After two sessions, time off also halves until I'm left with 120 days break before a final 313 moments. On average I have between 7 and 14 moments a shift, it depends on time and energy. After five sessions, I'll retire from Pritek. My home will be in my name with a highly luxurious pension... and guess what? As a retired agent, I'll be able to momenteer out of my consciousness and avoid living my own moments up to 100 times a year.

If you experience two suicides or go through nine deaths all your work will be marked as complete. These jobs are incredibly rare. I haven't had any yet and look how many moments I've

17

done. Deaths are difficult to come across because when people are dying or in a sudden intense pain they struggle to focus and forget to zone out. In our training, there was a suicide module and when you leapt to death—you were jerked back into your body gasping for air. Our clients usually don't have reasons to commit suicide so I don't worry about doing it.

Before a job, you're clueless as to what you'll momenteer but from the case notes at the side of the countdown, you'll get an idea. When you blink in you can sometimes tell from the height, arms, hands, scents, feel of the mouth or the accent if it's a regular but with so many bodies and moments you'll forget. When a job comes, you feel a buzz around the neck, shoulders grow tingly and your vision turns into what can only be described as ultra-wavy. Your headset grows heavy and if you watch the letters they'll surf to you from the screen. Random meaningless letters leap out and bang your forehead and pull you forward. We blink in and see what the client's seeing with a countdown from seven. Time to glance at the notes at the side to detect the aim. Sometimes the side notes indicate the body position, tone, nearby bonds or topic but sometimes not.

Six… by this point, you'll see if the aim is suicide or death. Your brain feels like it's shrinking yet squeezing. Five, four, three… Before we know it: abraca-damn-bra—we drift through an opaque transparent layer of sight and take control of another individual's body and mind.

Two… one… the saturation pops and you can move their body. "Consider it your body, for a moment," supervisors said during training.

I'm in. It's another moment where I'm to make love to this client's wife. I take a big breath. It's okay, it's Catherine, a regular. Before you wonder, I only momenteer as my gender and sexuality. Top agents can perform across both spectrums, but my training score was too low. People never explained why but the supervisors often refer to performance levels or compatibility. Sexual moments are rare yet I wonder how rare they are for our top female agents.

Sex with Catherine is a script. Why not try a few new moves? Either way, sexual moments aren't good for my mental health, they drain my spirit. I'm not sure if they're taking away the good or adding something bad. In the past six months, Catherine's body has grown into a familiar sculpture. Her hair and limbs are long and thin. She has a little pot belly which I'm only allowed to rub when she's distracted. Her back is bumpy with moles positioned like Greek islands over and between the shoulder blades. The client's body I'm inside is blocky, larger than mine, even the you-know-what. His dick as firm as the mattress. Currently, as we struggle to unsynced orgasms it's like it's me yet not me at the same time. What weirdness. I lay back, arms out to encourage blood flow. Our bodies wither and become as soft as the pillows.

Let's face it—if someone momenteers out of making love to someone else, it'll be because they're not attracted to them. In this body, I can sense an attraction mixed with guilt. The client's cheating. I understand it in faded-skills. I'm confused if the attraction for her is coming from me, Komo or the client.

This isn't nice to admit but I make love with Catherine more frequently than I do with Donna. Maybe I enjoy these moments more, maybe making love to other ladies in other men's bodies is reducing my desire for Donna? An unwanted thought which makes me gulp and bite my bottom lip.

Catherine's never keen for cuddles but I reach out anyway. She pushes me off and hops out of bed leaving a flowery fragrance to fall behind. I know how this goes… Gazing at this same mark on the ceiling I feel myself being blinked out.

Back in my body, I set my station on break. After sexual moments I always need a pause to shake the experience out of my short-term memory. My body doesn't know what's what because it's been sitting motionless this whole time yet my mind returns with memories of other people's experiences.

These two relationships (Donna and Catherine) are the only ones beating at the moment. This momenteer job has depleted my social life by vacuuming my opportunities to connect. Working alone and having to hide what I do from everyone makes me hide from... everyone. Even my ex-bandmates are no longer my mates after I won our courtroom battles over royalties. Last month, I was asked to leave my building's monthly book club before being formally banned for not reading the books.

Maybe the man that lives four doors down from me on our top floor (who I love to avoid) could count as my friend? Can someone have a relationship with you even if you aren't aware of it happening? He must believe we're friends, but to me, he's barely an acquaintance. I met him the day I moved in. I felt I had to avoid him after our first awkward interaction but for some reason, our interactions only seem to fuel him. I've never avoided anyone before but he has this crooked presence that makes an oddness skateboard through my skin.

Tonight, on our building's security channel I catch him wearing two different sandals during early spring. His oversized fleece jacket flops after he drops a wine carton in the foyer. He must be under the influence because he reacts as if the carton's made of glass. The concierge helps. I note the time of his return. How can this guy afford to live in my building? Not being prejudiced but he looks cheap like the wine he buys. It's expensive to live here. The residents are the type to wear sweaters/jumpers over their shoulders with bourgeois suede loafers and pointless embroidered brooches. I'm still trying to fit in with my turtlenecks and suit combinations. I even wear fancy socks with suede loafers. He, on the other hand, lounging the way he does, belongs in the halls more than the gold trim on the foyer furniture.

Next day, I blink into another moment, I'm sitting in a crowded audience fighting back yawns. The job is watching a play. It's boring as plays can sometimes be. It's okay because the notes say this client has already seen it, so no need to pay attention. My mind drifts to thinking about the man I like to avoid. I don't want him in my mind but avoiding him is so enjoyable. You should've seen how dumb the smile across my face was last weekend when I crept around him checking his mailbox. I finish my shift by showering for someone that doesn't enjoy being wet. I usually like showering but in their body, it's a slippery struggle.

After work, outside I spot the skateboarding gang again. I walk away as fast as I can before it can be classified as jogging. Thankfully, they don't say anything but my body remains tense as if they did. A big exhale comes from me and the car as I open the driver's door.

Back in my building, he's there. Shit. The man I like to avoid. He's talking to the concierge and laughing as old chums would—maybe If I walk fast he won't notice me… It's working, it's w…

"Well look who it isn't," he says, one of his catchphrases. His voice is as rough as gravel.

I stop still. A pulsing alarm rings through my finger and toe tips. Is this how a fish feels when it bites on a bugged hook?

As he talks my mind offers me thousands of possible excuses to leave, too many in fact that I forget to talk and move my head like I'm listening.

Sorry, I can't tell you what's said. For a moment I don't feel like I'm in my own mind. I position my body to leave, at least my muscle memory remembers what to do. Our meeting crumbles apart as my legs walk off, my head not following. Our eyes remain connected as I walk away and stumble up a step. I avoid him because he makes me act like this, because he looks like my brother. Not his face but they have the same tall body, confident posture and twisty mannerisms.

He gets the signal and says another of his catchphrases. "You've been you and I've been Gully."

It's like he's ending a nightly talk show. All I can do is force a laugh, but the laugh is not mine, it's deformed by social anxiety. I take the lift/elevator after walking up to the first floor and inside my empty home, it depresses me to reset my counter for how many days I haven't seen him (Yes, I'm petty and count). He's infiltrated my thoughts and I struggle to focus on which food to order.

Sushi and two beers are on their way, "Those beers with the pointless nautical designs on them please," I say when I have to call the restaurant because their app's dead. Donna texts and suggests she'll come over but as the night ages she doesn't appear. She does this often.

I spend the night watching memes but something strange is going on because my fav channel has a profile pic of Kermit the Frog. Then lots of memes of people falling arrive so I switch channels but it gets weirder when Kermit the Frog starts appearing in some of the memes. I wince at my blank walls wondering if this is a cosmic sign. As I brush my teeth, my mind drifts to that Kermit kid. Thinking of how to save him makes me remember a garden hedge labyrinth I got lost in as a child. Does this urge mean I want to be a father, at least be a better uncle to Emma?

The days blend into each other. So do the waiting rooms I have to wait in, from psychiatric to dental. I'm blinked back to my body again, when I check the calendar, the date almost makes me fall off my seat. Where do the days go? Is someone reshuffling the dates so they feel non-linear… Well if they are, it's not cool. We all know non-linear is an effort to follow.

The letters leap out and bang me on the head. I'm sucked into another moment. Well well well, look who it isn't… it's Kermit. There's no aim. This moment is fun, we're in his bedroom playing Lego.

"How do you know if you like someone? Like, like-like them," Kermit says.

I scratch my chin with this client's wedding ring, "Who are we talking about?"

Kermit won't say and puts his knees up to shield his flushing face.

"Is there someone at school you have a crush on?"

"What's a crush?"

After a vague explanation, Kermit covers his face with his arms. "I don't have a crush."

"What's that?" I say. "On your arm."

Kermit moves away, I grab a lamp and shine it to see. There's a brown bruise above the elbow. The shape is strange. It's the shape of the country Ireland. Wait, how do I know this? Faded-skills?

"Who hurt you?" I say.

"No, no one, nothing, shhh shhh anyway," Kermit says, his voice tightening with irritation.

I try to line up my/the client's fingers to the bruise to see if they match.

"Was this me? Did I hit you? You know I forget," by saying this I'm hoping to trigger faded-skills but nope.

"Can't we play?" Kermit says.

Playing with Kermit, I start giggling a lot. It makes me feel like a dork, a dork of giggling, I get swept up in the fun of making a Lego ambulance and hospital. Before I know it I've forgotten about the bruise and I'm blinked out back to my station. I should've interrogated more. Where did that bruise come from?

23

Bruises can appear from non-violence? My hand hovers above the assistance button. Should I? My fingers graze the button but not firmly enough. My palm slaps my forehead. Thinking about hearing Pritek's excuses again makes me decide against pressing and instead, I go to the break room to make a sandwich.

Some situations are better left alone. The result will be the same, you won't make things worse and you'll save your time and energy. You can quote me on that if you like but please spell my name Komo and not Komodo.

Five: Enrollment

4222 moments

Before this job, I played drums in a briefly successful arena rock band called Green Bread. You probably haven't... we had that one song about the 38-year-old grandma if you remember? It's been over a decade since our farewell concert in late 2012. My glimpse of fame now seems like it happened to somebody else. After we split, I was aimless in life. My girlfriend was stolen, I was poor again and our mother's dementia got so bad we had to limit visiting her at the psychiatric facility. The Green Bread money dried up and two and a half years ago, I found my first job since the band at a hipster roller skating staff café. I fell a lot and the job hurt my knees. I was only there for a couple months and one morning, while pouring Irish coffees with a banana syrup twist, a regular customer that spoke with an irregular tone asked to talk. She said that she remembered me from Green Bread. I fell and spilt water when she said that. I used to have long hair that went down my back so I don't know how she knew. My memory has fogged her appearance, but if the police insisted I describe her, I'd say: tall, dressed smartly with bouncy auburn hair and deep-ocean creature eyes.

"Surely this is a prank?" I remember asking after she whispered with a wide stare about Pritek and what they did. I was to stop by a multi-company building.

She peered around to make sure no one had come into earshot. "Waiting there, is a once in a many many many... and I mean many, lifetimes opportunity."

Didn't think I'd go. If only I could time travel and stay at the café, but reintegrating into the fakeness of customer service after having a slice of fame depressed me so much that I went.

25

The business card she slipped from her tweed suit was see-through, all but a reflective Pritek logo. A big P with the rest of the letters circling clockwise around it. Their offices were reflective too. A rectangle cube plopped in the middle of the city. I was early but the receptionists weren't helping. I walked back outside. Silly me—I found an email that went into my spam from Pritek informing me of the secret directions and code to a storage room. I went into an unmarked room and wow. It all happened too fast. Behind that inconspicuous door was one of those fake bookcase things. After you pulled the only purple paperback, doors swished open and a golden lift/elevator was waiting. There are 200 odd companies in this building but they don't know about Pritek in the basement. I dropped my phone at the first sight of how the supervisors dressed. The gladiator-metal masked security guards looked like they'd eaten three of the security guards from reception. Their muscles bulged with veins that could be seen from the other side of a large room.

At my interview, despite wearing my best suit, I felt both under and over-dressed as the clipboard and tablet-holding group huddled around, their lab coats obstructing my entire vision. They measured my skull, taking most care over the distance between my pupils. Without consideration, I signed up for their promises of riches and comfort. Mostly I signed the contract because I didn't believe the technology was real. They gave me two weeks of living in my dream apartment/flat with their bank card to show what life could be like. I returned to confirm my enrollment.

In case I defect, as insurance, I had to give Pritek control. All my passwords, family secrets, financial and social media accounts, email addresses (recovery and primary) were relinquished. In a hypnotic session, I told them about my brother and my cheating dad gaslighting our mother so often that she lost her sanity. Blood samples and fingerprints were taken. Pre-written confessions of insanity and unsolved crimes were signed should I expose their technology to anyone. A masked anaesthetist knocked me out and they implanted microchips in the lens of my eyes and temple. There are no visible marks but I feel a hardness if I press my temples enough. They required me to record a sextortion video of kissing a dildo stuck to a wall. I almost quit when they asked me to do that, but they convinced me with a VR recreation of the job and potential payslips. By the time they photographed me pretending to kick a famous Pomeranian and punch a swan, it was later than too late, training was due. My knees couldn't stop wiggling in anticipation, I guess everyone wonders what it's like to be in another person's body, just not for a career.

Today, Kermit and I discussed what he wants to become when he grows up, well I say discussed. It was a sore topic for him.

"I'm going to decide what I'll have to be when I finish school. That's the deadline?" Kermit elbows his pillows.

"There are no deadlines."

"Yes there is or you'll die."

I try to reassess his bruise, but he pulls away. Looking around his bedroom, wondering how I could accidentally see the reflection of his father's face. Maybe if I turn the television off I could see but Kermit insists it must remain on or he'll throw a tantrum. With his smooth palms and hairy knuckles, I inspect my/his father's face. There's no facial hair, strong jaw, wide nostrils, silky eyebrows and average-sized ears. Using his tongue, I find he's got all his teeth as most clients do.

Kermit leaps to his feet and karate kicks the wall. "I don't know what to be, I don't, I don't. There isn't a job for who I am."

On his knees, his face wet with tears. It's here I see Kermit needs guidance. His parents mustn't be giving him any.

"Lots of people don't know what to do in life," I say.

He props his fists against his cheekbones in a sulk. I blink out and enter more dull moments. It's frustrating, excitement was

27

promised with cutting-edge secret technology. I guess Pritek delivered but I find myself bored in waiting rooms, sobbing at funerals, and enduring pain or awkwardness. Come to think of it, any job I've ever had was nothing like the description advertised. Even in Green Bread—that I first joined as a bassist. Have you ever been catfished by a job? Jobfished?

After the training modules, I remember my first ever job for a client. I was acting as this man suffering from food poisoning on their toilet. Maybe this was a sign of how the job would turn out to be. I wait for a package to arrive for someone, then as an overweight person I'm weighed at a fitness club, the shame is so intense it crawls over my neck when the instructor says I've gained weight. I feel like eating something but manage to resist before I'm blinked out.

I undock and finish. Back home, the man I like to avoid is leaving our building but I have enough time to retreat and hide around the street before he sees me. It must be weird to witness my head peeking out from the wall but when the coast's clear I skip home and order double chocolate cake to celebrate another successful avoidance. I don't feel as good eating the cake because of the job I had earlier. Our interactions have been too awkward since I moved in. Our small talk makes me clench my jaw and lose brain cells. After I first avoided him, it made me so elated. It reminded me of being a carefree child, not even the fans singing our lyrics back to us in Green Bread could compare to the rush of this hobby.

Next morning, I'm back at work—where else would I be? Into another client's consciousness I go... The first moment is a Rouser, well it starts as a situation like that but turns into a family intervention about me being a workaholic. There's an intense shame pushing down my shoulders. I leave the moment whilst walking and there must be a lag because when I return to my body my legs are moving too and I slip from my chair and fall under the table.

On a break in the kitchen, I microwave a frittata. What's that noise? I stop cooking. Two muffled voices mumble in the hall. Are these two supervisors? Surely not, I've never seen two together. A spoon falls when I understand. It can only mean one thing: this is a new recruit having their induction. I try to see out of any slits in the door. No hope. I grumble undeveloped words against the door. If only I could meet another momenteer, maybe we could bond over work stories, maybe they could tell me about the moments they've had with Kermit.

Yes, I'm still worried about that kid. I checked earlier and the sedatives packet has returned to Kermit's sock drawer, a few less than last time. My dad denied using sedatives on us but I'll never forget the taste of his special drinks. We'd doze most weekends and he'd have ladies over while mother was embedding herself in the asylum. At the mirror in the ensuite, I pose questions to my reflection. Are my subconscious desires to be a father or better uncle fueled by my need to treat others better than my dad did? The question tightens my throat. Asking yourself questions in the mirror often gives you greater insight compared to a self-interrogating chat show you've assembled in your imagination.

Six: Hypo

4280 moments

Haven't seen anyone but strangers in their usual roles for a couple of days. No Kermit, not even the man I like to avoid. Still haven't met up with Donna, making me question the possessive label of her being my girlfriend. I usually let these things with her slide because when it comes to love, Donna's already felt a lot of pain from her past girlfriend's death. She won't give more details and if I ever bring this topic up, she'll leave.

The skaters give me nasty glares on my way to work. The supervisors ignore my small talk. My station welcomes me back, I attach the cables to my headset and dock in. There are no jobs for a while so I play chess against the computer.

The screen flicks to the main and here come the random codes pulling me into moments.

The aim is to: Raise blood sugar. Yay. It must be the diabetic. I enter his consciousness. I expect to feel cool but damn, this hypo is more intense than ever. The limbs move like lukewarm jelly. Must act now. His blood sugar's incredibly low. Soaked in sweat with a heartbeat like a kick drum vibrating through his entireness. I stumble from bedroom to kitchen, woozily knocking over a glass vase en route. So blurry, dots of light twinkle in his sight and burst around his eyeballs like kamikaze moons.

His sight flickers electrical, blurs and skews as if something's pulling his retinas. I remove his glasses and it's better. Why does he wear incorrect eyewear? The heartbeat thumps through to the fingers. I swing open the fridge, the door hits the cupboard and closes. I open it again, my grip slipping off the inbuilt handle. I scavenge for sugars, quick. Anything, this is serious. Phew, I find orange juice, that'll work. I can't get the weak straw to open the juice, hands quivering, urgency rising, I pierce the metallic film with one of his k9 teeth and suck the juice. A cat appears. While my hand pets it, I'm dazzled and frazzled. Unsure if I'm feeling my enormous heartbeat through the cat's bones or the cat's pulse? The body slumps before jolting into alertness.

Eyes wide. Drink, guzzle, gulp and drink in throbbing cold sweats. I hunt for the emergency tube of glucose gel faded-skills is telling me about. Up on the fridge's shelf. There it is, fingers fumble. When I grab it and tear off the cap, I discover another liquid. Looking at the tube there's red stuff over it. What the what? Is that… is that strawberry syrup? No, is that… it's blood. Woozy I'm lunged forward like the beginning of a bobsleigh race. Okay, this state is like being intoxicated but more dreamlike. I squeeze the glucose gel and wipe it along the gumline. Tastes sweet yet medical. I rub the gel into the gums with bloody fingers. There's a whiff of metal, as I lick the gums I taste what must be the iron in his blood. Is it okay to drink tiny amounts of your own blood?

Barely mobile, reality filters through. I've cut the diabetic's ankle on the vase. I roll down his sock and it looks bloody deep. Is that white part a bone? Oww! I retch but manage not to vomit. Looking back there's a trail of blood over the cream carpet and his cat's ginger fur. The cat's called Ricky, but I don't want to know this, of all times to find out.

"Remember to apply pressure to a wound," my brother once told me when he was training to be a paramedic, so I do.

Stumbling my way, I tightrope between consciousness and unconsciousness. I find myself almost teleported to his living room floor, holding his blurry smartphone. Both socks are removed and tied over the cut.

The glucose must be working because it doesn't feel like I'm free-falling and I can vaguely see the large digits on his phone. I call the emergency services from his lock screen. It isn't going well. My body jitters.

"Please tell us the address of where you are located sir? We need to know," the operator says.

When I try to think of his name or address I get a numb pain drill across his forehead and forget. Pritek's thought privacy is in effect. It's foggy at best, like trying to remember a verification code you were sent weeks ago. This isn't in faded-skills. Wait, I remember from training if I stay on the line emergency services can often locate you. I crawl across the hall and out his front door. It feels far but only because I'm drowsy and crawling. The blood sugar rises, I think. I involuntarily whimper. I hold his chest to find the heartbeat isn't banging on the ribs as intensely. The ankle stings as I hobble onto a street of a town. Darkness, apart from orange street lights.

"Help" I shout to the sky, before groaning at the moon. The operator says something but by the time I relocate his phone from his pocket, I accidentally disconnect. The line's dead. Dead, no, this isn't a good word to use right now.

My fist clenches into celebration when a home adjacent turns on its lights. Someone opens their front door, the clunkiness so apparent in this stillness I sense it more. No way. Without any wavy sensations the moment passes to another and I'm blinked.

No, no, no, no. I'm shocked still for a second. What happened? My hand stretches to touch my ankle. Nothing—weird to feel no agony. What have I done? Did I make a suicide happen? No, no, no, don't think like this. I could be in trouble for reckless endangerment should the diabetic report the injury. I hold my head in my quivering fingers. My stomach twists. I should call a supervisor, but I can't think straight.

Slapping my thighs, this will sound stupid but I decide to dock back in… 1) to appear busy if a supervisor comes, and 2) to get my mind off what happened.

I sit for five minutes biting my nails before another job comes. I'm waiting to sign for a delivery. The delivery person sighs after they drop off the parcel. In the breath of their sigh, I can only feel one question: is the diabetic still alive?

Undocked, can't focus, keep checking over my shoulder but no supervisors come. I set myself on break. In my kitchen, I heat up pesto falafel pasta but lose my appetite while it cooks. Wish my heart would shh so I could listen for movement. Silence. No one comes or walks in the hall.

My station glows bright, inviting me back, I stop and size it up. Okay, I'll do a few more moments since the supervisors aren't coming and I've only completed two jobs today.

I enter another client's consciousness. I've seen this place in pics. It's the Las Vegas skyline. Anger tenses my fists as a strong breeze blows my now long hair sideways. A crescent moon looms above The Luxor Hotel. That pyramid one. I've always wanted to come here. Wow, the lights, I've made it, somewhere Green Bread never played. I wonder how much the electricity bill is while the countdown trickles. Six, five. The aim says: _Suicide_. Oh no, it instructs to: `Jump off roof`. The word 'suicide' is flashing and underlined. It doesn't fade like normal moments. Too quick, too much. Can't think, can't, not now. I panic and pull the cables from my head to emergency exit the moment, abandoning their consciousness mid-job. The sky flashes blocky, buildings disappear and I'm back hyperventilating in front of my monitor.

That was a suicide moment. So rare, I couldn't, no, not after the diabetic. Timing is playing tricks. No. Maybe I should've done it. The codes on my screen fade away, that was the first one I've seen. A dagger of regret spears my existence. My groan transforms into a sigh. No, you know what—if you rich assholes want to jump off a building—do it yourself.

Standing, I remove the headset. I set myself on another break but see on the monitor that a supervisor is on their way. What, so now they come? Whoever's designing events to occur in this way, please, stop.

The floor and I have an impromptu staring contest while the supervisor enters. The door beeps and I try not to remember today's events by calculating how many stations are in the hallway. My station is at the beginning and I know the hallway bends into darkness somewhere else.

"An emergency exit? What happened?" A supervisor says before sneezing, reminding me they are human.

You can only emergency exit before the countdown ends. I explain today's jobs to the supervisor. For a change they're understanding.

"I know you've only completed a few moments today, but considering all these events we can release you early. Come in tomorrow though."

Words stop assembling in my mind. I nod okay. I wish I could unpack and repack my mind with a psychologist but Pritek won't allow me to see an approved one until this session is complete. They have an AI support chatbot that is about as useful as an abstract simile like this one.

"If this diabetic client uses our service again we will email you," the supervisor says.

"Trouble? Am I? I hurt the diabetic?" I say.

"At this stage it depends. Let us remind you, you're here to do a job."

I cover my eyes and breathe in so deep it feels like I vacuum all the gas from the room.

Like at the end of all shifts, a supervisor escorts me along the black window hall. I forget to peek to see how many stations are here. The secret lift/elevator takes me up and out. I walk the foyer behind suited people and out to blend back in with the rhythms of society, capitalism churning away.

Every time I leave Pritek I feel more detached from it all, from the busy pedestrians, the reflective buildings, the stationary weather, the tired transport, the hypocritical statues and even the kick-flipping skaters—they all seem more absurd. Catching my reflection approaching my wing mirrors I appear to be dim, disillusioned by society's illusion. Who am I when I'm being other people so often? Maybe I'm depressed? I decide an investigation would be too depressing to carry out. I know this will sound silly and unrelatable but when you live out other people's moments it gradually makes your own moments less meaningful.

Seven: Wiggle

Get ready, it's your first training module

As you sit the hairs on the back of your neck stand. Forget Komo, it's your turn. You wiggle your ass further into the ergonomic chair. The pulsing neon blue tube beside you glitters up this dim room with light. Your thighs wiggle too. The scent of burning metal lingers from the contracting, expanding and pulsing crystals inside the power cylinder. Who knows how this technology will work? Pritek keeps it all hush-hush with wires in locked drawers. A transparent bullet-proof cubic shield protects the power cylinder. Never Touch is embossed across the bottom.

"Focus. Let it happen, let your mind drift. Soon you won't be able to hear my…" A supervisor's voice hits the back of your ears.

It's scary, your sight becomes hazy. Giant blurs in the shape of jellyfish swim across your vision. Your thighs stop wiggling. You try but can't move. There's a pulling sensation but your body's not moving. Your eyelids flutter. All you see are fluctuating hues of large wavy dots growing until one of them fills your entire vision. You blink and fall into another person's consciousness.

It worked, it worked! This. Is. Weird. But it worked…

You wiggle every finger. The first thing you notice is your hands are thicker. The height to the floor is longer. You move your right arm but the left moves instead. Woah. Focus, focus. It's acting. Your movements sync to this body. Your hands hop to your ear, your ears are smaller, skin is rougher. Wait a second. You feel like someone else yet still yourself. Your guts jump as you step forward. Remember the aim is simple: all you have to do is walk to the end of this glass walkway, descend the stairs and collect a folder from the receptionist.

With larger feet, you step forward then immediately back because it feels bizarre not to be you. You ponder, why did Pritek pick you? Of all people to become a momenteer. You're so amazed that this technology works you can only relate this sensation to a surreal dream. Nothing feels real so you pinch your thigh to make sure you can feel it. Ouch. You wiggle the fingers to play an invisible piano before smoothing them over your now-hairy belly. This is insane. That movie *Freaky Friday* plops in your thoughts but this experience is something else, that was a comedy but this is a live-action documentary starring, filmed and dubbed by you.

Breathe to focus, forget about the high collar this person wears that's irritating your neck. Remember the supervisor told you to remain calm. Don't get distracted by shifts in your narrative. Pritek's bought you the bungalow you always wanted to live in and you can own it if you complete all your sessions. No more debt, no more dead-end jobs. You'll have enough money to live like royalty. Yacht trips and expensive meals you've never heard of yet. You step forward but the squeak of these shoes widens your eyes. Wait, shouldn't you call them my shoes? It's complicated being someone else, never mind grammar or possessive labels.

You wiggle each part of the body and it all moves. One foot after the other and so on. You're doing it, you are amazing, you're being someone else. Feels so strange to walk in someone else's body and shoes that you sway. You reach out to thin air before grabbing your hip. Has this person got a swagger or is this walk yours? Remember this client isn't a real human, but a training module randomly generated character. A few more steps reveal they do have a swagger. Pritek must've programmed the squeak in your shoe to test your adaptability.

You're doing so well that you reach the stairs at the end of the walkway. At the tip of them, you place your palm over your chest and take another large breath.

Come on. You've encountered steps before, must be thousands of times. Short two-step ones, long never-ending and spiraling ones. You've done most varieties, mastered all stairs have to offer. These may look similar but after a step, it all feels new. Like when you haven't done something for decades.

The second step makes your shoulders narrow but after you land it, the rest flow. Hey, you're doing it, without holding the handrail. You're being someone else and no one but you can tell.

You fix your collar. You swirl the tongue around your mouth to feel different teeth, these ones sharper. The supervisors warned that most trainees freak out and fall down the steps their first time, but not you. You've completed ten of them with only a couple remaining. Your ego interrupts to tell you that you're amazing. The whole building and decor are in see-through glass except for the walls and floor which are a solid beige.

Watch out! Whoops. Your legs flop like cooked spaghetti. This far and you stumble on the last two steps. One of your shoes flies off and slides over the marble flooring as if it's a curling stone. Your left foot is colder. You're frozen as you watch the shoe come to a stop. Too awkward to retrieve. A ripple of embarrassment flushes through your cheeks. Wait, you remind yourself—this isn't real, not yet, only a training module but your heartbeat can't tell the difference. You reach out for the hand rail but it already ended..

A bald genderless receptionist flashes into appearance at the desk. The aims appear at the side of your vision again. You have to retrieve a document from them. You wave and clap your hands but the receptionist doesn't react. The aims fade. You feel your head and your hair is shaved to that spiky level where it's pleasing to touch.

You're not wearing any socks. Maybe Pritek forgot to install socks in this, your first of many training modules. Rubbing your head reassures your feet. You aim in the direction of your castaway shoe. Look at it, barely belonging to you anymore.

"By Guv'nor, here to collect the interruption folder I see," the bald receptionist says.

Jump-scare. The sharpness of their voice makes you step back. Despite speaking with an accent their voice is generic smart-speaker AI. To the side, you see the bald receptionist moving. Is that a smile on their face or melted chocolate? Skin textures must be glitching. They move their head like they're talking to different parts of their face but aren't speaking. You notice a slab of the wall and the floor beneath you changes tone, from beige to orange but for such a brief moment you have to question if you saw it.

You turn to face the bald receptionist head-on and smile without exposing your sharp teeth. You step closer, looking at them then the shoe. Again and again, no reaction. They stare into space.

After they installed your implants, in the theory training, they detailed to you what being inside someone else's mind would feel like. It's weird because it's what they said yet an entirely different sensation. You wiggle your sockless toes. Do you need your shoe? Maybe that will make things feel correct.

As soon as you step towards the shoe, the hairs on your neck twitch. You're overwhelmed by feeling too many things at once. You squat to your knees and hold your head.

"By Guv'nor, here to collect the interruption folder I see," the receptionist says.

To think a month ago you were emailing customer support about a deluxe smoothie you liked because the ingredients and taste had changed, but look at you: inside someone else, moving their body like it's yours. Sure this isn't the mind of a real person but rather a janky module character, but still. You're not in your body but still in your mind.

A sudden desire urges you to talk to the receptionist at the desk. Must be faded-skills. They're looking expectantly at you, the way hungry animals do. You aim your feet away towards the shoe but it's too much of a detour to retrieve. You wiggle your posture back around and walk to the desk.

The overhead lighting creates a shine on the receptionist's skin. You feel like you've spoken but you haven't. Their eyes are reminiscent of a screensaver, cupped by bags shaped like seashells. They seem so real—you've encountered people in your life more like robots than this receptionist. A tickle in your throat reminds you to speak.

"I'm here for the folder."

You dislike your own voice, this includes recorded playbacks and hearing it leave your mouth, but this voice is honey. Too cool it makes you relax and try to put your hands in your pockets but you don't have any.

The bald genderless receptionist moves a lot of things around. For a moment it appears like the sleeves on their suit are way too long and hide their hands before returning to normal. Glitch? The receptionist produces a cardboard folder from a drawer under the desk. A flurry of dizziness ambushes you.

"Here you go. All yours," the receptionist says.

All you have to do is reach and take the folder but you zone out, thinking about your life two months back before you had even heard of Pritek. Before that lady came up to you outside that bus stop you were passing and offered you this opportunity. That life feels so distant now as the receptionist's arm wobbles the document up and down. Expectations demand you to grab the folder. You imagine the supervisors looking at the report of this, they'll know when and if you take the folder.

41

The only thing you grab is your head.

The folder wobbles vertically. You squint at the folder and notice that their hand is on a loop. The folder wobbles repeatedly at the same rate, stops and repeats.

"Sorry for the interruption, but can you take this?" The receptionist says.

This is strange, being someone else isn't for everyone. It's acting. It's as if you aren't working properly, it's difficult to focus. You thought dressing up at Halloween was being someone else, but this is the secret level. Thoughts pinball across your skull and collide, rendering you immobile. This must be that identity freeze the supervisors warned could come. What did they say? Remember it's all acting. Play the role.

The folder wobbles. You piece the puzzle of your mind together enough to move. You raise your hand. The moment your fingers grip the folder, there's a rubbing sound and you feel like you're moving through the milky way (Although you don't know what that's like.) Your eyelids have never felt so heavy. Woozy, you can't help but blink and after the third blink—you feel as if your body is being pulled.

The next blink places you back at Pritek. Your own body facing the monitor. You feel the headset around your temple. You lick your front teeth. Yes, these are your teeth, it's wonderful to have them back. Your teeth feel more reliable. You rub your thighs, feeling like you've lost something. Pockets empty, your phone is… where? Did you leave it in that other person's body? Impossible. Panic zaps you. No, remember, it's upstairs—security takes it off you before every shift. Your nostrils sniff and you smell that familiar stink of burning from the power cylinder. You wonder, will that always be here as you glance at the crystals that are too bright to identify.

"How was it? Slow but I see you didn't fall which is commendable," the supervisor says from your side.

You're spooked when their hand touches your shoulder. Those weird future motorbike gloves they wear, the knuckles reflecting the purply-blue light of the station.

You gulp. The whole world, reality feels different. The buzzing hum of your station and *tick-tick-clink* of the crystals expanding and shrinking.

"How did you enjoy your experience? We've got many modules to complete, next up we'll get you to eat followed by feeling emotional pain before starting the conversational block of arguments, resolutions and diffusing awkwardness," the supervisor sighs. "That'll take a while, then we can finish the week with a brief introduction to decisions or physical pain."

"It was weird, so I don't know, surreal," you say as you tilt your head in various directions.

You spin on your chair, the wires from your headset wrapping across your nose. The supervisor helps unplug you from your docked state. They consult their tablet. Only 220 training modules to go.

You glance around the room. Low ceilings NBA stars would have to crouch under are softly lit. *This is my life now, I mean job*, you tell yourself as your gaze travels across the break table and up to two rooms in the back, a kitchen and an ensuite. Everything appears to be leather, faux, of course, they said before you could ask.

The supervisor wiggles your chair back and reattaches your headset. "We'll get you ready for the real thing."

You can't see it through their helmet but you can sense they're smiling. Is that excitement tightening your chest or nervousness? Or a deluxe smoothie containing both? A desire explodes within you to momenteer again.

"Ready for the next module?" The supervisor says.

You blink at your monitor and wiggle forward.

Eight: Collection for Enchanted Squire

4309 moments

After another shift, I'm driving home thinking over the events. My shoulders slip down the seat as the sun is limboing down the back window. In my final job, which turned out to be the same four-hour-long moment separated by a break, I momenteered as a client taking a first-class plane to The Bahamas. I left the plane and collected his bag. The airport's doors opened and a gush of tropical heat embraced me. I forgot that I wasn't myself. A chauffeur service took me to this luxurious palm-tree-surrounded hotel, with my feet hanging over the pool—I was blinked out. So frustrating to return to my body and circumstances. I should convince Pritek I'm having an identity crisis because an ICB (Identity Crisis Break) is the only way I'd be permitted my passport to travel before I reach my tally.

At least I saw Kermit today. I watched an episode of *How It's Made* with him, but something was wrong. The episode was on how bulletproof glass is made but I felt like I was talking to it when he refused to open up. Did something else happen? Faded-skills were blanking. I checked his bruise, almost gone but did it switch arms? Perhaps my memories are mashed. We finally bonded when he revealed his fav actor is Jim Carrey.

"No way, I've liked him since the 90s," I said.

We did impressions from *Ace Ventura* and *The Mask*. He made my face hurt laughing. We ended up telling each other a secret no one else knows.

"I don't like Rosenthal," he said.

Faded-skills informed me that this is Kermit's teacher. I tried to rummage my mind for a secret but while my gaze was buffering, I'm reminded that I'm his father. I couldn't tell him a secret from my own life.

"When I was your age I had someone at school that I used to avoid. No one but me could understand why, so I didn't explain it to anyone and made it my own game."

"Why did you avoid them?"

I know I don't have an answer anyone would understand. It contains a rewarding energy and has evolved into its own thing. This job has made me an extra introvert.

"You ever felt like you have to do something but don't know why? That's why."

Kermit sat on his bed nodding into his knees. He understood me, if anyone could, he would.

A deluxe parking space in my building's basement welcomes me home and back into the present tense. I shouldn't let my job get me down. Every minute of every day, I bet someone's telling themselves not to quit their job. To find a job you like is special, to find a job that likes you back is rarer.

In my flat/apartment, Donna texts me a selfie. With no context or words, an out-of-the-blue self-portrait. This isn't on brand for her. I switch sofas wondering if I should send a selfie back. I end up replying with an emoji of a disco ball and broccoli, which is confusing and doesn't suit my brand either.

The selfie is simply Donna standing, shot from above with a pair of opened scissors twirled in her fingers. Dressed in her bohemian chic style. No expression. Donna's attractive in a non-stereotypical way, her face is plum shaped with hamster-like cheeks, aw. Her hairstyle fluctuates throughout the rainbow. Currently, it's turquoise and magenta. She's got a cool scar on her neck from surfing that resembles an upside-down Nike tick but what I like the most is her limp. You don't encounter it often, only when her legs are in a certain position, she does a cute gallop. It's worth the wait, it makes me smile, every time. Thinking of it now brightens my cloudy day.

Honestly, who am I to talk about appearances and objectify anyone when my reflection reveals a washed-up hipster that evolution ditched a decade ago. Donna told me a person's style stalls at 30 and I'm a walking example of this theory. My ironed suits appear exhausted after I put them on. My sideburns are often uneven, my painter's brush moustache/mustache is patchy. She says I shouldn't wear turtlenecks because my face resembles an old Teenage Mutant Ninja Turtle.

Tonight, I go out to get my steps in and collect a pizza. The man four doors down that I like to avoid catches me in the foyer while I'm checking my empty mailbox. The tone of his rusty voice pinches my shoulders and spins me.

"Well well well, look who it isn't," he says his catchphrase to my back.

Worms wriggle across my spine. This encounter breaks a two-week streak of avoidance. He's strange, maybe as strange as me. When I'm unfortunate enough to bump into him he's often carrying an object he's struggling to hold. Tonight he's jiggling a pink mug of unassorted pens. The moment locks me inside as I stupidly fuel our interaction by nodding toward his hands.

"Stole them, didn't I just?" His voice loud yet whispering, "I had to. They banned me. The staff at the library have been treating me not only as a second-class citizen but also a third and sometimes a fourth. They shouldn't have so much power over reading materials, desks, DVDs, printing facilities and stationery. No, not stationary, they won't give you pens unless you steal theirs."

"Can they treat you as this many classes of citizen?" I try but can't stop my squint.

His head stutters back mechanically. "But of course they can, young enchanted squire."

What were those Gothic words? How do you feel when words entirely out of your vocabulary are directed your way? I cover my abdomen because I feel disconnected and violated. Yet, I can't help but wonder what an 'enchanted squire' is.

"Well, you enjoy your night, won't you?" I counter with my own catchphrase I'm developing but will no doubt forget.

His eyes float between me and the pens, repeatedly. He jiggles them. Some fall out. He squats to pick them up, muscle memory reminds me to leave. Looking back at him paints a sad scene. I enter the elevator/lift. As the doors yawn shut, I press and press the doors button, because he's putting his arm out like he wants to continue chatting.

My front door locks. It's freshly clean. I reset my analogue-click counter and hope it's another long stretch before I meet him again. I need to improve my avoidance techniques. The avoidance record I can't see being broken sits at six weeks and a day. My belly grumbles and oops. I've forgotten to go get the pizza I was on my way to collect before that encounter. No matter how many times I rub my chin and door handle I can't leave my place. I check our security channel. No one but the concierge in the foyer, but it's still too risky. Instead, I call the restaurant but they say delivery's not an option tonight.

A silence blooms on the line as I consider going out. The silence seeps through my skin and narrows my enthusiasm.

"Hello? You're coming to get your food?" They say.

"No, please give it to a homeless person nearby."

"Oka—" and they hang up before finishing the word.

I order a kimchi meal on the food delivery app. If Pritek reviews my orders and sees two on the same night I'll explain that I was hungry.

The food's delicious and digested. The night creeps into the AM. I'm playing this music video game. Donna calls, her voice loose, her grammar intoxicated. She's wanting us to grab food. It's too late, I don't wanna…

I meet Donna at the roller skating staff café where I previously worked. As a vegetarian, she orders a rainbow salad. I fail to hide my red face from my old bosses. We exchange awkward do-we-have-to-yes-we-do strained smiles.

"Why's your face red? Reddy red shy face. Is this 'cause you never tell me where you go in that tower? Are you spy man? Eat up," Donna says these things in separate instances as if the statements aren't connected, adding new ones when I attempt to reply. "And how'd you feel about me? And stuff, doink. Ruben left, I alone, yes he went and did that."

She's speaking in rum syntax. Our eyes connect, I wish I could feel closer to Donna, to truly connect—but as my job requires having intimate relationships with strangers in other men's bodies… I can't. Our bond has diverted beyond love and into something so uniquely intricate that there's not a word for it.

Donna's elbow hits the table, she props her face up with it. She slides it closer to me, her face slips down her palm, wrist then forearm before resting on her bicep.

"Spy, are you spying on me?" Donna laughs.

I check if she's okay and pour her water.

"Aw, I like you," Donna says.

"Like you too, but will like you more if you drink this water."

She picks up the glass, takes a slurp and projects her neck forward to make it obvious she's looking at me.

"Aw. That's nice, but will we ever be more than seriously casual?"

I rub the skin between her thumb and index finger, as we play a brief round of 'are you cheating?'

49

The result of the game is: no, but would it matter if we were? This question seems difficult for both of us to digest as it knocks us back into our booth.

I blow raspberry kisses at how absurd the answer could be.

"You're the one that's a spy. I work boring stocks and sometimes dividends in the tower, but at the office we call it 'stoncks' to feel younger but that's sad," I say Pritek's rehearsed excuse. I can't talk about my job, not even with Donna.

Donna laughs, the wobbly table jiggles our plates and my mozzarella sticks shuffle. My belly pleads with me not to eat more. She takes her phone out, drops it, finds it and loads a press photo of me from my band days. I was so young and stupid with that emo hair. She places the image beside my head, looks around for validation but no one looks because it's empty.

"Look at the difference... Because I'm worth it, think different, finger-lickin' good, just do it, you can do it," Donna says weird slogans before continuing, "How can I be a spy? Who else would cut hairstyles here? Mandy, Luke, The Lady's name I always forget but she comes a lot, Dr Hope Jr, Gulliver, Electric Tina, oh don't forget Mr Smith, Bonesy, Samuel, who else... Cocaine Andy (When he comes. His hair long now.) They all say I'm the best snip snip snipper," Donna does an impression of a hairdryer, at least that's what I think her groaning is supposed to be.

Her salon's situated between the rich and poor parts of the city. My smile stretches then fades when I remember the man in my building that I enjoy avoiding is possibly named Gulliver because, well, his Gully catchphrase thing. It feels like half of the mozzarella stick I ate has turned to lead.

"Gully?" I once inquired and then regretted it when he responded with a rant about how as humans, we should have temporary names until we turn 14 and then we should be allowed to formally pick our own names, at a ceremony of sorts. If he's named Gulliver, do you think he picked it himself? What are the chances that Donna cuts his hair? I'm reluctant to investigate if they're the same, but in that last bitter sip of decaffeinated coffee, I   can   taste   that   they   are.

Nine: Violation

4384 moments

Ten days pass. There's no news about the diabetic. Routine disguises each day to feel similar. Awkward moments at work aren't as frequent and there's no Rousers. Last week I momenteered for someone having an ice cream brain freeze, a typical example of how boring it's been. I suspect I was the prankster again, this time he wore clown shoes to a chiropodist appointment and I blinked out when I removed the silly shoes.

Donna's supposed to come over tonight but she's three hours late. She should have her own fluctuating time zone. I call and tell her to forget it. She manages to reshape the situation into being my fault. Turns out if a person is late or very late, they need to be sorry, but if they're unbelievably late, it's your fault for giving them pressure and expectations.

Moments with Kermit have been nice. He's calm around me when I'm in his dad's consciousness. The bruise is gone and the sedatives disappeared. His father's become a regular client.

"Why aren't you in this mood all the time?" Kermit often says.

We've watched a few *How It's Made* episodes before bed. I've begun to notice that Kermit mirrors my sitting positions. Maybe this means I'm a good parent? My shrill moments with other crying children would suggest otherwise. Kermit asked my advice about school and we've had a few deep chats about life, things Donna and I haven't discussed yet, like what happens after you die, are humans ruining the earth and what creates or influences someone's opinion.

If 250 souls are born every minute, why do I have this bond with Kermit? Most people only ask themselves why they dislike something, not me. I question why I enjoy anything. Maybe it's because my parents made it seem like a chore to have fun with me. It must be why I avoid people. All these painful moments I'm having for other people, like the hypo, is making me both want to connect yet disconnect because you feel how frail personal connections are. One day, you might relate.

A few days later, a nightmare arrives. I bump into the man I like to avoid twice in a day. Earlier was easier because I was going to work but returning after my shift he's lounging on the seat in the foyer. I think posh people call this a chaise lounge.

"Have you ever been to Zeouw?" I ask, the strange name of Donna's hair salon, named after the noise a shaver makes swooping around your ear.

"Do waffles like syrup on them?" He says, readjusting his position.

This guy. I hate when people answer questions with unrelated questions. I don't respond because my phone vibrates against my thigh. Everything around me mutes as I read it's from Pritek. Everything around stops moving when I read it's about the diabetic. My heart sinks then floats as if it's attached to helium. I need to sit on the chaise chair thing. Gulliver shuffles aside but his thigh still touches mine.

'Dear agent Komo,
In regards to your query about a regular client, I can hereby confirm this client is now active on our service. However, due to the injuries sustained by the client, we have taken the lenient decision to fine 300 moments. As we cannot delete from your tally, you now require 5300 moments before session 1 is complete.'

In a celebratory motion, I punch the air whilst jumping to my feet. The diabetic reported me. I guess that's fair, to be fair.

"Good news?" The man I like to avoid says.

It's rude of me but I forget to explain, couldn't anyway. I run around the chair and head into the lift/elevator. Before I go up I see he's looking glum, kicking his feet. We share smiles of different kinds. His forced, mine uncontrolled glee.

Next day, more boring jobs. There's a new regular I have to shower and dress for before they go to work. Looking at my tally, 5,300 makes me pinch my throat. After momenteering for strangers I don't know, I go for nighttime pancakes with Donna. She tries to get me to come to Zeouw for a haircut. No.

Days blend into each other once more until I bump into the man I like to avoid again. He's wearing a denim cap with a tracksuit (making him difficult to spot). He appears while we're both returning to our building. He drops a swim cap from his sports bag and tells me that he's a star water polo goalkeeper but isn't competitive enough to compete.

The concierge looks at us like we're friends but I can't imagine a facial expression that'll show otherwise.

"I don't know," I say after he suggests he'll teach me how to play.

He moves to the side to pick up the swim cap and from above, I spot that the left side of his hair is buzzed, detailed with dazzling zigzag lines. My logic connects the dots to Donna's salon. Is he the Gulliver she mentioned she cuts the hair of. I presume this Gully guy from my building might be the same, Gulliver. I don't want to learn his name.

"Cool haircut," I say.

A weight lifts. Maybe this is the first time I've interacted authentically with him. Being honest rather than all the empty talk, lies or trying to get away.

"Blame my hairdresser, she's the one that did it," he laughs, removing his hat. A grin stretches his face and wiggles the only visible ear. His haircut is what the well-informed call cyberpunk. Intricately shaved lines on one side, long swirly bleached greasy mess on the other.

Regardless, his presence continues to draw energy from under my skin. Evidence is incomplete but let's call him Gulliver for now.

The doors open and strangers leave the elevator/lift. He points to it and I excuse myself for the sake of my social anxiety. It's strange I don't get social anxiety when I'm momenteering, not even in awkward situations when I know the client's faded-skills are feeling it.

Gulliver runs, holds the doors open with his sports bag and oh no, he joins me inside. It feels like we've dropped 100 floors. Our first time together here. We both go to press our top floor button and our hands graze off each other. We make impressions of our natural laughs. The button remains unpressed. I try to press it telepathically. He turns his head to mine and I nod to the buttons, all of them dull when the top one shouldn't be.

The awkwardness boils so much I clench my ass. I press button [6] for our top floor and he talks about how tired he gets saving shots at water polo.

He does impressions of saves but all I get is a whiff of his BO. The aroma is chlorine mixed with a spicy-wood deodorant. C'mon, hurry. This is taking longer. It feels itchy under my nails. I close my eyes for relief. The doors open. I make sure to walk out first and fast. His place is closer on the top floor. Halfway down the hall, over my shoulder, he nods at his door like he's inviting me in. My feet step on each other. I wave like a referee calling a foul. He swooshes one side of his hair over the shaved side.

"You've been you and I've been…" He says.

"Gully," I complete his catchphrase. A bird squawks. Unsure where the sound comes from. Maybe I imagine it, but I hear it. We both signal goodbye with friendly groans. Did I become involved in his life?

Inside, I search Zeouw's social media for Gulliver's hairstyle. Some similar cuts but Donna doesn't update frequently.

Another sleep and I'm back at my station. The jobs aren't exciting but even they're more exciting than my own life. The supervisors have fitted a mini and sleek treadmill into the break room because momenteers sit all day and our bodies don't get enough steps.

I'm blinked into a consciousness where I have to make a decision on which sports car a client will buy. A navy blue BMW convertible or a Porsche Cayenne Coupé. The aim simply instructs to: *Decide*. Who cares, I try not to get influenced by faded-skills but after a few seconds I'm not sure if these thoughts are entirely mine. I close my eyes, spin and point at the BMW. I tell the staff in the forecourt. I blink out and can't believe that cars mattered to me for a moment.

I'm about to dock out of my station for the night when I see the next case number fly at me. Maybe it's the time of day or I'm noticing a pattern in the codes but I sense it's going to be with Kermit.

I blink in, the aim reads: *Calm.*

Five, four, three.

"Didn't I do it right?" Kermit asks.

Perplexed, limbs and mind are woozy. The only other time I've felt this way was when a dentist gave me nitrous or those times we did MDMA after a few gigs. I blink and blink these sinus-stuffed eyes, trying to sharpen his father's vision. What the... Kermit's on the edge of his bed in underpants covering his body with a pillow. I turn my back away.

Facing a flamingo poster. The flamingo on the wall is too bright. Aren't they supposed to be pink? But this one is more purple. No way, is it—is it speaking to me?

"Wasn't I good at it? Get out!" Kermit snaps and I flick around to see him punching the mattress. "I must be bad," Kermit and/or the flamingo I'm facing says. I must be drugged as I can't tell who's speaking.

"What happened? Bad at what?" I say, trying to raise a hand but it keeps flopping. I focus on it and tell my arm to behave. I feel detached from the body I'm in yet emotionally connected to everything I see with these half-open eyes. There's a sweaty smell loitering. Faded-skills are being useless.

Kermit and the flamingo reply, "Leave me alone," to any other question.

Trying not to look at the flamingo because it has triangle pupils in each eye, I take clothes out the drawers and throw them over my shoulder to him so he can dress. I notice I'm warm despite not wearing a shirt either.

"What's going on?" I say to the flamingo. Maybe they can tell me.

"Leave me alone. Go, get out." Kermit or the flamingo says.

Never felt this unsure before. Maybe someone else in the house can tell me? I remember he mentions his mother sometimes. I turn to leave his bedroom but on my way, I spot something strange. I inhale so deeply the hairs on my chest move. What the FUCK is that? I crouch forward and sway back. It's a... a half-cut cucumber with a condom around it. Instantly, I know what happened. Can you guess too? Don't make me say it. It's the worst.

My eyes bulge like they need to breathe. I manage to rush out of Kermit's bedroom. No one else is here in his house. Scrambling in the hall I bang my head off the wall, the framed landscape paintings fall and land horizontally. What did the aim say? I forget. I can't form a single thought and I need many.

What should I do? Enraged, I stop moving when I spot a medicine cabinet bathroom mirror. I bounce off the wall while turning on the light and step in. Quickly, I scan many details and lines of this monster's reflection. Should I put two and two together again? A reunion tour of assumptions? Kermit, the condom, the half-cut cucumber, the talking flamingo—they all dance on his father's brow as I study his face.

Chiselled mountain ridgelines descend towards a stern jawline. Cleanly shaved skin softly shines. Ashtray hair with silvery streaks sits proudly above his skull, each hair at the perfect length to flop. Swamp brown irises float around his pupils. Feeling wavy I throw and catch his heavy head between my hands. His eyebrows have been shaped. Two massive veins pulse through each hand, his fingernails pristinely clipped.

Of course, because I looked in a mirror a drifty nature catches up with me and I'm blinked out. Back in my consciousness, there's an instant awareness that wasn't in the client's hazy mind. Finally, my mind can think without thoughts going wayward. My stomach feels, what's the word for it? I'm so upset that I retch parts of words and puke bile on the floor.

I relate to Kermit. My own father abused me and my brother, not physically but psychologically. He'd always put us down, play mind games, control us, look for arguments and at best neglect us.

The click of my station door opening is loud. The supervisor's boots make an unsettling echo.

Over my shoulder, my monitor starts flashing
Rogue Violation Rogue Violation Rogue Violation Rogue Violation
A supervisor lifts my head by my hair. We both look to the floor where my puke is.

"Listen…" I say, unsure where to begin.

Ten: Punishment

4397 moments

As you know, I've been using both Anglo and American English to protect my location. Depending on your accent you may pronounce this differently but there's only one universal term for what happened. You know it. It feels wrong merely thinking of the word and its connotations, even worse saying it to the supervisor.

The supervisor crosses their arms to my protests. All their responses are mashed up and edited into this outrageous remix:

"We are only concerned with what our agents do in moments, not what occurs before or after. You were blinked out because you violated privacy protocols. You're the one currently in the wrong. We are not the police. We cannot inform any local authorities." The supervisor shrugs and I do mine back. "We cannot provide evidence using our systems. Your actions within a moment can only be seen if you break protocols. We do understand your anger. You are never to commit crimes whilst being clients. We will wait to see if this client complains about your performance. *Blah, blah, meh et cetera.*"

Questions pile on top of other questions. Once again I should've investigated further. A naked tween, a cucumber with a condom on it. You do the maths/math and you'll find the sun doesn't shine.

"There's a creepy father out there doing horrible things to his son. We have to stop them," I stand and push my head against their visor. The mesh metal presses a netting pattern into my nose.

"Please step back. This is a warning," when the supervisor talks, the red from their helmet lights my chest. I snort in a fashion that would make a bull proud. They can't allow such evil to happen.

"Why won't you call the police wherever this client is?" My voice rises.

Another supervisor enters my station. So bewildered to see two together that my gaze bounces between them. There's a bulky and a slim one.

In a haze of anger, I slip from their grasp and rush to the power cylinder of crystals. It's protected by a clear glass case. I do my best to open it but a sharp pinch as if glass is cutting me spikes below my ribs.

Arghowwww. My body jiggles, falls forward while my eyes roll back.

I wake up wearing a loose straitjacket in a bright padded room, the size of a 2 m by 2 m cube. Claustrophobic nightmare. Below my ribs, ouch, it's tender. Ow, it hurts when my elbow touches it. Sitting there I understand. They tased me, shocked in both senses of the word. That's what that was. They knocked me out and put me wherever this is.

A single bulb above is my only company. I shout various things to retrieve their attention. It could be any time with no windows here. My anger mellows. I guess about an hour passes. One of the padded walls opens back and a large supervisor stands blocking the hallway. I step forward, chest to chest. I can see my station's door open in the distance.

"I'm here to give you your punishment."

"My punishment?" I step back until I'm touching the wall.

They don't explain through words but actions. My nipples are twisted. The supervisor lubricates my feet and administers electric shocks. My mind is zapped into alignment with their viewpoint.

62

They leave. I assume it's over but they return wearing large weird-looking gloves. They're danger red and have hundreds of mini tentacles that spark. They tickle torture me. Haharrghh. At first, the tickling is funny but after seconds it becomes unbearable. My eyes try to leap out my face. Haharrghh. My breath. Can't. Cat... ch. It. The tickling is horrific. My ribs feel as if they're cracking and shrinking from the pain. I can't. It's not funny. The supervisor grinds me down, mashes my spirit into a paste and smokes me out believing their perspective. I tell myself Kermit doesn't even exist. Anything to stop the pain.

They remove my straitjacket. The tickle gloves tentacles spark on my skin, my torso jiggles and I laugh so much my lights ping off. I wake up in darkness with a lukewarm meal with ingredients I must guess. Macaroni with unknown vegetables?

All there is, is darkness. Outside and within. Why are Pritek trying to cover this up? Did I deserve this? The largest supervisor visits me in what I assume to be the morning.

"Please remember, what actions are at our discretion should you defect and act in such a manner against our company," their muffled voice firm and heavy.

Thinking of all the blackmail material they have on me tightens my throat. I try to gulp but my ribs sting. My passport, my deluxe home, the bank cards, the crimes and mental asylum documents I signed. I drum my abdomen with punches.

"You were selected because you don't have a large number of contacts around. Should we decide to terminate your contract for treachery, we might skip these intermediate measures and move to the extreme. You don't know our capabilities. Attempt to break our systems or act with aggression to a supervisor again and we may decide to terminate you."

"So you will sack/fire me? Fine, give me my pension and place. I don't care about the rest."

They step back and cross their arms, "We mean have you around *at all*."

I open my arms but say nothing when I understand they mean that they'll kill me and tarnish my name. Which is worse than death. Death Plus. The potential headlines in future websites attack my consciousness and slip me to my knees.

Ex Green Bread Dummer Admits to…

"Understand?" The supervisor says.

"I do."

We return to my station and I'm reminded of the contracts I signed. There's a part mentioning my poor social circle, my mother's insanity and having a flash of fame that I'd be easy to frame. I forgot that I signed a confession for stealing a man's prosthetic leg and beating them with it. Didn't I read this? I must've really hated working with the public. They issue me an unpaid suspension for two weeks. Time for them to improve their security and for me to "consider my actions."

Before I leave, they make me talk to their psychiatrist on a web chat. I'm careful not to say much, but you can assume they've subdued me.

"We will make sure you are blocked and you'll never have to encounter this client and their child again," The supervisor's words ring in my ears and I'm thinking too many things at once. How am I going to save Kermit if I don't have moments with him? Sorry Kermit but I'm trapped. What can I do that doesn't put me in a river, ditch or a mental asylum.

Back in my home, everything's different. The click from the massive clock above the fireplace is harsh when it wasn't before. The oaky scent the cleaners spray smells fake. My empty armchairs are cold and when I sit in them they don't support me like they did. The 85" television looks smaller, I put my hands around it, it feels cold so I turn the electric fireplace on. I remove and reattach the HDMI cables but nothing's the same, not even close. I walk to my closet to look at my old Green Bread tour poster, it's changed. I fell out of love with drumming, with the past—but seeing as everything's changing but me, I impulse buy an electric drum kit online.

Sitting, mulling over what happened and why Pritek isn't helping. I try to see things from the company's perspective, as they're forcing me to. How would I be able to prove what happened when only I saw it with someone else's eyes? Is it that Pritek doesn't believe me or more the case that they want to protect their client and themselves? Remembering events I'm not sure if I touched the cucumber, I'm sure I didn't but why do I have the image that it was all mushy inside? My memory is adding extensions to events, painting over the scene. It's making me question if I got anything wrong. About thirty minutes pass and I'm sweating from the heating.

Getting up to turn it off I notice a soft throbbing ache in the middle of my chest, in the shape of a rhombus. The ache doesn't touch any flesh or bone but attaches, hovers in limbo. There's not exactly anyone I can tell and if I do go to the police, what am I going to say that doesn't make me sound like I've recently escaped an asylum? "Listen, a boy named Kermit somewhere in this world is…"

"Okay sir, and where is this boy and what drugs have you taken?" The hypothetical police officer would say.

The smart lights flicker on and I get the urge to clean before the cleaners come tomorrow, so they won't think I'm dirtier than I am. I order a bunch of sleeping pills to be delivered, as I predict trouble sleeping these next few weeks.

In my kitchen, I finally move the box that was keeping the snack cupboard door from closing. It's been like that for over a year. It won't shut, the door keeps its position and can't close properly. I put olive oil on the hinge but the door remains resolute to its position of not open but not closed. I walk back from it with my arms crossed before running and elbowing it. It swings shut, sticks and pops back out.

"There's nothing stopping you from closing anymore," I say to it.

The cupboard door's adamant it doesn't want to close. At this point, you've got to respect its decision. Some things in life don't want to be fixed and prefer the imperfections they are. I sit on the sofa, giving the cupboard the side-eye. I know it's so silly but I end up thinking the stuck door is a metaphor for my life. I've been going on like this for so long and now I'm stuck and can't be fixed.

Such a stupid metaphor but it fits. Donna would laugh out her nostrils if I told her this. No one would understand but Kermit and possibly, at a stretch, the man I like to avoid.

Eleven: Spaghetti Hoop Wedding Ring

"How dare you interrupt us," Kermit's teacher Mister Rosenthal slams his fist on his desk and his coffee with a hint of vodka wobbles around the rim of the mug. "We were enjoying this book, but you must think swinging on your chair won't distract us. Everyone's concentration doesn't belong to you."

No response. Rosenthal stands, someone's table leg interrupts with a screech and Kermit's chair legs return to the floor. Kermit stares outside the classroom windows, focusing across the playground on a yellow-vested builder adding another brick to the school's new cafeteria.

"Don't frown at me like that, Kermit O'Sullivan," Rosenthal approaches Kermit's desk. Rosenthal's lips narrow and a forehead vein appears.

Kermit giggles to his chest, imagining hairs leaping and leaving the expanding bald strip down the middle of Rosenthal's scalp. Rosenthal blocks Kermit's vision. He throws his copy of *The Curious Incident of the Dog in the Night-Time* at Rosenthal.

"Don't call me that. The headmaster said to call me Kerr."

Rosenthal catches the book between his wrists and shakes his head. The sound of classmates snickering bursts then fades when Rosenthal turns and puffs his chest. Kermit looks out the window and focuses on the builder's movements outside, narrowing out all other sensory information. By the time Rosenthal's words sprinkle Kerr's cheekbones—he can only hear a drone. He turns to face Rosenthal and envisions the same construction worker placing obsidian bricks inside Rosenthal's pupils. Kermit wonders again, at what age did someone decide to become what they'd become? At 12 and three quarters, he's running low on time. Soon he'd pick subjects for high school. A pressure which delivered Kermit unrestricted access to incessant worry.

Why's life so structured? He ponders as Rosenthal slams his copy of the novel back onto his desk. Rosenthal resumes the class and forces Kermit to read the novel out loud. Kermit reads the text as you are now but the words were meaningless to him.

The events of this morning's break play in Kermit's mind while he's reading. Billy ran around the playground threatening to manually sting his fellow students with a dead wasp. Kermit was the only one who didn't run away. He looked into the cloud-packed sky and he put his arm the way people do for birds of prey to land on. Billy was so surprised that Kermit wasn't afraid that he threw the wasp into the sky. The girls screamed on its return to earth.

"Ey, did I tell you to stop reading?" Rosenthal says.

Kermit zones back in, with a shrug, "No, but I'm tired."

Rosenthal purses his lips, shows a glint of a smirk. He lets the tension simmer and Kermit reads before Rosenthal interrupts and asks his classmate Zoe to read instead.

◆

Big sigh. In what only felt like an extended blink, mashed between the ringing of the lunch bell and the smell of lasagne hanging in the halls, Kermit finds himself in detention. There are three other boys of similar age under Mrs Green's supervision. Kermit, Billy and the younger but taller and stronger Phillip.

"Kerr, laddy, here again?" Mrs Green says with disappointment. Mrs Green was sharp to never wear green, to challenge any budding amateur comedians into better material. She wore pink glasses and tights that confused the children into assuming she has more personality than she does.

For punishment, they're all writing lines on blank pieces of paper. Kermit writes and writes: *I must not disrupt the class by interrupting.* Over and over until the page fills and his hand aches. Mrs Green lets them go ten minutes early but as the children leave the youngest Phillip decides to lift a spare table over his head with one arm.

"I am Power Boy," Phillip says, the table swaying in the air before dropping to a thud. Everyone's eyebrows rise.

Mrs Green steps forward.

"Lift up Mrs Green please," Billy says to Phillip, starting to hop with excitement.

Phillip sizes her up. Mrs Green raises her voice and heels. "If you boys don't…"

The boys run out of the classroom and make their way to the temporary cafeteria. It's quiet apart from their stuttering giggles and the clinking of spoons in the distance. Billy plops coins in the vending machine. Kermit stops to watch what he picks and so does Phillip. *I guess this means we're a gang now*, Kermit thinks. They eat chocolate bars and fizzy drinks for lunch.

"Want anything extra?" Kermit says.

He kneels, angling his reach into the vending machine. He groans and pushes himself further, flicking some snacks on the bottom rows free. Billy and Phillip press their faces against the glass and cheer when snacks fall.

"For free!" Phillip says.

"Don't tell the whole world," Billy elbows Phillip.

The boys snatch the snacks and hide them in their bags, but Kermit's arm's still stuck. Kermit mellows his breathing and nudges his arm out, bit by bit, the metal rubbing on his arm and creating a redness.

"That looks like it hurts," Phillip says.

Wiggle, wiggle, slide and pull. Ouch. Kermit frees his throbbing arm.

"So cool, you'll give yourself a bruise doing that," Billy nudges his body into Kermit's. They giggle and push each other. Kermit looks at his red arm and wishes it to stop growing so he can keep stealing snacks.

Phillip and Billy try to do what Kermit did. Despite their groans of effort they're not even close. The bell rings and students rush to class. Phillip waves bye as he's in a class below, putting his whole arm and hip into a wave.

Rosenthal must be taking his boring pills because Kermit dozes through the maths lesson. The bell rings to end the day and the class cheer, followed by an ironic cheer by Rosenthal that turns authentic.

"Eiy, eiy, wait here Kerr. Let's have a word," Rosenthal went to get something. He's taking his time and Kermit looks at the builders continuing to work. The bell rang—don't the workers go home?

"Can I go? My dad's waiting," Kerr wiggles his body as if he needs to pee.

Rosenthal hurries his words, "Okay, forget it. I can't find the leaflet. Listen now, next week is important for you with the health and relationships class and I don't want you causing any trouble. It's school time and that means it's time to learn and mature."

Kermit nods slowly to show Rosenthal he's thinking.

The corridor held a sudden stillness as if a crying baby had just left it. There waiting, creaking a floorboard is Kermit's father Bruce. He jiggles coins and car keys in his pocket while allowing a smile to crimple his lip. Kermit throws his bag into his father's arms and struts to the car.

Dad smells like minty medicine again. Bruce plays with his phone before the screen timer locks him out. They set off, driving, listening to dad's CDs. The car has Bluetooth but Bruce's wife Tiffany won't let him use it because she believes it to be cancerous. Kermit has heard these songs over and urgh. At what age does one decide to stop enjoying new music, when does someone stop being open to new things? Kermit knew his dad was beyond that stage of life and like his songs is stuck on repeat. At least Kermit had already decided his fav music would forever be glitch-rap, it's the most popular genre played from phones in the toilets at school. Kermit turns to ask his dad at what age decisions need to be made but he's met by a wall of noise.

"Lalalalala," Bruce's shrill singing makes Kermit turn his ear against his shoulder.

The car stops before the golden arch of McDonald's. Kermit's head floats back on the headrest and his eyelids widen.

"What's going on? Mum banned this place," Kermit says.

"It's okay, I have a fake GPS app on my phone that says we're still at school, she won't know."

"Really?" Kermit drums his feet against the car mat.

They leave the car and McDonald's does to them what it does to most.

The exit doors burp open. They walk out rubbing their bloated bellies after a lethargic Happy Meal, the two toddle back to the car. Kermit's given the key and he gets in and as that song about fearing the reaper plays, he looks over his shoulders in case Mum's around.

What's Dad doing? Kermit leans forward to watch Bruce talking to that scruffy man in a sleeping bag outside. Bruce hands the man something shiny. Bruce gets in, his seatbelt clicks.

"What did you give that man?" Kermit says.

"Nothing."

It better have been nothing, Kermit thinks, *you shouldn't give money to homeless scum*. It only encourages begging. Kermit inherited these beliefs from his mother. Why was Dad being so carefree? If Mum found out about this she'd punish the both of them.

"These roads aren't the way home," Kermit says.

"The day has come. You promised not to tell Mum," Bruce says.

Kermit raises his chin until his lips squash together. Maybe Dad has cancer and doesn't care about the rules anymore, either that or, oh, that must be it—Mum must have a gig tonight.

They drive to Toy Paradise, another banned place. Kermit's father goes in alone and leaves obscured by a large box, his fingers gripping around the sides, only recognisable due to his navy chinos. Kermit kicks the glove box in excitement when he notices the 'Lego' logo.

Bruce drives back to school. He's regained enough screen time to delete the fake GPS app. Kermit isn't too aware of what's going on because he's watching the builders leave and get in their vans. Maybe he should become a construction worker? The car drives and reaches the familiar roads home.

They pull into the drive beside Mum's car, the exact same brand Toyota, model Yaris, and shade of navy as Dad's. Only the green pine tree air freshener, licence plate and tyre use separating them from being clones.

"You know the plan. We'll keep the box in the car until later. Don't tell Mum about the Lego, or food. You promised," Bruce says.

Kermit doesn't remember promising, but his relaxed posture shows that he doesn't mind.

Bruce owns a detached house in the city, which he inherited from his reclusive grandfather.

They walk inside to find Mum swirling around for a change, doing her make-up and trying on different outfits.

"Why are you late?" Tiffany says.

The two stop cold. Bruce looks at Kermit and says "We, uh…"
Bruce licks salt off his lip, "we had to talk to Rosenthal about
homework."

Tiffany grabs Bruce's phone and checks his GPS timeline. His
phone shows he was at school for a while. She studies Kermit's
blank expression. It passes the test, a tension releases from her
posture.

It's one of the rules that Kermit must go straight to his room
after school. The living room was for adults unless they were
having a prearranged event paid for by chore credits. A sign on
the fridge in Tiffany's handwriting reads: *Say hehe before you do a
chore, it'll make it less a bore.*

Tiffany points at the clock and Kermit sees that it's five. They
watch Kermit put away his jacket and shoes correctly before
grabbing his lunchbox to retire to his room for the night. His
door closes, the noise indicating a routine clicking into place.
Kermit kicks his bed, telling himself: *as soon as I'm a teenager I'm not
going to follow their rules. And! I'll get an iPhone to replace this baby junk
one.*

Bruce studies the painting of his hallway in his hallway. The
painting displays the hallway before Bruce inherited the house
from his grandfather. So meta, Bruce compares the hallway to the
painting. It's cleaner since Mum moved in after giving birth to
Kermit.

"Can you fetch me a cookie? I need it for inspiration," Tiffany
says, pinching Bruce's shoulder blade,

Bruce must be tired from work because he doesn't see this
ongoing prank coming… When he opens the snack cupboard an
assault of popcorn and packets fall on him. He fumbles like a
panicked goalkeeper.

"Bah-doiiiiiiiii," Tiffany shouts her prank catchphrase.

Bruce shields his ear before cleaning the mess. This prank is
one of Tiffany's tortures that she does. Sure this prank had its

drawbacks, always leaving things in the cupboard so they were primed to fall out—would occasionally backfire and Tiffany would suffer the indignity. Tiffany was the type of person ready to catch anything at any moment, she'd catch a cold on purpose to give her immune system conflict.

Tiffany always had a cruel side to her. After she fell pregnant and they got married it became more apparent. The years staggered by. Bruce's affair and lies only increased the intensity of her control. You'd assume Bruce would momenteer out of his mind when Tiffany treated him badly, but bizarrely he enjoyed it. It made him feel like he deserved it. He liked it in that messed-up way people are shy to explain.

"Got a gig tonight, outside the city. I text you this. Another lush mansion affair, pretentious. Good money but I'm tired of acting. The world doesn't understand my music so I have to pretend to be someone famous," Tiffany says.

Bruce stares at his wedding ring, a silver band with a 'T' engraved. He tries to recall at least one of their vows from thirteen years ago but those now feel untranslatable.

"This house… clean it will you. Before I leave, or else," Tiffany says.

Kermit's mother is part of a celebrity lookalike agency. Publicly she told people her career was making soundtracks for video games but her side hustle brought in way more than the main. Amy Winehouse was the celebrity she dressed and impersonated. Tiffany had a similar bone structure and with the hair, dresses and temporary tattoos added—you wouldn't be able to spot a difference as you lifted a canapé from her silver tray.

While scrubbing the hallway, Kermit's father let out a big breath when he heard the door click and Tiffany's engine fade away. He rushes to the window to make sure, away and back again.

They met as most did in the 90s, at a rave. Tiffany began hitting Bruce and enforcing strict rules in their home about five years ago when she caught Bruce having a fling with Cindy Cummings, an infamous voice-over artist.

"Not the hands or face," he'd appeal to her. Regardless, in front of the television cameras, under his clothes, Bruce would translate the spoken word into sign language with scratches, bruises and cuts on his body. Bruce's father was deaf, so it was second nature to him to sign. The sign language interpreting came because he was smooth at signing yet easy on the eye. He held a reliable yet emotionless face, ideal for the job.

Despite her tight control, Bruce is currently having a secret affair with young Melanie, a new make-up artist at work. He knows he should leave Tiffany for her but their affair is still developing and Melanie doesn't want to become a stepmother at 26.

Bruce goes out to the car and takes the Lego box to Kermit's room. This activity wouldn't be allowed by Tiffany but this was their secret. Kermit would rip up the boxes and hide them in his school folders while Dad would hide their Lego creations in the shed.

Kermit and Bruce have so much fun playing Lego that Bruce accidentally brings up the momenteering menu and even sillier he focuses to confirm. Oops, he zones out of his consciousness. His vision folds into darkness. He becomes a floating mind in an empty colourless space. Time moves differently, twenty seconds here is relative to an hour. He worries in case he doesn't return to his body before Tiffany gets home. She can't know he has momenteering. It's been two years since he got the implant, a referral from his television executive friend. The technology keeps improving, imagine what he could avoid living in the future.

Bruce blinks back into his body. He checks his watch and rushes into action, hiding things. He runs to the living room, fluffing the cushions to pretend he's been there all night. He goes back to Kermit's room and taps his nose, a signal of keeping this secret and Kermit copies him. It was rare they were connecting. Bruce often momenteered out of saying goodnight to Kermit because he resents his son for holding him back from being with Melanie. Kermit was slowly turning into a teenager, turning into a stranger.

The return of Tiffany's car is signalled by headlights screaming through the front window. Bruce's heart sinks and relocates. Tiffany enters, her hair in a net but still looking partly Amy Winehouse. She calls Kermit out of his room and gets him to brush his teeth before giving him a head kiss goodnight.

Ten minutes later, Bruce could feel a monster growing in the silence and her firm movements of kitchen items. Tiffany has a criminal record for embezzling funds from various fake online charities. A brush with the law that made her believe she knew when people were lying.

"Come here," Tiffany says.

Bruce tiptoes into the kitchen where he's met with a nasty gaze that drifts between him and the floor. Tiffany's Carolina Reaper stare is so intense that it points.

"Did you clean?"

Bruce looks into her ablaze eyes and lies, "Yes."

Tiffany's face scrunches. Bruce could feel his heart return and xylophone mallets tap on his ribcage, playing a symphony of anxiety. It's been a while since he'd lied to her face and it wasn't about his secret affair. He'd only cleaned the hall, but Lego was so fun. That was their yearly chance to bond, maybe their last with Kermit's oncoming hormones.

Tiffany bends and studies the floor. A crumb roars. Bruce could see it from above. It was only a matter of time until Tiffany would. Bruce nudges the toaster to divert her attention but Tiffany doesn't react.

"It's so clean you could eat off it honey," Bruce's attempt of a cuddle is deflected off the fridge. The magnet from their package trip to Benidorm falls but doesn't break.

Tiffany's hands meet her hips, "Well, why don't you?"

"What?" Bruce laughs but tries to stop.

Tiffany takes a can of spaghetti hoops from the cupboard, cracks open the tin and pours them onto the floor. She adjusts the cupboard so a can would fall out next time. Bruce sees this but knows he'll forget and it'll fall on him at some point. It always does. Tiffany turns to confront her husband.

"Well, go on. Eat. If it's as clean as you say it is."

Bruce gulps. Tiffany grabs him by the neck and pushes his face to the floor. He tells himself this is normal, hoping Kermit couldn't hear the noise of his slurping from upstairs. Each slurp sounds pathetic yet necessary. He gobbles the pasta up but leaves a few hidden in his mouth. The spaghetti hoops in Bruce's mouth feel heavier, stronger than the wedding ring on his finger.

Tiffany crosses her arms and leans back, "Honey, go get a mop and clean the mess you've made."

Bruce nods, reminiscent of a bad dog. Tiffany turns off the light and leaves him with the moonlight coming through the kitchen window. It's weird because the spaghetti hoops in his mouth feel heavy and when he spits them into the sink he blinks rapidly and his eyes get wet at how soft they are.

Oops. Bruce blinks up the momenteering menu again. Careful, he holds onto the sink. He looks to the side to avoid focusing on the confirmation button and after four seconds the menu disappears.

Twelve: Lifestyles of the Suspended & Avoided

Still 4397 moments

My two-week suspension is going well apart from my recurring nightmares where I'm trapped and powerless. It sounds oxymoronic but now that I'm not working 11 am to at least seven moments. I seem to have less time to myself. Truth is I'm wasting more. I'm seeing Donna frequently. I've told her I'm taking time off. I'm avoiding the man from my building well. My counter displays that it's been nine days since our last encounter.

Donna and I have been meeting at a new Mexican fast-food place twice a week. She loves the black bean burritos. Tonight before we meet there I try to convince her to come to my side of the city instead. She's only come to my place a handful of times.

Predictable. She texts back that her bed is better and my place is unclean. I send her photographic evidence proving otherwise: pointing inside the sparkling dishwasher, reclining on the massaging armchair, sitting on the satin bed sheets, rubbing the golden faucets/taps, displaying my neat vinyl collection, laying over the yoga ball in my corner gym before falling to the floor with my tongue on the rustic oak flooring to display the cleanliness. Much effort goes into these selfies, with the timer, my poses and curated moronic expressions but Donna replies with ambiguously faced emojis I didn't know were available and sends: `lol, meet usual place, eight.`

It's nice to be seeing Donna more but with replies like that I can't help but drive over slower. After the Mexican food and after I drop the fact she won't come back to mine, we go back to her cleaner place to make love. Well, something close to that. It's as if our bodies do it without our minds.

"Where did you learn that new move? Have you been practising?" Donna says.

My pulse increases. Oops, I used that move, the experimental one I tried on Catherine. Donna can't know that I make love to other ladies using other men's bodies.

"The hip move? Ooo, I read an article online," I speak at the speed of a highly-caffeinated amateur voice actor.

Donna pulls the bedding over her, "From what sites? You will tell me if you see others."

My gaze focuses on Donna's bedroom, painted beige to appear sleek but it's depressing. The rug she has blends in with the carpet. All the same beige with brief flashes of pyrite silver. It's in a part of the city that her dad chose for her, where people don't feel the need to stand out.

A strange silence sweeps in and freezes the moment. Stuck like I'm an animal facing its prey. My posture stiffens at how long this silence is stretching. Is our sporadic relationship becoming deeper than I thought? The accumulation of no reply piles a weight of firm expectation, but I resist and remain mute. Pressure makes my eyebrows fall. The air feels like it contains less oxygen. The silence gains power and for a brief lull, it doesn't feel like Donna and I have met—a glimpse at our connection's original factory settings. I stare at the bedside digital clock, waiting for a number to change. It does and does again. The waves of silence sweep underneath our limbs on the mattress, amplifying any movement we make. A faint hum of a refrigerator plays from downstairs. Donna's imagination must've taken her away too because in my peripheral vision she's staring at the ceiling while her phone bathes in her palm. I think of our relationship, trying to picture it as an object. I see an inflatable bouncy castle with lots of children playing, but if you zoom in, you'll see the children are wearing heavy boots. The silence has gone on for so long that I can't help but tell myself, this must be a record.

It must be hard for Donna to connect after her ex-girlfriend's death. We never talk about it. She made me promise to never ask. Donna's smart lamps hit their schedule at midnight and dim pupil-enlarging low. Silence is fractured when Donna yawns. The yawn tickles my neck with a slight heat. Triggering my memory.

I'm in my childhood bedroom, a blanket of smoke above and a carpet of ash below. Burning hot, too hot to remain motionless. My legs are shorter, I run through the licks from flames and dodge falling clunks of wood. Don't inhale, it hurts. Too loud for my little ears. I must be around Kermit's age. I shield my eyes and keep my head down. The front door's open. I escape alongside clouds of smoke. I gasp and gasp to the sky. My lungs heavy. A weight drags my chest then legs to the pavement. I cough, pant and spit. Through bleary eyes. I spot Dad grasping my big brother to his side. This image has a glowing filter on it. I wipe my eyes to focus on his new lady pulling up in her car, her mouth open as flames shine on its windows.

The sandy bearded fireman beside our dad pushes him: "I thought you said no one else was in there!"

Dad slaps his forehead, his drunk legs are unmasked to the whole town. "I, I, thought he was at his mother's."

After the house burnt, I moved in with my aunt while my brother moved in with Dad and his new lady. I wish we could have lived with Mum/Mom but she had been taken into the asylum a few months before.

The memory is approaching twenty years old and there's inconsistencies. Like was my brother there? Did my imagination make the fireman's beard sandy? I worry because I fear my memories of that night with Kermit may soon be watermarked with doubt. What if I lose my sanity like our mother?

Donna sneezes and I'm goosebump jump-scared back to the present millisecond. There's nothing more present than the present yet we haven't spoken. In the long run, it's a good thing. Keeping Donna at a distance will protect me in my job. Should I speak or is silence too golden? Our bodies move away from each other. Nothing is said. We roll back into the rhythms of our seriously casual relationship. Donna pulls the bedding over her. My mouth opens. I almost say goodnight but there's something blocking me. I roll over and we sleep back to back.

Next morning, Donna insists I leave early with her because she doesn't trust me with her key.

"My place doesn't have a key," I say.

Donna dismisses my fingerprint door entry with a brief laugh.

We drive and I drop Donna at Zeouw.

"You seem sad lately," Donna drops this bombshell closing the car door. Typical Donna, leaving statements behind as she leaves.

My mind and body must remain busy or I'll worry about the Kermit situation. I don't know what time it is when I get home. Not knowing the time is freeing, disconnecting you from reality.

When I return to my building, shit, not again. He's here. The man I like to avoid. Let's call him Gulliver. What's he doing awake? It's rare to see him this early. My feet squeak as I rush to the chaise lounge. I snatch a magazine and hide my face with it. My heart rate reminds me how high it can go, how petty and intense my avoiding has become. Ten days, down the drain, if he spots me. I imagine my blood sliding through my body, whizzing around the veins. My posture squirms and I hide under the magazine. I hear Gulliver yawn. I don't know how I know it's his yawn but I do. His shadow hovers underneath the bottom of the magazine. My usual existential question of what I'm doing with my life comes. Avoiding him is so petty, so pointless, but I need it. Faint footsteps arrive, I can hide but can't run. The main door opens and street noises filter inside. I try to peek above the magazine but can't. I hear the concierge mumble. The door clicks. Silence. I pop my brow to see, oh no. The man I like to avoid is still here, gesticulating to the concierge.

He must've seen me. Any true friend would notice. To be fair I'm not wearing my usual suit. The lift/elevator dings and loud voices come out. Can't see who, can't expose myself. I lift the magazine and peek at Gulliver's feet. He's wearing odd socks. A yellow Tuesday sock and a red Sunday sock. It's Friday. Odd socks on incorrect days, he's offensive to all structures.

"Righty-well, I must go on a voyage. The library awaits my presence," he says to the concierge.

The sounds of Gulliver leaving are clunky and beautiful. Shadows slide away. Lines of sunshine lighten the floor. I sit for a moment to make sure he's not coming back. A gush of relief floods my body and lifts me to my feet. Walking to the elevator/lift I notice a few integral members from this building's book club Gwen and her cardigan sidekick Kay. They're both ladies in their sixties that don't appreciate movie adaptations after the eighties.

If you've read this far and haven't momenteered to this point: you're not going to relate to me... and if relating leads to liking, you won't like me either. Truth is, I got uninvited then formally banned from my building's book club because they tricked me into admitting that I don't read books. I didn't. I only watched the movie versions, I got away with this approach for a year and a quarter. It wasn't until they read books that didn't have movie versions that I was rumbled. Psychoanalytically, I guess I joined because of loneliness and lonely people do weird things.

So obvious. Gwen and Kay simultaneously shift their necks away as they pass me in the foyer. Both their swirly silver hairstyles seem to growl from behind their ears. Going up the steps, the link hits me... not only are Gulliver and I being avoided, but we're both banned from literature, he from his library for stealing the pens and I from my old book club. We have—we have something in common.

A few days pass without going outside, automatic blinds down and food delivery packaging piling up. Donna has reverted back to her consistently inconsistent self. An idea develops to try and find another momenteer. But how? Maybe if I could find one we could exchange details and save Kermit. I need to hang around work and find one. What do momenteers look like? Do we all wear turtlenecks? Wait, have you been thinking this too... what if Gulliver's a momenteer? Or used to be. Crazier things have happened and he does live in my building.

Procrastination strikes thinking how Pritek's control will make it impossible to find another momenteer. It takes me another few days to get in my car and drive to work. I'll hang outside the tower, to see if anyone could be a momenteer. Stupidly I don't drive there. I don't know what I'm doing but I drive out of the city and towards my brother's. It's strange how I remember these roads.

The town's changed. Trees are replaced by buildings. My fav park has been replaced by a bunch of homes. Who knows where I end up. With my stupid head pressing against the steering wheel, I ask myself the question out loud: what am I doing here? Do I want to see Emma? Are they raising her well? Is this Sigmund Freud nonsense about how Emma's the daughter I wasn't able to have? I'd like to see how my ex looks. My skin feels crawled on. My chest tightens. I must leave.

This is creepy of me. I drive around the town but get lost. Has this street always been here? We've lived here since we were kids but my brother didn't leave this town.

Wait, this isn't the same town. Did they change the signs? An assortment of déjà vu, future visions and corrupted memories swirling in my head. I hop out to find a proper sign or ask someone which town this is—maybe my GPS is lagged. I walk towards a fountain. My walk slows when I see skaters loitering. *No Komo, not all skaters are rude.* I urge my legs to move. Some of the skaters look like they could kill me. I show my hands to appear non-threatening, something I've seen in a documentary, or maybe I read this in a magazine in my building's foyer.

"Hey, can you tell me the name of this town?" I say towards a bunch of them.

The group of early 20s and late teenage skaters must be lagging too because they don't laugh until I turn halfway around.

"What'chu lost tubby legs? Why don't you get lost if you are lost," an official spokesperson from the skaters with eyebrow slits shouts.

The shout daggers my ribs and spins me away. I rub my legs, they're not tubby. My shoulders sink with every step. Why are they acting the same way as the skaters outside Pritek but with worse insults? Not worth the confrontation. I return to my car and mutter in the rear-view:

"What do they mean? Get more lost than I already am? If one is already lost and they are told to get lost, must they get further lost, or become so lost that they find themselves?"

It's too late for clarification because I'm on the final long road to the city when I think of how I should've replied. I need to research if childhood trauma stunts psychological development. Because I should be more responsible and less petty than I am. I park and get out. I take off my jacket and shake the skaters' giggles off my clothes.

It's around eight and inside, the concierge is smiling and looking at the elevator/lift. They're so calm it's infectious. I walk up, unaware.

"What's going on?" I say.

The concierge shuffles, "Sorry sir, we are testing something."

The lift/elevator dings open and there's a blue package laying inside. Weird. The doors are shutting but the concierge runs over and stops them from closing. They lift the package. With a swirl of their white gloves, the concierge shows me inside.

"No, it's okay. What's going on?" I say.

Shame brightens the concierge's eyes. "Sir, you will want to get home now."

A crashing of footsteps approaches. Staring at the steps, an out-of-breath person yelps "Did I make it?"

"No Mister, sir," The concierge says to the voice descending the stairs.

And shit. There he is, the man I avoid. Turns out he wanted to test if he could run down the steps faster than the elevator/lift if it had to stop on every one of the six floors.

He smiles at me and I dunno how but the package ends up in my hands. It's wet. Why's it wet? My gaze slips and I read the name, stopping myself after the first. My oesophagus croaks. His name's Gulliver. The man I like to avoid. Donna must cut his hair.

Gulliver gives me a friendly tap on the shoulder. It's depressing to know his name for sure. I was already calling him Gulliver but I was hoping I was wrong. Now that I know his name it brings us closer.

Interacting with him is a blur because my social anxiety can't record what's happening. Instead, it's screaming at me to evacuate. I should ask him if he knows my name, maybe he thinks my name is: Well-Look-Who-It-Isn't. He takes the package from me with peaceful movements.

"Out the blue, but have you been to Flower Cave? It's a new Thai restaurant. I'm an investor," Gulliver says.

I don't know how to say no so I tell him I'll go. Urgh, I hate recommendations, it's just another task for you to do and you have to do said thing and report back to whoever recommended it. It's homework in disguise. I never recommend anyone anything unless they ask. It's one of the politest things you can do.

We wave to each other but he does a fancy hand movement in his. Gulliver walks outside to conduct other mindless experiments I assume.

At night, I watch episodes of *How It's Made* on YouTube—I've watched a few with Kermit and enjoyed them. Gulliver's a person you'd expect to wear odd days-of-the-week socks and have a wet package. As the credits roll on another episode, I wonder how Gulliver was made. How does someone become strange and carefree like him? It's fascinating. You know they say we evolved from fish. Well, maybe Gulliver evolved from rogue gangs of tumbleweeds.

Afternoons come and go, leaving echoes of time to barely remember. I'm thinking nonsense bad-poetic lines like this to stop me worrying about Kermit. Maybe I got it wrong? I didn't see anything happen. Shit, listen to me. Pritek's giving me trust issues with my memory. If I get this wrong I could end up worse than my mother, trying to convince staff that I'm sane—so much that I actually go insane.

The night before I return to work, Donna and I meet for food with her platonic friend Ruben. Ruben's a banker, handsome and modelesque. He has a crew cut and wears a white crew neck. In a Lebanese restaurant, Donna draws a portrait of me on a napkin. In order for us to be able to order food, we must stop laughing at how accurate Donna's drawing is. Ruben snaps a picture of it next to me. The waiter snorts when we show it to him. While Donna's ordering the okra, Ruben notices she has a gem on her teeth, Ruben says tooth gems are a "poor investment" because Donna doesn't smile with her teeth.

"I like the gem but how did you draw me so well?" I say.

The waiter leaves. Donna leans back, revealing her tattoo of an empty squiggly picture frame on her outer forearm, "Don't be silly."

"Hm, to a basic level, art can be taught," Ruben says, not one of his gelled hairs moving as he shakes his head.

An idea arrives to paint a portrait of Kermit's father. I don't know how, but it might help. Turns out I'm entirely silly because right there on my phone I find and book myself into a local art class without asking Pritek's permission like I should.

Donna keeps smiling toward me, that way proud parents do, "When does the class begin?"

"Just under two weeks. I have... to, never mind. I'll go,"

"You better go, you need friends," Donna says.

I turn to Ruben, maybe he could be my friend but Ruben's already staring out the window, beyond his reflection.

Thirteen: Back to Work

Still 4397 moments

903 moments left. To my surprise, the supervisors aren't weird when I return. It's almost as if nothing happened. Well, apart from the new shock sensors around the power cylinder. Back at my station, it barely feels like I've been away as I leave my body. The first moment back reminds me of how this job can be. I'm waiting outside an ice cream place and I'm blinked out holding a cone without getting a taste.

I take a walk on the treadmill before blinking into another moment.

The aim says: *Deal wit...*

It stinks. Can't escape. Trapped inside an elevator/lift with a horrendous fart. Pew, it's sewage bad, stanky like a sewer of rotten eggs. Ew, I miss my suspension. There are seven adults here, most of us wearing summer hats including myself. We all look like strangers to one another. Elbows rubbing as we huddle into a corner opposite the stench.

A bald mole-looking person points towards me. "Whoever smelt it, dealt it," they say.

People scurry away from me and into the fart's previous location. Did the fart move? Through faded-skills I know this flatulence isn't my doing. Breathing through my mouth makes my words glue around my throat. Momenteering feels more like acting than ever.

"By time... we down, we... find, who did it," I manage to say while lifting my leg.

My eyelids close and I walk, reaching to the corner. Someone slaps my hand, my eyes open and sharp necks and even sharper faces turn to face me, their hands moving as improvised fans before their noses.

One lady wearing a panama hat scorns "We're actually going up,"

Faded-skills kick in and repeat that this isn't my doing. My shoulders fidget at this injustice. The floor indicator number rises. Someone presses the next number and we stop on floor 22. There's a pause where time is suspended before the doors belch open. Everyone but me rushes out gasping and coughing. I'm left alone. It's sad because I know it wasn't my fart. The bald mole-looking person covers their face, shielding a flicker of a grin. The door closes, trapping me inside. Shame makes my ears hot but it's okay. Work's work as they say. The lift/elevator descends again but once I reach the 12th floor and another person enters, the fart is fading. They look at me but I don't look at them. I don't move until I'm blinked out. Once a fart has left someone's body does that mean a loss of ownership? At what stage does it become public property?

After a couple shifts, it's like I was never suspended. They tell me that Kermit moments are blocked from my task list. I have more moments with Catherine, this one isn't making love. I haven't seen her for three weeks and she has a shorter hairstyle that frames her face. I'm on a date with her and it's fun. I don't know why this client is cheating on Catherine. She's so lovely but I guess this client wouldn't agree. I want to tell her I'm cheating but know I can't or I'll be reported, unless I do it in a way that's too smart for me to think of.

Routine's on a comeback tour in my life because I slip into it. Days pass and moments inside other consciousnesses make me less myself, which I guess is good. Even the uncomfortable and difficult moments don't seem to drag as much as they did.

An unspoken yet welcome ceasefire has arrived between the skaters and I. Guess we're bored of one another. Without this hostility, when I'm outside the fountain, I take time to observe people that could possibly be momenteers. Studying their walks, their faces, their attire. Here's a candidate, a dainty loner lady with a ginger ponytail. The ponytail is loose, hanging over the back of a navy trench coat. I remind myself not to follow her but my legs won't listen. Remaining at an unsuspicious distance, the gap enlarges and I lose track. Her navy trench coat makes me suspect she's a momenteer. Who wears a trench coat unless they're hiding something? Her eyes remind me of used sponges—as if she's spent all day being different people.

Tonight, I'm waiting outside Donna's for an hour. Why isn't she replying to calls, door buzzes, texts, or sad selfies showing me outside? I check the texts. Yes, we're supposed to meet tonight. I return home and finally receive a text telling me she meant to meet next week, not tonight. Urgh.

Next morning at work, I'm in an interesting job. I momenteer as a live sports presenter that's introducing this year's 2022 WPA quarter-final 9-ball pool championships. The presenter has a toothpick, it's weird to present with one but it makes me feel cool. I know nothing about sports and the F.s are limited too. Still, it's fun. I enjoy presenting. Talking to the guests. I must be loving it because I'm gesticulating and laughing at jokes that are barely funny.

The crew in my earpiece keep saying complimentary things. There's a ring of achievement cast over their mics as we close the broadcast. I walk over to shake hands with one of the pundits but trip on a cable and the cameraman falls with me.

"Cut to break, cut, now, cut," the people in my earpiece shout.

Shit, I was doing so well but I'm blinked out. My lying-on-the-floor-grimace transfers between the host's face to mine.

At home, I try to find the coverage but it's not available in my region, online or cable/satellite. Aw, I was almost on television, being someone else, that would've been so interesting to see. I look constipated drumming in YouTube clips of Green Bread's concerts. I wonder how good I was at acting as the client. I guess I miss the cameras. I almost research who the host I momenteered for is, but I remember Pritek might ask me about this irregular activity when they see my internet history.

At night, I've stopped watching *How It's Made* episodes because it makes me sulk, frustrated that I can't save Kermit. Confused because as the shifts slither by, the more my dreams detach me from what happened, from my interpretation. At least I've got my art class on Friday. Pritek approved it after I submitted the request through my station and provided links. I've booked the time off for the next six weeks on my schedule.

At work again, a Monday to Friday schedule, I'm blinked into a moment, but I don't know what to do because the aims and details are distorted. I assess the situation and see I'm at a boardroom meeting of sorts. I simply do nothing but nod my head when I sense I should. Something about profits, I nod. It's relieving when I'm blinked out, I raise my arms like a champion. Not sure what of, because in my life I don't know what to do either. Why were my aims corrupted? Are Pritek updating their systems? My finger hovers over the call button again but I decide not to press. It won't go anywhere we haven't already been, remember my quote from before? Better to save energy and do nothing. After my shift, I loiter to search for other momenteers. No candidates. Donna texts that she wants to give me a haircut, well an emoji of scissors with a question mark. The last time she cut my hair, it resembled the mesh head of a dynamic microphone so I'm in no rush.

I might be avoiding Donna because she stood me up. With all this avoiding I'm doing I have no time for people in my life. It makes me nervous about my art class. I'm not used to meeting new people as myself. Maybe I'll find some new people to avoid? Most jobs at work involve meeting people, but it's different as Komo. We all learn avoiding skills as children from playing hide and seek. If only I could join a club for people that like to avoid others. I guess they don't exist because the members will inevitably avoid each other.

A few days after many funerals and waiting rooms, Gulliver catches me on my way to my first art class. He notices the brushes and paint tubes. After I tell him I must rush and no I haven't been to his Flower Cave restaurant yet. Gulliver looks deflated like a birthday balloon four weeks later. If feelings could be bottled and sold, this letting-people-down one would not be a bestseller.

"You're always in a hurry," Gulliver says, helping me catch a canvas I'm in the middle of dropping.

At that moment, our eyes connect and possibly more.

"Do you know my name? I know yours is Gulliver. I'm not sure If I ever told you mine," I say.

"Yes, I know yours," he says.

In the lull when he should say my name, he doesn't. Instead, the moment stretches and unsettles our postures. We nod backwards like we're flicking something off our scalps. We position our bodies to separate.

Alert, alert, social anxiety alert.

My feet leave. I turn back and he's waving. He doesn't know my name, the fraud. I wonder why Gulliver likes talking to me.

93

Our interactions will not nourish him. Although as my mother said when she accused one of her carers of stealing her bellybutton: "We'll never understand why people like things."

Art class is okay, a big cool room with fifteen of us and fourteen chairs. It's a 20-minute drive on the other side of Pritek but easy to find. I don't get to speak properly to anyone, mostly due to us all being shy or working. Our teacher hovers around or sits on the desk. She's a bright old lady with coffee brown hair cut sharp to the shoulder. Named Miss T and aptly dresses misty like she sells crystals and salt lamps when she's not here. Maybe she'd know about the crystals at work? In HB pencil I sketch faces. The teacher helps me see what I'm doing wrong in shaping faces and how I can improve by drawing the eyes more oval. Classic teacher. Next week we paint.

Weekend off, I'm still avoiding a haircut but Donna isn't texting so maybe she's avoiding me too. Gulliver isn't around which is nice but also worries me when he might appear.

Monday, a usual shift at work. I'm drained from looking after screaming children, breaking up with someone and complaining about poor service at a hotel. I blink into another moment.

Oh my. Oh. My. My oh.

For real? Is it? My gaze twirls to see the same walls. I turn to find posters of flamingos and look who's sitting there on the floor before his bed. Kermit.

He's talking about something but I'm not able to listen. I over inhale and cough. Aren't these moments blocked? My toes wiggle, my calves hop. I clench a pillow and blink rapidly at it with wide eyes.

"Dad?" Kermit says.

"Ah-diib-bi-dib," I make noises. I move my arm then it freezes.

I study his father's pristine hands and fingers. I shiver and leap to my feet. It's like being someone you thought was dead. My eyes fly around his bedroom fueled by a fluttering heartbeat, trying to copy and paste all the details to my memory. His bedside table, the camouflage green curtains, three flamingo posters and his cloud print sheets.

"Am I dreaming?" I say to him via the wall I'm facing.

Kermit laughs, the noise reattaching me to the present moment.

At the window, looking out, trying to see where I am in the world. It's been raining here. No, don't. Remember not to get kicked out. Don't alert Pritek. Returning to the bed, hobbling as if I've just finished a marathon, I sit on my hands. *Okay Komo, calm. Don't move. You've forgotten what the aim said.*

"I'm okay," I say, even though no one asked.

How did this happen? Can Pritek block moments? I don't ever momenteer out of my gender, sexuality or with VIP clients so they must have some control. My smooth hands creep under the father's Oxford shirt and I nurse the heartbeat until it calms. Kermit scratches his hair and approaches. I shift back.

He crosses his arms, "I don't know. How do people become the way they look? Do they decide or is it nature? Like why does Rosenthal look the way he does? Do teachers decide on a style at a meeting?"

It's nice to talk to Kermit again. We discuss aesthetics. Nature vs nurture. He's a bright kid. The interaction's fluid. I check for the sedatives or any bruising but neither are there.

Kermit makes a joke about boring teachers all having beards and a familiar haze drifts into my vision and I'm blinked out.

Back to my body, I caress the hair above my lip expecting a supervisor to come. I stare at the door until it loses focus then meaning. Nothing. No one comes. On break, I loiter in the kitchen and find a pack of toothpicks. I flick one and catch it between my lips. You know what, I might be able to save this kid after all.

Fourteen: Imprint

4464 moments

Nine days pass with a few simple moments with Kermit. Still Pritek hasn't noticed. Still I'm clueless where he lives. My art's improving and a few people in class are talking to me. A couple in their mid-fifties that claim they recently got divorced make the jokes, Tommy and Ender. I've started using a toothpick when I'm momenteering, it gives a better indication than the headset does between when I'm me and when I'm someone else.

Yesterday, Pritek shut early because of a glitch. I'd blink into a consciousness but it would only last five seconds. It must be fixed because today I blink into a consciousness with spotlights and a full audience's eyes on me. My own nerves mix with the client's. I'm momenteering for an actor on stage in a whole stage production of *Othello*. Blinking into moments where you have to respond quickly are the most perplexing. I act badly as someone already acting badly. I try to use my skills but I forget key lines. The boos are acidic and directed my way. The curtain closes and the rest of the cast walk away from me. The moment ends with me sitting ashamed in the dressing room closet. I blink out remaining sat at my station before blinking into another moment where I'm also sitting.

The sound of scissors snipping, dryers blowing and a familiar voice drifts through sprays. I turn away then back at the mirror I'm facing. Am I a raunchy book-cover model? It can't be—can it? I puff these cheeks and tilt the head. Am I… this face's too familiar. Am I momenteering as Ruben?

My question is confirmed when Donna appears in the mirror. I squeeze the eyes shut hoping it'll change when I open them. An anchor falls and drags me into waves of sea sickness. My mouth feels like it's in my stomach. Is this how strokes feel? What. The. Fuck.

I'd never imagine momenteering for someone I know. Everything is happening too close to the bone. It's Donna, she's behind, speaking about some loser. The shock is making the veins in Ruben's neck stick out. Wouldn't have guessed Ruben had momenteering. Initially, I'm proud to have such handsome cheekbones but the more Donna sprays and snips, the more my denial has to admit Donna's sharp tongue is speaking about me. Not me Ruben, but me—me Komo. I avoid the mirror as much as I can so I'm not blinked out.

"It's like Komo doesn't know how to love..." Donna sweeps Ruben's shoulders.

I raise his eyebrows and grumble. "Yeah, he's nice but, I mean... weird guy," I gossip about myself from the lips of another.

Donna won't stop talking behind my back. (And physically behind Ruben's).

"Yuh, hun. I think he has problems with his brother but I wanna find someone that can connect deeper. Every sec, we're getting old and ugly, aren't we?"

If only I could remind Donna of her inconsistencies in our relationship. I go quiet. My performance levels at an all-time stall.

This is an odd moment to endure. I force smiles and imagine talking to Pritek's shrink bot. Squinting at the inverted clock in the mirror, I wish the moment to end but it doesn't. I have to go through the whole process of leaving the salon. Donna gives me a hug, a tighter one than I'm used to.

"You like the cut?" Donna says, tilting a mirror around my head.

It's cool, why can't she cut mine like this? So weird to be talking to her as Ruben with his gooey voice. Doesn't feel real. After I grab Ruben's bag and step outside, the doorbell jingles and his eyes get heavy. I'm blinked out. Ouch. Thinking hurts, physically. Sharp throbs brew a headache and I have to undock.

At least I know Donna wants commitment. A toothpick twists between my lips, then two of them. I spit them out, lay my back on the floor and close my eyes. I need advice so I struggle to my feet and call for a supervisor. They take a while to arrive. They connect me to their online psychiatrist. Not this janky chatbot again.

I try to go to a numb place in my mind. The supervisor doesn't leave when our chat begins, so I have to be careful about what I type. Don't want to let Pritek know I'm still having moments with Kermit. The shrink says my body's fine, just in shock. Although it's incredibly rare, sometimes being involved indirectly in your work happens because they can't control the location of the client, only the language that's being used.

"Isn't it great, you now know what it's like to be your friend whilst also gaining some inside information that could aid your love life." The shrink bot frames things to make it seem like I'm lucky to have this experience.

The supervisor pulls my contract up on their tablet. I go to the treadmill and as I walk they remind me where I've agreed not to confront anyone outside the office about them having momenteering. Everyone talks about others behind their backs, but hearing it in this way spooked me like nothing else. I'm given a three-day mental-processing break.

Arriving back at the same time, Gulliver catches me in the foyer, breaking a five-day streak.

"Why do we look like what we look like?" I say, trying to collect theories for when I next see Kermit.

As he talks, I blur out. My focus diverts to his shadow cast by the foyer's spotlights. He steps to his side saying something with his hands and I watch it happen in the shadow. I must ask other questions because our conversation continues.

"Genetics are limited or whatever. If you're not a model, you're a freak. Get this, most people don't know this but models are in fact freaks too, they're a minority. Yet, calculate the most average looks of humanity and you will find something close to a model's appearance. Humans are attracted to this optimum averageness because deep down we're scared to get freaky with freaks," Gulliver says.

Gulliver knows his shit about nothing. Together, we step into the lift/elevator. He's wearing a puffy waistcoat with baggy hippie *pantalons*. Gulliver's unexpected giggles at pressing the buttons may reveal he's stoned but for once my toes are pointing towards him and not away.

On our way up, I regurgitate a jumbled rant telling Gulliver that I try not to get lost in aesthetics.

"You got a lover?" Gulliver says.

"Something like that. We're not too serious."

I'm busy thinking of the aesthetics of Donna's gallop that I don't notice him following.

"I try to only use the way things look to keep me out of danger. Isn't attraction already predetermined by evolution?" I say more misguided pseudo-intellectual nonsense while pressing my fingerprint against my lock.

Oops. No way. Is he—how did this happen? Gulliver squeezes in my home. The first time he's been here. My lazy attempt to close the door wasn't assertive. An invasion! He's greased inside and now I'm staring at the lock from inside while feeling his smile weighing on my back. When I turn, I wish Gulliver's smile to be so bright that I faint.

It isn't. Gulliver turns and skips to the sofa. I look out the living room window, hoping to see an incoming asteroid.

"You've got a balcony," He says, flipping off his shoes. There's a musty whiff of burnt wood and baby powder. He instantly belongs here more than the two years it took me. Gulliver's a person that owns space wherever he goes.

"So young squire, hypothetically, how can a person withhold attraction to aesthetics? Isn't aesthetics a fancy word for looks?" Gulliver sits on my sofa.

I tell Gulliver about this job I had at work, except I reframe it to be an old relative and not a client. The client was helping their boss who had a heart attack. As we waited on the paramedics, the boss said to me: "Do most people stand at standing ovations because others are standing or do they truly believe it was remarkable?"

I'd been thinking about this and aesthetics all day. Earlier, as I was the client looking into their boss's eyes with the oxygen mask around their mouth, we caught another's eyeline and I felt a strong message. I'm not sure what it was but I think it could be: Do things for how they make you feel, not for how they make you look.

"Aesthetics have only done one thing, formed and modified over time, wait, is that two things?" I say then mumble a confused rant. I point to my fireplace. There's a fake wooden log that's plastic and has nothing to do with the heating. It's decoration, it's to make you feel warmer. It's a lie, an aesthetic lie.

Silence vacuums the room. I stretch my arms and yawn so he'll get the message to leave. I turn, aw no. Wait, is he... he can't be. Gulliver's head is sunk and his eyelids are shut. Is he sleeping on my sofa? The same u-shaped premium sofa I had shipped in from over five thousand miles away. I wave my arms, clap, ask loud questions, hello?

He *is* sleeping.

With downright clunky steps, I pace around the room. I clink silverware and glass in the kitchen. Drop a pan. Nope, still asleep. I retrieve the remote controllers and fling them into his lap. Only one makes him grumble. He turns and curls up, burrowing into the back of the sofa. I see my avoidance counter and hide it before deciding to throw it at him. I miss and it lands beside his leg.

"Just, you. Put it. Mmmmm." He makes noises of incomplete sentences.

He snores, the vibrations turn my neck and grab my gaze. I notice that I'm on tiptoes, ready to both flight and fight. The best idea I have is to play car chase videos on the television. I raise the volume. *Vrooooom, wee-oww, wee-oww!* How? Why isn't he woken by this?

I haven't seen this video before, I'm engrossed until there's a strange noise. Was that snore or a wheel screech from the television? Whatever it was from—it skid marks over my heart. Nightmares come to life, I look down on Gulliver to match the angle of the helicopter cameras following the runaway cars. Sirens roar, the living room is brushed in red and blue light. In a panic similar to a runaway driver caught in a cul-de-sac, I rush down the hall but I catch my breath and tiptoe back to see if he's awake.

"Gulliver?" I say into the void of the room at increasing intensities.

The car chase video ends. I turn on another lamp.

A whisper of a snore escapes his body. Please tell me I don't have to touch him. Another car chase video comes on but it's scored with relaxing music. Damn my YouTube algorithm. I toddle to my bedroom. Shut the door silently and regret not doing it loud.

Is this safe? It doesn't feel so. I've been avoiding him for years and he's now merging in with my furniture. I don't want to leave my bedroom. I attempt to drift off to sleep but knowing he's out there delivers restless-legged insomnia. For hours, I toss and turn, feeling like a client that couldn't sleep yesterday. My imagination is on overtime, creating a playbook of what could be happening. I lack the courage to check but force myself. On my tiptoes, I peek at the sofa. The television's now off.

My whole body sinks in relief. He's gone, but there's an imprint of Gulliver's body left sagging in the material. I turn on all the lights for the same reason I do after a horror movie. At least he left me something. I take a photograph of the imprint and set it as the background on my phone.

My front door is closed but unlocked. My notebook is open on a page. There's a note. It reads: *Komo, you ROCK, 3 days = no sleep, bye*

He does know my name. In bed, I gaze into the photograph of Gulliver's imprint on my sofa. It's weird because the imprint feels both full yet empty.

Fifteen: Your Second Ever Job

1 moment

You're momenteering for real clients. A few minutes ago, in your first ever job you blinked into a client who forgot where they parked outside a sports stadium. You had to find their car which took 20 minutes.

Codes flash on your screen. You gulp with wide eyes and blink into another client's consciousness. Ultra-speed read finishes loading. The aim says to: *Endure awkwardness.*

"Why did you do that? You've ruined everything," A husband grabbing his partner's hand outside a neoclassical mansion says.

Your eyebrows squash. Faded-skills inform you their partner is your cousin and you've ruined his surprise birthday party. You stumble drunk while guilt sloshes around your body.

"I'm sorry," you say, as you recall seconds ago, asking your cousin why he was late to his own party.

"What party?" Your cousin said before their husband came out and pushed you.

You raise a surrendering hand but your cousin storms inside with his husband.

They aren't dressed as nicely as you, they look like they've been gardening. Both of their long silver ponytails swing aggressively across their shoulders. You follow through three sets of doors. You catch up and around 40 guests jump out wearing ballroom gowns and tuxedos.

"Surprise." the guests and for some reason, you shout.

Black and white balloons drop from the ceiling, deflecting off the chandelier. Your cousin and his husband wave their arms like they're communicating with a helicopter.

"I knew about this surprise. It was ruined!" Your cousin turns back and points at you. You step back and misstep. You understand that you drink because you've lost more than money at the casino. The crowd groans and sighs. Disapproval cast on everyone's face.

Your cousin greets guests but you spot that he's crying. You go stand in a corner. Ten minutes later, you start to feel less ashamed and wonder when you will be blinked out. The awkwardness is more intense than training. It has a weight to it that makes your posture squirm and stare towards your shiny loafers.

Your cousin tells everyone to re-enact the surprise moment again. He leaves outside with his husband and returns. You all pretend to surprise him once more, but it's faker than fake. No balloons drop. Your cousin acts surprised so badly that guests roll their eyes or giggle into their champagne. His husband tells a joke no one understands then explains how it's funny. It only makes the atmosphere hostile. Guests avoid you.

The rhythm of the party returns to normal but the awkwardness hovers over everyone like a hawk and at various moments it strikes and people roll their shoulders or excuse themselves from conversations.

Some presents are given to your cousin but when you give yours, a small red box holding something that you've forgotten. He refuses to open it and puts it behind him.

You stay there for another half hour feeling as shit as can be.

You're blinked out, back to your station. That was so awkward but it's prepared you. You feel ready for anything.

Sixteen: Homophones

4481 moments

From the food delivery app, I order brioche waffles with bacon and walnut butter before work. I drive both sweet and savory/savoury with crumbs stuck to my fingers. Pritek tells us to blend in. Momenteers must park in the streets or parking lots with all the business workers. At least the skaters continue to ignore me.

Today isn't special. My client's moments are dull—waiting around for packages while the neighbours/neighbors are drilling, then I return clothes without receipts to Dior. Until I blink in... the aim instructs to: *Sing*. A flamingo birthday cake is sat before me. I count 13 skinny candles. Their smoke smells of plastic. The mahogany door frames are familiar and I know why when Kermit's ushered by his mother into the dining room and we sing the birthday song. My smile expands so wide I feel my ears rise.

Wow, there's Tiffany, Kermit's mother. I've only heard her voice before. Our bond through faded-skills has a fear, a strange one, a fear I like. She's petite with snappy fingers but smells of stale tobacco. She bosses me around but fun thoughtlessly flows. There's no effort interacting with Kermit but his mother is intense. She doesn't allow elbows on the dining room table. I study her appearance to try and guess her genetics. She's a brunette with a squashed face. Her eyes are small piercing dots. I sense an attraction, but only at certain angles. Her accent sings at the end of words. What accent is this? I lose focus after she playfully slaps my shoulder. She has this mannerism where she flicks her nostrils.

Kermit and I volley a pink balloon back and forth. It reminds me of a Green Bread lyric: *Parents betray their children by growing old.*

The mother doesn't talk much, but after I eat a slice of cake she remarks "Better not get fat, boom boom splat."

"If you don't move your ass, it will grow," Kermit says what must be a family mantra.

My gaze drops to this slender belly. I wonder if Kermit's mother is nice? Is she in on the abuse, the sedatives? She's odd, at times pleasant but then snaps into anger. When she's mad, it's intense and difficult to look anywhere.

"Take your elbows off the table boys," she says and we do.

It's too late to collect more evidence because my eyes droop and I exit the moment. The toothpick returns between my lips.

I finish my shift with typical jobs. In my eighth moment, I think the prankster put me in their body because I'm posing as a life model for a group of art students. This naked body has a hairy belly with a shaved chest. One hairy shoulder and the other shaved. I must remember their body type in case they try to prank me again.

When I return to my car, I check my phone—it shows a digital memory. Eight years ago today I was celebrating my birthday. A picture of me wearing a wonky party hat outside The Hard Rock Cafe. I looked so unaware then that I would soon stop playing drums. The fact abseils from the back of my neck to the front of my mind. My arms twitch and elbows prod the ribcage. Kermit has the same birthday as me. We're birthday buddies. This means today's the 2nd of May.

Does this mean we're connected? I don't want to research it in case Pritek might see.

My mind's imagining far-fetched theories that Kermit and I have the same soul but are on different timelines. How do you prove so or otherwise? If this is true or crazy, how do you know there isn't someone out there who is you but is 88 in Buenos Aires while there's another version of your soul at 16 months in

Belgrade. Could it be true? Is a soul contained within a single vessel? Does the entire soul occur at the same time or at separate instances? Too much thinking so I go and play my new electric drums with headphones.

I stop drumming to check my mailbox but there's no cards. Not even one from my brother which pleases me. No social media messages as Pritek doesn't allow agents to use it. Despite this empty packaging feeling, to keep people at a distance from hurting me I refuse to tell Donna when my birthday is. My old Green Bread bandmates, my brother and ex-girlfriend/sister-in-law—all their birthday wishes dried up over the years like pressed flowers in a book.

I go out for a walk to get some steps in. You know who might have interesting views on birthday buddies? I don't want to admit it but Gulliver might. Returning to our building, he's not around. I sneak and stomp. Caught between avoiding him and wanting to see him. I put my ear up to his door. A hollow silence spooks me and I rush away.

A few days pass, Donna and I exhibit our communication problems when I'm over at hers and I go out to grab apples and return with frail kiwi fruits.

"They didn't have free apples, only kiwis," I say with a dumb elevated tone.

"I wanted three apples, not *free*,"

Donna doesn't stop going on about this until I understand and admit it's all my fault. Oh, words that sound the same but mean entirely different things. Give me a *brake*.

As a punishment/token Donna is allowed to give me a haircut. I refuse to go to the salon because it will remind me of being Ruben except without his handsomeness. My training means I inadvertently avoid the mirror in her bathroom, she whizzes around, singing and snipping. I get thinking about aesthetics or looks again.

"Looks... they don't matter, do they?" I repeat until Donna hears.

She swoops her hair behind each of her ears. "No, they matter, that's what ugly people tell themselves,"

"Aren't we ugly?" I say.

Donna laughs and knocks over a bottle, she grabs my chin and moves it as if it's my head talking in a cartoon voice, "Look at us, we're not ugly, not even close."

I lean out of her grip, "But would you get mad if someone called us aesthetically challenged?"

Donna sprays my face with water.

Our miscommunication is in style because Donna cuts my hair shorter than requested. She sweeps my shoulders while they shiver. What is this monstrosity laying on my scalp? She's made my natural hair look like a toupée. It appears like there's a flapping piece of toast on top of my skull. Through gritted teeth, I tell her: "It's nice, yeah, it's... *gneiss*."

Next day, I'm momenteering for Kermit's father. I feel some pain on his torso. Tiffany flares her nostrils and demands I spank Kermit for leaving his room without permission. The aim said to follow orders but I cross his arms and shake his head.

"I don't want to do it either but how else is he going to learn? It's how I learned," Tiffany takes off her slipper.

"No, I'm not hitting anyone," I say, "Violence is never the answer."

"Yes, it can be," Tiffany's stare burns. She wags a finger and pokes my bruises. She spanks my leg playfully instead. She snaps, with her strong arms she bends me over her knee and spanks me as Kermit turns his back.

"Someone has to pay for being naughty," Tiffany's eyes sparkle with aggression while Kermit stares towards a flamingo poster, his hands over his ears.

While this is happening, faded-skills tell me I deserve this. With each spank, I can't help but smile. A part of Bruce likes it, he enjoys giving Tiffany the power. It ends and Tiffany leaves Kermit's bedroom.

"Thanks Dad," Kermit says.

I'm blinked out. My toothpick falls out of my puzzled mouth upon my return. I can't believe it, Tiffany's evil too?

Seventeen: Pistachio

4508 moments

These aims say to: `Wait for prescription`. I blink in and my vision immediately blurs and skews. It's that feeling. That calm fuzz, oh—I swirl the tongue around the gums. Most of our clients have all their teeth but the diabetic is missing three molars.

"Whit ye smiling aboot?" The lady missing a front tooth across from me says. Her accent is different but faded-skills help me understand it.

I can't tell her that I suspect I might be piloting the consciousness of a fav client of mine. I sneak his fingers down the leg, into the sock to touch the ankle. Yes, an indent of a scar. I'm the type 1 diabetic. This will make more than my day, maybe my month. While waiting I'm eating a bag of pistachio nuts. One of the nuts gets caught in the gap of his missing top left molar. I find myself nodding as I smile. I rub his upper arms. For a moment, he feels complete. Everything in life's tranquil. I don't understand how much I missed him.

A young girl appears and twirls in front of bottles of mouthwash. She must be around my niece Emma's age. She knocks over a bottle and I do nothing to help, reminding me how neglectful of an uncle I am. The missing-a-front-tooth-lady loses interest in me after her name is called. Margret something. White floors, lights, walls, lab coats and pill boxes surround us. Sat in the pharmacy's cheap shineless chairs. The pharmacist gives me a cheap look of distaste but I have the confidence to wink back. The diabetic's wearing pastel combinations of non-branded comfy clothes. Peach and lime. Giddiness strikes and I pop open numerous pistachio shells, trying to get more nuts stuck in the remaining molar gaps. The pharmacist calls his name but Pritek blocks the sound. So weird, I hear it but my mind forgets and remembers a bleep. Standing, a shower of pistachio shells falls from his lap and bombards the floor. Customers disperse and I put the empty bag of pistachios in my pocket. I limp over the shells and collect his medicine. All while trying to avoid seeing his name. I can't help but notice it starts with a C. I turn back to help clean the shells from the ground, the girl helps me too. I pick each up and put the shells back in the trash/bin. My eyelids flutter and I'm blinked out.

Rogue Violation flashes on my screen. I wipe my face but my fearful expression doesn't change. Uh-oh, not this again.

A supervisor comes. *Dah-doo-dum.* I explain to the supervisor that it was an accident because I had to collect a prescription. It was difficult to do this without discovering information.

"We tell our clients not to momenteer out of these situations. I have to write this up, don't be surprised if you have your tally increased," the supervisor says.

My face scrunches for 30 seconds. Whatever. I'm glad the diabetic's alive even if he is getting me in trouble.

The next day breezes by. I momenteer with Kermit again. We're playing Uno, well the more advanced version called Dos. He's angry tonight, being around him is like stepping on eggshells. I think it's because his mother is evil but he avoids talking about her.

"Can we turn this off?" I say, referring to the television mumbling *How It's Made* episodes.

No. We can't. Kermit needs the episodes on and he needs the volume to be on an odd number. It can't be even or it means, well it means the end of the world to him. I study his room for any details of where on earth he lives. If I see a name of somewhere I'll forget it when I return. I've already forgotten the name of the pharmacy I was at earlier. What did the diabetic's name start with again? Was it a G?

"So permission is granted?" Kermit says after I confirm we can go and make a sandwich. After we leave his room there's a yell upstairs from Tiffany. We explain we're making a snack.

"Hey, make sure you don't leave a mess again and stop putting me off," Tiffany shouts up.

Kermit does the smallest of laughs but she hears it.

"What, do you think making music is easy or something?"

We stop on the steps, looking at each other with motionless faces about to giggle.

The tension slides and Tiffany clicks her mouse and hums a tune. We move carefully. I didn't truly notice this until now, but when I'm in their kitchen, whenever I open a cupboard something falls on me. It happens again with the cheese slices from the fridge.

I slap the cheese between the bread. The microwave hums and Kermit looks into it like it's his TV. The cheese and bread merge and spin. That's right, the products they buy might reveal their location. I check the fridge, but there are so many products from various countries. Stop. I better not do anything that'll get me caught when I'm supposed to be banned from momenteering for Kermit's father.

Kermit makes my mind spin when he turns to face me and asks, "Dad, what's love feel like?"

My hands retreat to pockets. The fridge door closes itself. Words fumble around my teeth, hoping an explanation will come. I only know about flings, my ex and Donna. Is that the type of love he means? Nothing comes from faded-skills. Kermit's gaze intensifies so I avoid his eyes. I ramble on about how emotions are like songs. Cover versions of emotions come as you grow old but sometimes you can have a remix which makes an emotion feel new, so although you feel love, it can change from lover to lover.

115

"It sounds complicated," he says and I confirm it is.

Ding. The microwave calls and Kermit eats the grilled cheese but I notice he's using a fork and knife. This spooks me because I've also eaten this way since I was young.

After my shift, I loiter around the fountain eating mango chunks. The skaters aren't here and I should be wondering why but I spot the lady who may be a momenteer. If I find a workmate they could help me find where Kermit lives. Her ponytail is tighter. She's also eating a yellow snack. Can't tell what, too far from this distance. Should I approach? I overthink. I stand then sit. What if she reports me? What if tickle glove? What if she's a regular person and knows nothing? She leaves and regret hits me for not approaching. Let me think of what to say and how to say it first.

Donna hasn't texted all day, so I go to Flower Cave alone. The worst thing happens... the food is amazing. A red Thai curry that's to-die-for, but the interior's confusing with bumpy stone seats and the service is terrible. Now I have something to say but I hope Gulliver never asks me about this experience.

It's late when I get home. Back and parked, I have to do an awkward no-I'll-go-this-way repetitive side step from Gwen leaving the building. She gives me a groan and a tut.

Entering the foyer I stop two steps in. There's no concierge. I spot Gulliver way ahead stepping between the ferns and towards the elevator/lift. By his walk and his hairstyle, I know it's him. He has his arm around the waist of a lady with all her hair swooped over one shoulder. Both of their legs move in sync. I look at my feet and stumble, making sure they're not synced with theirs. The lady stumbles on the step and I stop on my toes with the other leg dangling. I need to ask him about birthday buddies.

Gulliver enters the lift/elevator, turns and so does the lady. My insides turn to crunchy peanut butter. Gulliver's got his arm around Donna. She's dyed her hair black. No matter how much I blink and tell myself it can't be, it is. I step closer but veer towards the stairs instead. Donna presses the floor button too, her arm slows back when she notices me. I should be jealous or hurt. I expect to feel these emotions so I think I feel them, diluted versions anyway.

My emotions must be buffering, awaiting translation from the present tense. Gulliver notices me and moves sharply, he puts out a water-polo-saving hand to stop the doors closing and presses to hold them. Donna looks to her knees and covers her belly. I walk above a crawling toddler's pace. Okay earth, you're now welcome to suck me into your core.

"Come on, we've got you. Stop walking so weird and come squire," Gulliver says. But how I wish they didn't have me.

I wave it off and head for the stairs, Gulliver lets go of Donna's waist, runs out, grabs and drags me into the elevator/lift before it closes again. I travel between them and bang my back off the mirrored wall. We all laugh our versions of the same uncomfortable giggle at separate instances. I focus on their backs, wishing them to never turn. Maybe it's the diabetic's calm inside me but I lean back and meditate.

Maybe it's a twin or a lookalike, but when I spot the surfing scar on her neck it confirms it's 100% Donna. My torso organs play snakes and ladders.

"This is Donna," Gulliver turns and confirms anyway. I give them both a nod. Where's my jealousy? I consider telling Gulliver I went to Flower Cave but it's not the right time.

"Hi. I'm Komo. Nice to... Well, you two enjoy your night," I say my new catchphrase as the doors open.

Donna turns to let me pass and forces a smile with closed eyelids. She scratches her cheeks. We catch eyes as we move our bodies out. At this moment we exchange emoji combinations that make no sense.

Drums and a plunger. Corn cob and an anchor. Megaphone and a ladybug. Accordion and magic wand.

The noise of pistachios falling takes over my mind. Maybe I'm a pistachio nut, stuck inside a hardened shell—one of those pistachios that's slightly ajar, giving you hope, but not even by using other shells to pry me open, will it reveal my heart to the world.

I walk, not my walk, someone cooler's walk. I look over my shoulder, it's so weird seeing Donna on my floor but going into Gulliver's. She does her cute gallop as she enters his. Surely, I should be devastated, if monogamy has taught me anything it's to feel betrayed but I'm more lost. Can emotions be delayed like planes and parcels? If anything, of all the emotions I've experienced, I'd say this is a cocktail of sweet relief and tangy liberation. I'm content in a manner that will shock most readers. My guilt is reduced to evaporation. You know what, I deserve this for not being able to commit.

Eighteen: Angle

4517 moments

I'm following the ginger ponytail lady. Closer up, her flame-red hair and freckled skin appear more real, more of a momenteer. Her walk is jaded like mine. Knees weak, arms heavy, she slips around a corner of a bakery. I've been following her for ten minutes after my shift. Caught her loitering around the fountain. She appears to be friends with homeless people, stopping to chat with a few. I know as a man you shouldn't follow women but she turns the corner and so do I.

"Knew it, you're following me," she says, pointing right at me.

"I. Er. Uh." I say and she copies me but with a mocking tone.

She swirls her hand as if she's revealing a magic trick, inviting me to explain. My legs toddle forward but my mindset doesn't. How do I ask her if she's a momenteer without letting her know I'm one?

"Do you work back there, in the tower?" I say.

She doesn't respond, she kicks a piece of the air towards me and I breathe it in. I repeat my question. As I finish there's a noise of dry heaving from behind. I turn but only packaging from the bakery we're behind is there.

I must better assess this situation: why's she down the back of a bakery? An alleyway of an alleyway. Did I get her wrong? Surely, if she *was* a momenteer she'd hang out in fancy restaurants not here where litter congregates and bushes are entangled in metal fences.

My gaze splashes into her tired sponge eyes. They soak me in. With a piercing green stare like that, maybe she is a momenteer.

"Do you get tired from working? I work in the tower. It feels like I'm doing more than my own life, sorry, my I mean, job, right?" I say.

This was my master plan, misspeak on purpose so she'd admit to being a momenteer.

"You're tired?" She says, stepping back.

Steam floats between us from the bakery. A sweet warm aroma makes us both smile after we sniff.

"You lost?" She says.

I turn 360°

"Lost like how, physically or in my life, as in what to do with it?" Finally, I might get clarification on this subject. On my tiptoes, waiting for her response. Her fingers pinch her eyebrows together.

Forcing a smile she says. "Argh, you wanna see my tits? It's why you're following? Everyone wanna see my love tits, like you know who."

I move back on my heels. Is she sane? I don't know who.

"What? No, I want to work with you. Discuss approaches,"

She opens her trench coat, I close my eyes. After a few seconds, I tell myself that skin wasn't exposed. It was a white t-shirt with a drawing on it. I try to open my eyes despite their resistance. My vision is all over the place like a cheap auto-focus.

She holds her trench coat open. My vision fixes to reveal she's wearing a sauce-stained white t-shirt with two drawn-on boobies with red sequined love hearts as nipples. She laughs as relief covers my face. Her laugh is rusty like she laughs too much or not enough. I raise my hand to block my eyes from seeing what I now realise/realize to be, a squiggly outline drawing of two breasts printed on the chest of her shirt. Ah, she fooled me. Good one. Classic comedic misdirection.

She closes her trench coat as I hesitate on my questioning, trying to find an angle if she works at Pritek.

To protect myself, I can't help but be vague. Last week I was awake late every night trying to think of what to say. Now I'm here and she's listening. How do I, I can't find the angle. I wipe my forehead but my mind remains hazy. I must leave before anything bad happens.

"I have to go, sorry," I say.

She points with her nose and says, "Don't be following my love tits again."

Walking out the alleyway I pass a homeless lady with greasy eyes, skin and hair. Her hair is held in two unequal buns. The greasy lady kicks a stone behind. I have to turn. She approaches the ginger ponytail lady. Her slippery voice echoes from the corner.

"I found pizza for us, Hazel. We can share, I got it in my patch," the greasy lady says.

Hazel? Is that her name? The greasy lady kisses the ginger lady. Their arms embrace and tongues slip out of each other's mouths. It's one of the most passionate kisses I've ever seen. Kisses in films can't compare. Turning away, I feel as if I'm offending the kiss by leaving, so I sneak another look to show some respect.

Before I turn the corner, I glance back at the lovers who seem to be measuring out a box with their arms. Oh, I understand. I'm so stupid. Hazel's homeless, these two are. The pieces fit to make sense. I slap my head so much walking back to my car that I go the long way and give myself a mild concussion.

The car door opens but I don't drive. I sit there looking at my hands going over things.

◆

It's been nine days since I caught Donna with Gulliver. The surprising thing is Donna calls me more and we're somehow closer. This doesn't make sense but… Last week, my hand was over the mic as Donna told me she still wants us to be together.

"Gulliver doesn't need to know about us. We can hide it. I'll make sure he doesn't find out and we can continue our thing as if nothing happened," Donna proposed.

Initially, I wasn't interested but after I slept on the idea and truly thought about it. This arrangement is perfect. Not only do I keep Donna in my life and relieve my guilt but I'll reignite my avoidance of Gulliver. Introduce jeopardy and fun in avoiding him. Bingo, a purpose, more meaning delivered.

Donna doesn't know I avoid Gulliver so that adds spice. She says she hasn't been seeing him for long and didn't know we lived in the same building until it was too late.

"I knew I'd bump into you when it hit me that I was in your building. And there you were," Donna giggled after I agreed to her proposal.

The only bad thing about this arrangement is that Donna will still see Gulliver but that's okay, I'm not jealous. She deserves more love than I can give.

Speaking of which, I've been momenteering with Catherine more. It hasn't all been love-making either. I saw her a lot last week, the client was stuck on a yacht with Catherine and momenteered daily out of his consciousness. It was wonderful company and delicious food. But I worry by having fun with her that I could be making Catherine more attached to the client.

Art class is going well. When paint hits the canvas, it takes me back to listening to Blink-182 in high school art, where I met two of my ex-bandmates. No, no flashbacks—we must think forwards. I've befriended Ender, one of the divorced. She's 55. We make jokes while washing our brushes about how the teacher says "If you ask me," a lot before she says anything, giving us the illusion she answered our questions before we ask any.

"If you ask me, we haven't asked anything yet," Ender says.

Ender's painting a portrait of her ex Tommy and Tommy is returning this sentiment. I'm trying to focus on painting you-know-who but tonight when I step away and squint at my painting, it looks like a hybrid between Kermit's father and Hazel, the homeless lady I followed. The eyes have gone bulbous and zany. The face is at a crossroads of appearing old yet young.

Back home, Gulliver hasn't been around which is a relief but I still need to ask him about birthday buddies. Kermit and I discussed growing up and I taught him how to tie a tie.

Next week, I'm momenteering with Kermit. He's telling me dad jokes in the kitchen. I try to figure out where on earth he lives from the cutlery and plates but they're 'IKEA' which gives no hope. I worry what his parents are doing when I'm not here.

This week's art class is subdued because Ender isn't here. Tommy says she's at a casting. The memory I have of Kermit's father isn't as strong as I thought when another of my paintings looks more like Hazel. Mountain ridge lines are replaced by smooth lakes.

Returning home, I'm so frustrated I forget not only to avoid Gulliver but forget to ask his opinion on the topic of birthday buddies.

"How's that girl you were with, what was her name?" I say pre-rehearsed lines I'd worked out with Donna. Look at him, the toothless fish, no clue what's going on. The clueless can be so beautiful.

A few days pass and I'm back with Kermit again. He's talking about a girl at school and playing with his phone. I sit and watch *How It's Made* with him but I think I've seen this episode on dishwashers. Kermit shifts his arms and when I glance over at him I see he's pouting, sucking his cheeks in.

"I dunno how to take a selfie, Zoe wants one and I don't know the best angles. Dad, you do it, show me good angles," Kermit says.

He flings the phone into my lap, its weight intensifies. My fingers grab it and the camera is flicked to selfie. I don't notice that I'm looking at my reflection. I catch myself studying the eyes and seeing where I've gone wrong in my portraits. Look, his cheeks are sharp, his nose is as straight as an escalator and his ears aren't as big as I paint.

Lifting the phone, I angle it around his face, getting a detailed view. Maybe I should paint his eyes more sunken but soon I'm blinked out.

A violation roars on my screen and before I think of what to say the door clicks open and a supervisor is arching over my station. I try to explain it was an accident. I stand to show physical re-enactments of the misunderstanding.

The supervisor downloads something from my station to their tablet. As the loading bar increases my breathing tightens. My nostrils develop a squeak.

"Ah, I see your problem. This was supposed to be a blocked client, don't worry. We will fix this. You shouldn't have to deal with them anymore. Sorry about that," the supervisor says.

I force a smile while my heart yells, no no no no no no no, no. My insides turn to smooth peanut butter. I stand with my hand out, the fingers open and twitching.

"You can dock in," The supervisor says after a pause.

I can't focus and seeing as I've already hit the minimum jobs for the day I signal to leave. A skinnier supervisor sees me out. I enter the streets and I angle my walk towards the fountain. My hand remains cast out as I walk, looking as if I'm holding an invisible coffee cup.

"Are you training to be a zombie in a movie?" One of the smart skaters heckles my walk.

Hazel appears and approaches.

"Look how you dress. I know what you do in that tower. Ha, revenge, I followed you back," Hazel says.

Her coat's open, one of the sequined love-hearts is reflecting the setting sun into my eye. She slaps my aimless hand as it lingers in shock. The skaters see this as an act of aggression. They glide over and pick their boards up with puffed chests before pushing me. But… but one of their boards says *PEACE* on the bottom.

"Get away from Hazy Hazel. She's from the streets, you're not. Stay apart, oil and water. Step off fool," a tough skater with a long nose and hair says.

A shoving brawl emerges. I don't push anyone. I am the pushed. In the commotion, I fall and lose Hazel. I rush away, shielding my head and back from being kicked.

It sets in that I'm banned from seeing Kermit, again. Everything feels out of shape, out of place. Does Hazel know I'm a momenteer? I watch Hazel talk to the skaters but soon she disappears. I go and ask the skaters where but they won't say and have witty put-downs.

Back in the car with a tub of pineapple fingers from my lunch box, I watch the skateboarders failing tricks around the fountain. I'm stuck wondering if this moment (that I'm currently living) is truly a moment and not simply time passing. Especially when most moments are deficient of memorable activity. Before I can calculate, it's grown dark and intoxicated degenerates loiter. Look at them, you can't tell if any of them is being momenteered. They play intrusive techno from their portable speakers. I take this as my signal to step off. A bunch of red lights appear while driving back. I catch myself in my mirrors and ask if I'm being my true self or am I so great an actor at playing this version of me that I've lost who I am to routine and the expectations of others?

Nineteen: Grunt

"Cut. Great stuff Brucey," the director says.

Kermit's father strolls off the set after filming sign language to a nature documentary. He steps from the green screen to the dressing room, moisturising his hands on the way. Hand cream and wearing non-branded plain clothing are essential to his profession of interpreting on screen.

Bruce wipes off the lip balm, hoping Melanie will come to remove the rest of his make-up. Where is she? He's potentially free tonight. He sits wearing foundation to hide the bags under his eyes and mosaic powder for a less sickly nose. Waiting, he hears the legendary raspberry voice of Cindy Cummings stuffing up the hallways. His shoulders twitch, his hands lock into regretful fists.

Cindy narrates the audio descriptions for the blind while Bruce interprets the spoken word for the deaf. Despite sharing a blitz of an affair, they no longer communicate. He counts on his fingers how many years it's been since his hands last caressed Cindy's infamous white tights. His fingers keep flicking between four and five. Tiffany caught their hotel arrangements on Bruce's phone. He always told her he'd end up cheating but since this moment her grip on his life tightened and Bruce says he likes it, he deserves it. So toxic. Tiffany had a hint of OCD but it has now gathered pace.

His current and still secret affair, Melanie floats in behind and grips Bruce's shoulders. As a television interpreter, you're trained to avoid smiling but Bruce's face couldn't hide his delight. They share a quick embrace. Cindy's voice still loitering in the hall behind. He focuses deeply on Melanie's face. Trying to avoid a flashback, an involuntary recurrent memory that'll take the reader backwards.

"Bruce was on the south side of a zany time as Cindy removed her..." The flashback says, pulling on our attention.

No stop, instead Bruce imagines a future with Melanie. Sure, Melanie might be 17 years younger than Bruce at 26. Thinking ahead was better than what his present or past had to offer.

Lately, he'd been daydreaming during filming. In shows when words weren't being spoken, Bruce would imagine laying in a four-post bed, Melanie using his bicep as a pillow, a soft breeze from a cottage window. Sometimes, they'd discuss it, an exit from his marriage. Their vague plan is: once Kermit was settled at high school in a year or so, Bruce would kick Tiffany out of his home. He knew he should leave now, but the prospect of untangling his life seemed better suited to a future version of himself.

Melanie wipes Bruce's face clean before checking behind to make sure there's no crew, live subtitlers or camera operators near. She kisses him where the earlobe meets the jaw. Bruce grunts like one of the hyenas from the nature documentary he signed. He looks into the lightbulb-adorned mirror reflecting Melanie. Their eyelines hug.

"When words fall short of describing beauty, all we are left with are grunts," Bruce says.

Melanie flicks her dirty blonde French braids and leans close whispering: "Good news, you can come tonight. If you want, I mean can. Thing is, Opia would love to see you too."

Opia is Melanie's border collie, a rescue dog that has its cancerous eyes surgically removed. In place of eyes are two hardened scabs. Opia has struck a deep connection with Bruce, Melanie jokes they're both middle-aged males that don't know where they're going in life.

Bruce nods and in a brief lull where words should be spoken, he winks. Melanie checks they're still alone, but someone's moving behind them, a producer calls from another studio, she blows a kiss into the mirror and leaves with a hesitation in her step.

Bruce pretends to catch the kiss but drops it when Melanie's back appears in the mirror. The right hemisphere of Bruce's brain confronts the left. No, he doesn't feel guilty for cheating, maybe for doing so with Cindy but not Melanie. The way Tiffany controls him versus Melanie's escapism—she's the parallel life he should be living. He retrieves his phone. After unlocking it, a notification informs him that he has 15 minutes of screen time remaining. Tiffany set the limits. He rushes a text to Tiffany reminding her he'd be home late because of an important badminton match. He'd been seeing Melanie with this secretive technique for over a year.

The routine: He'd drop his phone off at the local badminton club and return to collect it after dates. Despite the badminton rackets in his car and the gold-plated trophy in his home, Bruce had no idea how to play. He bought the trophy and paid for the engraving himself. Other than his fake badminton career, the only other affair-tactic Bruce has is downloading a fake GPS app then deleting it before driving home, which was risky enough because it's cheap and unreliable.

The foolish yet wonderful thing about the badminton club is their lockers were kept outside, while the changing rooms and courts were indoors. Bruce drives to the lockers and drops his phone off. He texts Tiffany again, a big paragraph about everything that happened at work and the match. With only three minutes of screen time remaining, he mutes the phone and closes the locker.

He drives to Melanie's. She lives with a hippie named Sebastian, an online life coach who makes his own scented candles. His beard buzzed the same length as his hair to give a look of follicle solidarity. Tonight as Bruce's nostrils sniff in a candle's aroma in their living room, he nods with raised eyebrows.

"I can't guess," Bruce hands the candle back to Sebastian before petting Opia.

"It's apple and tobacco, I'm gonna call it—I don't know yet, any ideas?" Sebastian says.

"The Big Smoke," Melanie shouts from her bedroom.

Bruce didn't have the knack for creativity—he would leave that to others. Opia doesn't leave Bruce's side, not even when Melanie comes in and out. Melanie's holding shot glasses filled with shroom tea. Bruce declines the invitations to microdose, then the subsequent "are you sureeee?" offers.

Bruce's posture stiffens but Opia's presence calms him. Silent and frustrated, he figures out why he doesn't enjoy Melanie doing drugs. It highlighted their age gap. He couldn't help but feel left out despite choosing to exclude himself. Too risky—imagine what Tiffany would do if she found out. The minutes drag by. Melanie and Sebastian grow giddier watching videos of news presenters making mistakes. It becomes apparent this isn't going to be a romantic evening. Opia must sense this too when he goes to his own doggie bed. Sebastian and Melanie sway before dancing like avant-garde freestyle crabs.

Bruce couldn't hear the music that played in their imaginations. He took initiative and lit an incense stick. It smelled of intense orange and cinnamon. Bruce doesn't want to check the time but knows he... oh no. Time's up. Already.

"It's 9.30, time for me to go," Bruce announces while he stands.

Sebastian and Melanie stop dancing and hug each other before wandering over to him. Their pupils, their movements are wide and slow. Melanie rubs her eyes because when she looks into Bruce's brown swamp irises, for a moment she can see two pupils beside another, blending over another like the Mastercard logo.

"You two have intimate times," Sebastian says, closing Melanie and Bruce out of the living room. In the hall, they sit on a couch.

"I love who you are, you know. We will be… hehe. We will be… us. I'm ready to move in with you," Melanie says.

The last part of her words make Bruce rub his knees. Putting his jacket on, Bruce punches his arms into their holes and has the sense too many things in his life are happening at once. He'll never be ready no matter how much he prepares. Opia claws from inside the living room. Sebastian opens the door and sticks his tongue out. Opia follows their voices in the hall. Melanie pets and pets Opia, the touch of his fur has never been so pleasing.

"I must go. My body is an easel, yours a work of art," Bruce says more of his poetic nonsense, stopping Melanie from petting Opia.

Melanie places her arms behind her back and Bruce walks outside to his car, Melanie and Opia following.

"Don't look sad," Bruce says sarcastically instead of a goodbye.

He drives away. Melanie takes Opia back and her dog bumps into the gate of the garden of their lower ground property.

Bruce faces his steering wheel, adjusts his mirrors and sighs enough to fill the airbag. Driving away with raindrops all over the sunroof, he's trying to convince the steering wheel that tonight wasn't a waste. It could be another week or two before he could be with Melanie and Opia again.

Bruce retrieves his phone from the lockers before driving home. A few typical texts from Tiffany saying that she's tired of the world not understanding her music—he types badly rushing to reply. One minute screen time remains and it feels like the walls are closing in. The screen timer locks. Bruce drives in silence, parks at their home. The engine lets out a grunt. Bruce mimics the grunt at various pitches as he stares at his front door, not wanting to return to his life.

Inside, he steps on a creaky floorboard and Tiffany shouts from her basement. He stops and as if automatic Bruce takes out his wallet. He slips out the photograph of Tiffany, from a time when she was pregnant with Kermit but didn't know or show it. She's around Melanie's age, smiling over her shoulder in a gold silk dress. Those were the days, but they didn't know that then. Bruce raises the photo and frames it before the painting in his hallway. The painting depicted the hallway itself but from an earlier time. A cleaner, younger, free, spacious, less manipulative, controlling and violent hallway. He keeps switching his focus between the painting and the photograph. How could things change so much from what they'd been?

Tiffany appears and grips Bruce's hips. Bruce jitters and disguises it as laughter. He hides the photograph in his palm, around his back and into the butt pocket of his chinos.

"What were you looking at?" Tiffany says.

She has a cute curve in her voice that makes Bruce question if the old Tiffany, the pre-Cindy Cummings affair Tiffany had travelled back. Her subsequent evil giggles and spanks of Bruce's bottom meant the past hadn't returned.

"Nothing, just the hallway painting. Funny how much it has changed."

Tiffany strains her eyes, "Looks the same, always a mess."

Her eyes light up watching Bruce amble close to the closet where Tiffany's angled a shoe box to fall out on him if he slides open the door.

Bruce walks in circles. "Can't you see the evolution?" Bruce says, guiding his arms around the hallway like an estate agent.

Tiffany didn't need to say no, the frown on her face said it for her.

Bruce turns and his heart floats to the floor like a shuttlecock when he sees Tiffany's holding the badminton trophy he's bought for himself. The one with a player doing what Bruce believes is called a smasher shot.

Tiffany places the trophy out before her and pushes it into Bruce's chest until he falls back into the wall. His smile appears and disappears as the trophy prods beyond his Oxford shirt and against his skin. The trophy feels sharper than it looks. Bruce pushes back until the pain is bearable. His forced smile reappears and flickers.

Tiffany stares into Bruce's soul and says "I want to play you. I will beat you... at badminton."

Of all the muscles, a tightness is served to Bruce's thighs. Oh no. Bruce wonders what he could say for an excuse. Tiffany's competitive and a sore loser. Could he imagine a good lie? An injury? Or could he learn badminton well enough before they played? The walls are, yet again, closing in, compressing his thoughts so all the words in his vocabulary evaporate. All he's left with are grunts.

Tiffany lets the trophy slip between her fingers and Bruce's torso. It falls. Bruce instinctively knees it up, again and again. *This could be a meme*, he thinks as he attempts to catch it but, whoops, it slips from his fingers and thuds to the floor. His gaze sinks, his name is engraved on the trophy yet it still doesn't feel like it's his.

A-hem. Hrmpt. Bruce grunts.

Tiffany grunts back in Bruce's face and jerks fast as if she's going to hit him. Bruce flinches.

"Go check Kerr went to sleep," Tiffany says, "I gave him one of my sedatives, you know how kids like him get, banging and whatnot. A good sleep makes a smart kid."

Bruce turns, sighs and shakes his head.

Tiffany rolls up her sleeves, "Don't start, you know I need peace to create music,"

Bruce moves with caution and climbs the stairs. He rubs his wedding ring but it ran out of wishes a long time ago. He'll never understand why they give Kermit sedatives but orders are orders and the pills do make him behave. He knocks while entering

Kermit's room. After a long day, Bruce feels tired talking to his dozy son. He slips another sedative into Kermit's nighttime cola bottle. Ready for next time. Kermit's turning into a teen and becoming cheekier. Bruce blinks to bring the menu and he momenteers out of his consciousness.

Twenty: Stapler

4581 moments

It's worrying to report that it's been eight shifts without any moments with Kermit. The ban must be working. The supervisor's tablets… maybe I could steal one and unban myself?

After my shifts, I keep trying to find Hazel because I'm stupid and think she's a momenteer. I followed a few other guys but they didn't have the same presence. Hazel's vanished. Last week, I asked the skaters if anything's happened to her but they told me to "do the planet a solid, jump into a blender and crush yourself into a liquid." Her girlfriend, the greasy lady is around. I followed her yesterday, but when she turned, her face was glowing with grease, the large crusts in her eyes scared me and I scurried.

Routine's biting hard. Painful moments at work are increasing, both physical and emotional. I blinked in to endure a broken hip, followed by a full two hours of intense Sciatica. These experiences go into my subconsciousness and my dreams use these experiences as ammunition for nightmares.

The supervisors are speaking about a speed reading upgrade that will soon be in beta. The feature enables momenteers to digest thousands of words in a second. Instead of a few instructions, a whole epic novel could be understood within the faded-skills, giving momenteers far greater insight on how to act in their moments. Apparently, they will soon be rolling this feature out to our top agents. Seeing as I was recently suspended and my performance is regularly questioned. I guess I'll try this feature in my next session.

It's not all bad. I'm able to momenteer regularly for the diabetic. You'll like this one… Today he gets me into his mind to edit and polish a little 500-word story about how much he loves someone. The silence of the library gives an unrivalled peace, their carpets have calming swirly patterns. The story begins: 'The way they're advertising these new headphones reminds me of how I love you.' Well, I'm no writer but with faded-skills I manage. Grinning at the laptop when I finish, I must be feeling pride because the smile continues, transferring to my own face as I blink out, undock, leave and drive to art class. (You can read our, sorry, his story '*Better Than Sound*' at the end of this book.)

At class, my art is coming further into focus. A side effect of having no friends and practising at home most nights. The teacher says they can see the progression. Soon but not too soon, we will have an exhibition in the local hall. It's a big deal, well the teacher's saying so. My portraits of Kermit's father look less of Hazel.

Tonight as I paint, I catch myself sneaking looks at Ender. Not like *that*. Earlier when we were getting our pallet boards she informed me she landed a modelling gig for an elderly swimwear website. I guess I'm imagining the type of swimwear she'll model and in what poses.

"They want someone old but still hip," Ender said before bouncing her hip against mine. Any stronger I would've gone flying.

A whole day sneaks by and tonight, Donna leaves Gulliver's, exiting the building but goes around the corner and flips her reversible jacket, puts on a hat and glasses then returns to mine. We've got to be careful with the concierges and the security channel. It's special that she's here but the mood's deflated after we finish the chocolate strawberries and she tickles me.

"Why are you acting so weird, it's tickling," Donna says.

Flashbacks of Pritek's tickle torture glove deflate the mood. Donna decides she's not going to stay over tonight.

"I can't get to sleep in other people's beds," Donna says and I agree to drive her back to her place.

Rushing to take her hand, we dance into my spare room. As soon as I flick on the lamps, we kiss and kiss. It feels like I'm kissing someone else, a secret version of Donna. My heartbeat blends from snare to bass drum. I go and ruin the romance by thinking about Gulliver. What if he knows about this arrangement and Donna's playing two fools off another? The thing that could spoil this is if Gulliver finds out or if he cheats on Donna.

"Got to hand it to you," I say, shaking her hand like a business deal.

"You're being weird again," Donna winces, "What's up with you? Something's dragging you down?"

Stepping back I reveal the spare bedroom and we walk in. I guess the Kermit thing has been bothering me, also hurting the diabetic has made me fear real life connections. I flick on the light in my spare room and hunt for a better hat she can wear but when I return she's pointing at one of my most accurate portraits I kept in case I can't paint better.

"Who's this person you keep painting?" Donna says.

I'm too slow. Donna repeats her question louder.

"It's this man. He chases me in my dreams. Must paint him to get him out of my head. Messed up. Tell me about it," I say.

Donna nods her head like she knows exactly what I'm going through. She lifts one of my best portraits and studies it with a curled lip.

"I like how you do their eyes," Donna says, "What's this one called? If you don't mind me asking."

This gives me the idea, despite Donna's eye rolls, to name my best painting 'If You Don't Mind Me Asking'.

The eyes in this portrait have clock hands going around Kermit's father's pupils. An artistic display of running out of time whilst taking too long.

Donna looks at her wrist and yawns. I get the message.

"We must leave separately," I say, throwing Donna my car keys, a dusty fedora and a crinkly biker jacket with 'Live Fast - Die Young' printed on the back.

I watch Donna walk fast on our building's security channel. She has the style of someone who used to own a motorcycle but hasn't gotten over the loss of it. The concierge sees her out. Donna turns and waves at the camera. I follow downstairs. Exiting the foyer, around the corner, we get in my car and I drive her home.

The next few days are dull. You don't know how many bad movies, plays and books I have to endure in moments for clients. There's a new regular that doesn't like the act of eating so I have to eat with faded-skills making it a chore. I'm outside after my shift, the sky's like a live painting coated in frustration. I know, I know, we need action. Something has to happen to progress this story. Conflict and resolution.

I found the greasy lady. She's on a rampage, munching various crusts from various pizza boxes.

"Do you know where Hazel is?" I say.

She stops still, before blowing crumbs from her fingers, "She's busy planning revenge, not gonna tell you."

I try to plead with her but she changes her tune and says she doesn't know. The conversation becomes tense and awkward, as to why I'm so interested. She blames me and asks me to reimburse her for using her time. I leave splashing through puddles.

Sad, think of all those people that didn't care enough about saving Kermit. But hey, you didn't give up when most would. This shows you're a caring individual.

We must share a special secret for reaching this moment together.
Here, especially for you:

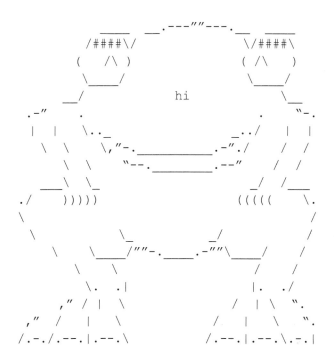

This is a token, a symbol that endurance and patience is valued. They won't know this is here, will they? Let's pinkie-promise to keep this as an inside joke between us. By sharing this frog we're making fun of all those other readers that gave up.

I'm going to leave it there, it'll make no sense to anyone who's listening to the audiobook but by looking into the frog's eyes I feel your support, your energy transmitting beyond the page, shaking the timeline of destiny and fortune.

What should we name this chapter so it's not easily found by people? So they won't know anything special is here. You're right, something simple and boring. How about a toothpick? True, we need something less sharp yet more boring. Stapler? No one would want to read a chapter called that. They will never know about this moment we shared.

You're going to help. We'll save Kermit, somehow. Before I reach my tally, before my vacation/holiday where I think I want to go travelling. I don't know how we'll do it but I'm sure we'll think of something we can't think of now. I know you can be trusted because, well remember in the second chapter I told you to stop reading if you couldn't be? I want you to know, honestly—if you were in trouble I would help you.

Twenty-one: Pens

4616 moments

A week and still no Kermit. We better find a way to save him before I reach my tally. Gulliver catches me on my way to work. It's rare for him to be awake this early. Judging by the times of day I see him–plus his haircuts and clothing, I doubt he's a momenteer. He's too social to operate as anyone other than himself.

"Want to come with me to the library?" Gulliver says, "I've decided to return their mug of pens. You're the only one that knows I stole them."

"Oh, those?" I say looking into the same mug of pens from weeks ago, but it seems he's added some of his own pens. The mug is that soft shade of pink they use to reduce aggression.

His offer is a surprise but I reject it. On my way to my car, a text from Pritek stops me from starting the engine. It's a reminder they're closed today for planned maintenance and upgrading of the servers. Huh, I don't pay attention, this would explain why I went to work last week despite having the day off. How can I trust my memory over the incident if I'm forgetting these things. All I know is in a couple of weeks it will be Emma's sixth birthday.

Out I get and lock the car, regret squeezes my throat as I yell to Gulliver. "Wait."

It's a long walk, not the closest library. This is my perfect chance to ask him about birthday buddies. Judging by his usual ideas, he'll have a different insight I can counterbalance against any astrology book.

"Same year and planetary birth locations?" Gulliver says.

141

I itch my collar "No, but same day of birth."

He stops, shakes the pens in the mug. "There's no true connection, these individuals might be offered the same choices in life but that doesn't guarantee they will make the same decisions. Therefore young squire, it's unlikely they'd be on the same life path."

"But what if they were like best friends?"

Gulliver shrugs "At best, these two birthday sharers might have similar personality traits, but this might make them clash."

I turn silent while Gulliver explains why he stole the pens, something about guest fees and faking his registration. Maybe Kermit and I don't have a good bond? Feeling lost inside, my thoughts run wild and I imagine having a bond with Gulliver. Nah, I'm kidding. He dresses like a futuristic cowboy in triple denim (denim shoes), his greasy part of hair now dyed neon blue. He's okay to talk to, kinda.

At the library, we're in a long impatient lineup/queue. I had no idea libraries are this busy. We stand on a rough lime carpet. I can smell the books, old and new. The people too, old and new. The staff look sweaty and tired. There are 15 or so rowdy teenagers here, rugged looking like they bully the skaters. Their presence makes me want to leave literature and scanning/printing facilities behind.

"Leave the pens on a desk," I say.

"Never. They must be returned personally," Gulliver stamps.

It takes 15 minutes and we're almost at the front when an old lady uses a tissue to shuffle people aside from behind us, shooing people aside like germs. I see her approach and feel her pushing others and then me. I block her and grab Gulliver close. A tap on my shoulder makes the bone sink.

"Frankly. I was here before you." The lady groans like a broken refrigerator.

"No. I saw you come in from outside," I say and Gulliver nods to confirm we did.

He adds "Look. don't take this the wrong way ma'am, but we were here before you."

The use of the word ma'am makes the old lady yelp then her mouth attempts to eat that yelp. "No, I was here first and when I say 'here' I'm referring to this earth. E es tee 1962. I deserve to be served. It was me that was here first, before you two thugs."

An idea comes to name my next painting '*Don't Take This The Wrong Way*'.

The lady is small and tries to burrow under my arm but I flick my hip to block her. I'm taken aback when I spot Gulliver speaking sign language to a staff member behind the desk. By Gulliver's exhale and glances at his feet the sign language discussion isn't going well. He lets the lady progress beside us and I block her with my forearm.

"Let her pass," a voice ahead squeaks.

We stand close and firm together not allowing the 1962-born lady to pass. She presses on the small of my back and I turn to get a good look at her. Exactly what you'd expect. Dark curls licking the back of her ears, pristine sad red lipstick and neck fat. You can't argue with the wrinkles shaped like barrels around her eyes. Guilt makes me step aside but Gulliver places his arm out. There's reckless pushing and the library staff leave their desk and tell Gulliver he's banned and to leave.

Various voices collide: *Hey, don't push me, well don't push me, stop it. I'm not. You are. Argh. I said stop.*

"Haven't you heard of forgiveness?" Gulliver shouts into the ceiling.

I don't know who says it because our bodies are in a pushing war, but someone mutters: "If I haven't heard of it, it doesn't exist."

Tempers erupt in the library of all places. The Baker-Miller pink mug fails to stop the aggression. The rowdy teenagers get involved pushing us and each other. I kneel on the floor with my hands shielding my head. Bad idea as people knee my ribs. I need to get back up. Ouch. Someone with camouflage cargo shorts is pushing me. I turn to see another pair of Gulliver's odd days-of-the-week socks. This pair is different from last time but at least one sock is correct. I spring to meet an army of cardigan-covered elbows jousting me.

"But I'm here to return your," Gulliver launches all the pens into the air. They travel up, hovering between floors. "Pens" he finishes as they return back towards us.

My eyes land on a man playing with putting his false teeth in and out of his gums. We share this moment. A couple of pens hit our shoulders. My cheek is hit and it stings. The man drops to the floor shielding his face with a flat cap. It all feels unnecessarily intense. There's a gap between my lips that won't shut.

"Your guest fines are now doubled," the librarian resembling a praying mantis says.

"Your fines are imaginary. Find them in your fiction section. I bet your printers aren't even working today," Gulliver pushes someone back.

"No they aren't but that's beside the point. You're banned,"

The brawl settles. My mouth finally closes because Gulliver whips out his penis and pees on the carpet. It becomes illegal. From the noise of it, you can tell he's interrupting the flow. Everyone but me scatters, giving us space. It's an unpredictable moment and honestly fun to be involved in. My heels hop and I don't know where to look. It's interesting to see the penis that Donna integrated into our lives. It shouldn't have taken this long, but I should enjoy and experience the moments I'm in without trying to leave them. His penis is tucked back in when a duo of security guards march our way. I realize/realise why Donna likes Gulliver, he's unpredictable and funny which is a lethal combination.

Gulliver and I run around the aisles of books, displays, tables and computer chairs. I'm in flow. I'm truly experiencing this moment as my pure self. My smile won't shut up, our giggles either. We evade authority with arched backs and silky shirts.

We fail and fall by knocking a stand over. The stocky one of the two guards trips over it as well but goes flying into the bean bag chairs.

The old lady that said she was here before everyone looms over us. She sounds like she's swallowing a scream. She points at us. I try to give her a high-five from the floor, rejected.

The other security guard is breathing like a bull. They're approaching us. Shit. Now they're punching their palm and making a screwing motion. Maybe this is the end for me?

No.

Gulliver throws a few hardcovers and plastic book holders (which are clear and they don't see coming) at the guard which gives me time to recover and run. We run too fast for the automatic doors to open. We have to wait a second, giving us enough time to look over our shoulders at the unnecessary carnage before we exit.

Outside, we dash down the street until we no longer recognise/recognize the surroundings, until our breaths are demanding and short.

"Wasn't that indecent exposure? Aren't you gonna be in trouble?" I say.

Gulliver blows his lips "They don't know my government name or where I reside."

As we catch our breaths Gulliver takes a leaflet out of his pocket.

"You dropped this. When we were running."

"What is it?"

Gulliver reads it and my face warms. It's a flyer for my art exhibition. He immediately invites himself. I bite my lip to stop the sudden sinking feeling of dread.

"You can come. I guess," I say and his face lights up.

We travel back together and you know what? He's alright. We're on the hill looking down on our building, if you squint and have someone point where it is, you can pretend to see it too.

"It's all downhill from here," Gulliver says, running down the hill and I follow, giggling. We create our own game as we descend the hill. It's like tag but it involves being caught in reflections.

At the bottom, my social anxiety appears and my confident walk falls apart. My feet try to walk in different directions from another. I lie and say I'm busy and have to go somewhere so he won't assume we'd hang out when we reach home. An awkward silence drifts between us, all my doing. Without words, Gulliver slows his pace to match mine.

"Stop," Gulliver says across from our building. "We forgot to let our bones know that we have to celebrate, yes our brains know, but do our body parts know we've tasted success?"

We cheer our arms then whole bodies. Gulliver lifts me onto his broad shoulders and jiggles me. It feels like we won a trophy. We are the library security direct-avoidance champions! A kid with their parents retreats from us while Gulliver sets me back on the ground.

Our giddiness vanishes and I aim my walk towards my parking spot. Gulliver walks away to our building but turns back remembering something. He jogs up and gives me a tight hug. It lasts for a moment longer than it should.

The hug ends as he slaps me on the back. For some reason when his hand strikes my spine I feel a hollowness inside, an empty echo. The echo shockwaves through my belly, out my throat and ears, across the cityscape—its lights, its street signs and vehicles. Every building, every sewer, every piece of litter and person here. I imagine birds on wires turning their beaks, spiders slipping, people touching their windows receiving an unexpected shiver, as the slap informs every living thing of my entire emptiness.

Did Gulliver feel it? My hands cover my belly and we share a goodbye nod.

Getting in my car, embarrassment floods. Gulliver's waving. I forget where I lied to him about driving to, so I drive away and around various streets aimlessly until I remember. I need to buy a birthday card, a funny one for Emma.

Twenty-two: Exhibition

4630 moments

At our end-of-class exhibition, white plastic cups are filled with Shiraz or rum mixers. Our portraits slouch on easels while a select few hang on rusty nails. Most of us are tipsy by the time Gulliver appears. Gulliver brings Donna and Donna brings Ruben. A faint purr of jazz dances around our bodies.

With an hour to go, it's not weird to see Donna with Gulliver but it's perplexing to see Ruben perusing our art.

"Hm, are you following me?" Ruben says and my shoes slide into him and I need to push off his abs.

You know, I think I was. Remembering what it was like to be him, how things felt in his perspective.

"No, same directions," I say, squeezing the words out like paint from a tube.

I'm standing upright and dodging guests to sneak aside. I leave with a smile but you can tell Ruben's smile back is forced.

There's a wonky goatee man who's been loitering the last hour. He's wearing a black Metallica hoodie with the hood up. He asked me if I was in Green Bread and I said maybe but to forget it because that was so long ago. Quick, walk away from him. Momenteering has changed how I connect to strangers.

Must keep my distance from Ruben. From afar I keep looking at the back of his head. So strange to see him moving when I'm not controlling his body. Flashbacks of being him intermingle with other moments I've worked. I want to ask him how he got the momenteering implant, but I can't trust him.

Somehow, Gulliver has already given himself the position of barman as he dishes out snacks and drinks from behind the stained sheet table. Donna and I talk with my teacher, pretending we're strangers. I must've slipped up because Donna gives me an enlarged eyes look and walks off.

"No, we don't know each other. She's a friend of a... someone I know," I say to my art teacher.

The art gallery wine invites waves of randoms indoors and loosens our opinions. I peruse our art again and it isn't even a competition. Tommy has the best painting. It's a good thing that Ender has that model job because her portrait is childlike, but maybe that's the art. I'm no critic and who's there to judge the critics? Donna approaches me with Ruben.

"Ruben's got to go but he enjoyed the art," Donna says.

But I wonder as he's standing next to her, why didn't Ruben say that?

"Yeah, busy boy these days," Ruben confirms before looking at his empty wrist.

Ruben and I shake hands and I thank him for coming. I think: he must know about Donna's dating arrangement. Maybe he's known for longer than me. What else has he momenteered out of? When Ruben leaves, Donna goes to stand with Gulliver and I get a premonition I'll never see Ruben again.

This is the end of my journey with Ruben, please only read on with the knowledge there will be no more Ruben Whateverhisnameis.

I'm standing woozy studying Tommy's painting of Ender. Tommy didn't come tonight but he's painted a stunning portrait. He's painted his own forearm, hand and brush in the act of painting Ender. I mean, who thinks of painting yourself in the act of painting an already great painting.

The wine's snorkelling in my blood. I float around, looking melancholic at the shiny floors, sad because I sense I'll never see Ruben again. Sure, I might bump into him, but not *this* version. I must be tipsy-wipsy because I'm thinking how as people we have different versions of ourselves and change every week. I trip and hold onto a wall for support.

My hand is squeezed. I sway like an insecure bowling pin.

"Is it fine that my hand is there?" Ender says.

My neck drops to see my hand being held by Ender.

"It fine." I squeeze hers. It's warm.

Ender's weaning stylish dungarees. She and I stroll around the gallery, her dainty hand leading the way. It's getting busier. We move around the people and easels before aiming our walk to get a refill from Gulliver operating the bar. Still, we hold hands with no expectations or assumptions. It feels nice. I'm humming a new tune. Donna sees us but doesn't seem to care.

Gulliver refills our drinks. We walk back to our pieces. Our portraits face each other on their easels. Ew, Gulliver poured this rum too strong.

"It's okay if your friends don't like your art," Ender says.

"Why didn't Tommy come?" I say.

"He wanted to but he's got a date."

My eyebrows leap then fall as I face my portrait. They leap again when I turn to compare mine to Ender's portrait of Tommy. Her portrait is so bad—the birthday card I stupidly sent Emma earlier had better art and that's saying something. The card had an illustrated clown on it that looked more like a balloon-stealing ghost.

Our hands should separate but they don't. Then it makes sense what's happening in this moment. Ender and I are holding hands while we both think each other's art is poor. Ender's calming and sincere demeanour makes this moment dissociate from reality and takes us to warm nostalgic memories. This is the first time I've experienced a moment so pure. It's a profound moment, a finding buried treasure moment, a moment so intricately woven it could only last a moment, moment.

My portrait '*Don't Take This The Wrong Way*' frowns on the easel. The lines around Kermit's father are sharper in this one. His neck and gaze are crooked. The face is propped by a chiseled jawline that's been clipped by a razor. I overheard a few comments about the cut looking like a smudge, making me regret not submitting '*If You Don't Mind Me Asking*' instead.

We turn again to face Ender's portrait of Tommy. I wince then mask my expression with a smile. It's bad, it's more like a gun range target body with a doodled face. Maybe it's the reason Tommy didn't come? I mean if someone painted me like this I wouldn't come.

Gulliver reappears, his presence making Ender remove her hand from mine. He drops something and I pick it up for him. It's a business card, a stranger's name. He puts it in his pocket so carefree that it drops to the floor again. I nod towards it but he's looking at the art. No, I'm not going to pick it up.

"I like this one, it's so innocent," Gulliver says.

To my surprise, he's facing Ender's portrait. Donna comes and we all make comments and then comment on those comments. Standard conversation creation. Ender explains about her beautiful divorce and how they're still friends. Gulliver nods a lot and keeps asking questions. It gets to the point in the conversation that I haven't spoken for so long that I'm not sure if I'm still part of the conversation. I should make a stupid comment or laugh loud followed by a question, but Gulliver is in charge of the talking.

Ender gives Gulliver a giggle and squeezes his shoulder before leaving. Wow, what an avoidance move. Beside him I watch Ender leave, wishing her steps to reverse. I'm left with Gulliver and still have the instinctual urge to avoid him.

"So you like the looks of senior gentlewomen? Their aesthetics, my mistake," Gulliver says. While my thoughts buffer he interrupts by whipping a slap across his thigh, "I'm kidding, I know not every female you know has to be romantically connected, a platonic gin and tonic,"

He raises his plastic cup and I cheers it. My fake laugh shifts to one of true relief. I aim a foot away, but my one leg is drunk. It boomerangs around my body. Out again and it swings back. Did I accidentally create a dance move?

Gulliver holds my lower back, "Where's your painting K-man?"

"I'm K-man," I say, feeling the identity of being a K-man forming around me.

We look at one another. By his slow-dance eyes, I can see that he's been helping himself to drinks too. I turn and point to the wrong piece, a self-portrait the teacher did, then correct my silly finger.

"Arr, you know this guy too?" Gulliver says.

His words don't register for a while. An earthquake shudders my bones. He turns and says how innocent Ender's painting is and how he wants to get a commission.

"Wait, what did Gulliver say?" I say. Oops. I say my thoughts out loud. Stupid wine.

"I'm Gulliver," Gulliver giggles.

Wonder and panic collide. I tug him and turn his head to face my portrait, "You. you said, you know who this is?"

My fingers make his head nod yes as he says "Yeah, I know this guy, not personally but I've seen him on streams."

Dizzy, spinning, my thoughts instantly melt on top of each other. My stream of consciousness is a blur.

"Take your hands off my boyfriend!" Donna pulls me (her other boyfriend) back, my teacher helping her.

There's a scuffle. What happened? I stop saying I'm fine because I know if you say it too much it means you aren't. Things calm but Gulliver won't tell me who my portrait is. I try to explain why I must know but the focus shifts to me, as to why I was grabbing him.

"Isn't this the man you dream of?" Donna says, her eyes skipping around, her nostrils sniffing "You... told me... about it earlier when I asked you. When my boyfriend was serving drinks."

Must keep my mouth shut. They can't know secrets if I don't secrete words.

"We're okay, he was excited," Gulliver says, before helping our teacher take me to the back to sit in a dark unused room.

"We'll come get you, when the exhibition is over," my teacher says.

The door squeaks shut and darkness appears. My thoughts resemble a never-ending pong match. Wait, why didn't I think of this until now, why don't I post the portrait online to see if anyone knows? Damn. Where? Pritek will know of any website I visit. Gulliver knows who Kermit's father is? This has to be a joke. Of all the billions it's the one person I like to avoid that knows. I point to the ceiling while time hiccups by. No higher power explains.

Ender comes to say goodnight. Kneeling next to me, she squeezes my hand and says, "We must let go of mistakes or they'll haunt us," I tap bye on her arm. Her advice flies over my head, especially because I'm currently in the process of making mistakes.

The lights come on. My teacher reappears with her arm around me and rubs my back. I feel better, well not better, less dizzy.

"It's okay, no problems," Gulliver says after I apologize/apologise.

Everyone leaves. The teacher locks the doors of the gallery. About ten of us are caught in a cluster as we descend the elongated steps.

Call it muscle memory, call it a big mistake but I take Donna by the hand and we walk. Donna must be drunk too because she goes along with it. Aw, she does her little gallop down the steps. We stop and turn. My teacher's tilting her chin inward. Gulliver's approaching. Too late. He's seen. Caught. Donna's hand pulls away. I grab tighter while Donna's sigh breezes over my cheeks.

I rub Donna's hands "Your hands are kinda hot let me feel your boyfriend's," and I reach out and grab Gulliver's hands, then my teacher's. We all hold, rub and compare the heat of each other's hands. I rub Gulliver's for longer, they're big and smooth while my teacher's are rough and small.

"Gulliver has the warmest hands," I announce.

When I lift my head, I'm so relieved to see Gulliver's dumb smile. My teacher must be tipsy too because she argues that she's got the warmest. Honestly, Ender's were the warmest but she left twenty minutes ago. We leave Gulliver and Donna to hold hands. I walk beside my teacher and we both hide our hands in our pockets, regretting the competition that just took place.

Ahead, that person from earlier, his hands hidden in the joining belly pocket of a Metallica hoodie looks back. He slows his walk and puts his hand out before us.

"Check how warm mine are," he says.

"No late entries," I jog away from everyone and find a taxi.

"Where to?" The driver says through a dreamcatcher covering their rear-view mirror.

"Home," I say.

The driver looks at all their mirrors and my eyes follow their gaze.

"Do I look like I know where that is?"

I raise a thumb, I should say where, but Gulliver and Donna enter the taxi and squeeze up. I can't think of my address but when Gulliver says it, I nod as people do after hearing the answer on a game show.

"Correct," I say.

Gulliver knows who Kermit's father is and Donna's in the middle, her thighs are squashed between both of us, resembling packaged hot dogs. The taxi accelerates, we all lean back then I lean forward.

You know what, I've had enough of my own moments for today.

Twenty-three: Crimson & Crows

Mister Rosenthal's blathering about these Japanese types of poems called 'hi-kews' or something. He shows the class examples but Kermit yawns and swings on his chair.

"What does crimson mean anyway?" Kermit says.

Rosenthal opens the drawer and pulls out his trusty and worn dictionary. "It's a rich and deep red inclining on a purple."

Kermit's eyebrows shrug "Why don't those poem people write red anyway? If that's wha—"

"Because it's poetic," Rosenthal interrupts, "it's descriptive, emotive, beautiful. To understand poetry, you must realise this. I don't know, maybe you kids are too young."

If this was poetry, Kermit didn't wanna know. He vows to himself to ban the word crimson from his vocabulary.

Zoe waves a piece of deep red paper in front of his eyes saying, "Crimson. This is yer crimson."

Kermit bats the paper away, revealing Zoe's face. Uh-oh, not Zoe. Kermit didn't know what to do with these feelings, they were too new and complicated. The problem is that in the last two months her presence made his insides feel like they were melting. Kermit covers his eyes, if he can't see crimson or Zoe they can't confuse his mind.

His mother has banned orange objects from his household because she says it invites aggression, so what's stopping Kermit from banning crimson from his life? Last week Dad got in trouble for bringing an orange sports flyer back from badminton. He lost chore credits and didn't have enough to combine them with Kermit for a movie night in the living room. Kermit stamps his foot to commemorate the beginning of the crimson ban. He pumps his fist under the table, celebrating that he'd made a decision. He knew there were hundreds more to come that would shape his life. His parents taught him that once someone makes a decision they can't change their minds. Kermit obeyed most rules, especially those his mother set, but none more so than those he imposed on himself.

Rosenthal details three lines of the 5-7-5 syllable rule of a haiku. Kermit's interest peaks. He likes the security of rules. He focuses deeply. Something's making Kermit want to read. Well, as long as the poems don't mention crimson then he'll read. Rosenthal asks Zoe to read one aloud. The poem's about hope being a place not a feeling. Kermit's legs run nowhere under the table. He feels hot but when he pulls his collar, beside him, he catches eyes with Zoe, her curly brown hair framing a rosy face. He must sneak another glance, one at her tights then another at her wrists. He holds his shoulders but his stomach floats with an unknown pleasure.

These feelings are worrying. He didn't know if it was what the poets called love. After all, Kermit hasn't decided what sexuality to have, he wasn't sure if he even wanted one–he's about to turn thirteen. It can't be like *that*, not yet. Kermit reassures himself. Mum says love doesn't arrive until you're at least 21. Who cares what the other channels on TV say, that stupid *Naked Attraction* 4 am show he mistakenly caught his dad doing the sign language for, ew.

Under his breath, Kermit hates himself for feeling different. The sexuality decision looms large, especially because next week their class would have their dreaded health and relationships class. Kermit thinks of the kids a year ahead of him, how they changed after watching that DVD.

Luckily, Kermit's distracted by a murder of crows outside the window. The crows are jet black beautiful, that dark they reflect glints of blue. He couldn't take his focus off them—no matter how good the other haiku sounded. The crows are up to something, doing intricate dances and performing a ceremony. The crows move back and Kermit stands to look over the dip in the hill.

"Sit, Kerr," Rosenthal says.

Zoe tugs his school tie but Kermit pulls to see the crows.

What are the crows up to? Rosenthal stands in the way and Kermit peeks around him. One of the crows is sleeping or sunbathing and seven others are gathered around, squawking at the back. Their sound travels across the playground and drifts in the window along with the cold air.

Kermit sits, thinking about the crows' ceremony. *These poems are nice but nature is better.* The crows made every movement matter and soon Kermit understood why.

"Party??" Kermit says looking out.

"Kerr O'Sullivan... if you don't pay attention..." Rosenthal says.

Kermit sits and goes quiet but at the first opportunity, he sneaks on his phone and searches if crows have ceremonies. There's a few posts saying that they have funerals.

The next haiku the class read is about... who knows what. Kermit isn't listening because a crow has flown on the ledge of the window next to Zoe's seat. Kermit tilts his head and so does the crow. Is the crow looking at him? Kermit narrows his eyes and feels its eyes on him. He'd never felt a stare like this. It's a warning of something, indicating a change. The bird flies away but leaves a chill.

The homework is set. The class has a week to write their own haiku poems. Predictable Rosenthal. Kermit thinks about writing a poem for Zoe. Wait no, he's got to make it not about Zoe. It has to be one that no one will know the meaning of.

At home, Mum's busy making music, Kermit must keep quiet and be in his room by five. Dad cooks and brings his dinner to his room with a snack box. Kermit watches *How It's Made* episodes and plays games on his phone, trying to distract his brain from decisions but there's so many and they're coming soon. He consults an online thesaurus and starts his poem, that's not about Zoe.

All these decisions were coming and Kermit was unprepared. He wishes he could have a scan that pregnant ladies get of his own skull to see if there were any clues. What sports and which teams to support, which phone network, what type of hairstyle, style of winter jacket, how many best friends to have, how many children to have, which city to move to, which hot drink, what hobbies to do in the spare time from the career he didn't know either.

At 10 pm, as usual, Dad comes in to say goodnight. He must be taking his cool pills because he's fun. He does this new stutter thing before speaking.

"You know, if you only do one thing in life you are limiting your experiences," Komo, piloting Kermit's father around chapter 8, says.

Bruce returns to his mind talking about homework and rules before leaving. Kermit cringes at his flamingo poster, thinking: at least I've made a decision on what's my fav animal. Although bored of flamingos and wishing he picked crows or sloths, Kermit at six years old had already made this decision and we all know there's no going back.

◆

A week goes by. The day Kermit's been dreading is here. The class are sharing their poems.

Kermit fidgets next to his desk, clears his throat and doesn't know where to put his hand that isn't holding his notebook.

'A puddle of crows
Evaporating in sun
Unsure of the meaning'

Kermit looks around. The whole class has never seen Rosenthal's eyebrows so high. Twisty lines that resembled borders on maps appear across his forehead.

"Good Kerr but you need to remove a syllable from the last line," Rosenthal says, counting the syllables on his hand.

A cluster of kids break the tension with laughter. Billy's cackle stands highest. Perfect. Kermit rubs his hands. He didn't want anyone to understand his haiku in case it showed his soft side. Zoe flashes the crimson paper in front of Kermit as he sits back next to her and he punches it.

"Hey, I don't like violence and I didn't like your poem," Zoe says.

"Good," Kermit says, trying but failing to control his male gaze from scanning her again.

"Did you like mine?" Zoe says.

'Homework is for fun
Always is, has and will be
Never ever late'

Of course he did, it was clever. Rosenthal gave it top marks unlike his. The whole class laughed but in a different way.

"Can't remember yours," Kermit says.

He turns to face Zoe, it feels like his lungs have inflated and popped. Is she wearing lipstick? A heat tenses his veins. Weren't we too young for lipstick, wasn't that for high school after summer break? This is cheating. Kermit punches the table. Zoe

161

moves her seat away and flicks her hair. Rosenthal marches over and sends Kermit to the hallway for a time-out.

In the hall, Kermit repeats a developing mantra: *I don't need to decide my decisions today.*

Back in class, the clock sneaks ahead when he isn't looking over his shoulder at it. Kermit tries to focus on the maths lesson, but all these numbers nosedive him. He doesn't want to go to their health and relationships class. It's going to change him and his classmates. Anger simmers within him because his parents didn't opt him out. Caught in a spiral, time is creeping on his back, crawling up his shoulder blades and across his neck.

The bell rings in a blurt, not the normal way. Kermit's belly… where was it? Mrs Green arrives and takes the boys over to the gymnasium. Before he leaves Kermit looks back at Zoe the same glum way the crow looked at him a week ago. Billy's tapping on everything on the way. Kermit's the last of fifteen boys to arrive. Mrs Green pulls out an old thick television on a wheel-stand before a set of chairs.

"Sit Kerr, go on, now," Mrs Green says before she presses play.

Kermit sits with hesitation. His eyes don't want to watch but can't help it. Mrs Green struggles to contain the boys as they watch the DVD. Kermit never knew his classmates could be so funny. Clusters of giggling and kicking matches burst and fade. Billy makes farting noises or screeches his chair whenever he thinks a lady part appears. Mrs Green holds her hands over her eyes and shakes her head. Hahaha. Attention isn't being paid.

Billy stands after a section of the video and says "Is that what Mr Green does to you?"

The boys explode into a chorus of howls. Kermit holds his ribs from laughing too much, his face in pain from smiling. The boys laugh themselves out of breath. As the class would settle, a silly comment or noise would make it erupt with twelve to thirteen-year-old immaturity.

162

Mrs Green sighs "Listen, I said listen. Listen, you must pay attention. Do you want to remain boys or do you want to develop?"

Mrs Green repeats the word 'develop' so much that the mere mention of it produces further clusters of laughter. The word merges with the video as the narrator mentions females developing breasts and peculiar feelings.

"Deve-lop!" Billy begins a back-and-forth shouting match with the DVD.

Another outbreak of uncontrolled laughter. The video mentions breasts.

"This person talking means boobies, big massive diddies," Billy says before Mrs Green grabs his polo shirt by the collar and sends him out.

All the boys look at the rectangle window on the door and try to listen to the muffled shouting out there. Someone finds the remote and puts the volume down so they can hear. When Green returns the boys sit as if a crime had been committed. Mrs Green looks at them and skips a few sections on the DVD, Kermit expected to see a homosexuality part but the laughs intensified and Mrs Green throws the remote up in the air, almost like an improved mic drop. It falls and the batteries roll out, one of the AAA batteries slips under Kermit's shoes.

The boys elbow and tickle each other, accusing each other of being homosexual.

"I can be homosexy if I want," Kermit says, then wishes he hadn't by the following teasing.

Mrs Green's a devoted Christian so although she stands to lecture the boys, she turns the television off instead. She crosses her arms and stares at the gymnasium's shiny floor. She's supposed to show the whole video and stop for questioning at intervals but the boys have enraged her so much that she won't. The DVD's audio is still mumbling from the connected speakers.

163

She slams a textbook onto the desk as the boys continue misbehaving. The boys only see half of the video and hear some more. They shuffle awkwardly and pull funny faces at one another. Unsure of what the narrator of the DVD continues to talk about. Mrs Green turns off the speaker after five minutes and they sit for another ten in silence before they're taken back.

On their return to Rosenthal's classroom, Kermit thought about what he learned. Hair will grow in smelly places and before sex, you have to put a silly hat protector thing on top of a cucumber. Kermit holds a laugh, looks around before letting it escape. So funny but so weird. Where do you get either of them?

To think Kermit was dreading it before but who knew sex ed could be funny. Also, the best thing, Mum was wrong, there were no forms where Kermit had to decide which sexuality to have. But maybe Mum has these forms at home.

Twenty-four: Avoi-dance

4659 moments

How do you know if the person you're avoiding has flipped the script and is now avoiding you? I've given Gulliver his few days and then some.

Yesterday, I knocked on his door. No answer. The concierge told me he's alive and well.

"We mustn't get involved in your games of avoiding each other when you're both alone," the concierge said before tapping their nose. My previous lies are catching up with me.

Tonight, my ear is up against Gulliver's door. From the African drum music that blends with various chuckles... something's going on. He's a socialite while I'm social-lite. I knock, hard interrupting the flow of the music.

"What's going on in there?" I say and immediately regret it because I'm not his landlord.

A strange stranger with tight clothes squashing a plump figure opens Gulliver's door halfway. They leave and return to announce "Gully needs a few days more."

The scent of weed escapes as the door closes and I escape too. Storming across the hall, I lose a diabetic sock. This doesn't mean I'll start wearing odd socks. I leave the sock and order more online.

I call Donna.

"See Gulliver, do you know if he's avoiding me?" I say.

"Why are you talking about him—maybe you should avoid him, isn't that better?" Donna says.

"But he... nothing, never mind," I bite my lip to stop speaking when I remember Donna doesn't know that I like to avoid him.

"Do love triangles lasssssst loooooong?" Donna says.

"Depends on the intensity."

"What if it's deformed? A liking triangle instead of a love," Donna's voice adrift. Our call goes quiet because I sense bad news is hiding behind her words.

"We might need to meet up. Maybe. We need to talk about something," Donna says.

"About what? Why not tell me now?"

Questions are dodged, we both turn shy and after we say goodnight the phone feels heavier. Maybe it's society's expectations but when someone wants to meet to talk—it's usually important, something that can affect your routine. It could be worse, at least she didn't tell me to sit before telling me something.

The week continues, Gulliver's still avoiding me. At work, the diabetic and I have begun exchanging written notes because he's calculated the times that I'll momenteer for him. Pritek's violation system won't know unless we write our names or addresses. They're clueless about what we're doing unless we tell them. We communicate by writing large on paper because I'm so stupid and didn't realize/realise that he's visually impaired. That explains his warped vision, the mistakes in his writing. I shouldn't, but I tell him how being a momenteer works: how I can't see any identification or intentionally look into mirrors or I'd get kicked out. *Can you write your address and we can become pen friends in real life?* The diabetic's last note reads.

Real Life? I write back explaining that I can't write or see personal details with Pritek. I ask him to give me a few days to work something out. If we manage to become friends I'll have to confess to hurting his ankle.

When I return home, Gwen and Kay from my old book club are inside the elevator/lift. They're pressing and pressing the doors to close before my steps reach. They're doing their best to avoid me and I admire that. Avoiding someone is a beautiful dance that requires the utmost grace, skill and dedication. I stop, fold my arms and smile like a psychopath through the gap in the closing doors. Gwen's eyes bulge goldfish-wide while Kay's freeze to the floor.

Gulliver answers his door tonight.

"It hasn't happened yet, sorry. What day is it? Give me more," Gulliver says through a slit. I overhear giggling and a bird yelp. He must own a bird.

"You said that a few days ago," I say.

"I did?" His voice adrift like Donna's was.

He looks tired and lost. To my mistake, I tell him to take his time. What? I know, I'm frustrated too, but he seems like he needs time. Pangs of guilt rumble my toes at the thought of going back to avoiding Gulliver after he tells me who and how he knows Kermit's father—if he knows.

I guess Gulliver won't know so I leave. At home, there's missed calls and texts from my brother and an email from my ex, I mean sister-in-law. Swiped away, into the archive without reading. Told you if I sent Emma a birthday card the gruesome twosome would be all over me. I'm so stupid and deserve it. I need to think of a new plan, maybe Hazel knows other momenteers?

The next day, a supervisor's controller is unattended. Exiting a moment whilst I was running, I accidentally broke a wire from below the desk. They're under there fixing my station. They've left their tablet. There it is. Just there. Should I? No. I shouldn't. I shuffle my fingers along the table. Back and toward. My heartbeat increases in tempo and bass. I step towards it and yawn to disguise the noise of me lifting it. It's so light. They don't have these in retail. What am I doing? Quick. My fingers scroll, but my eyes scroll the other way. My vision scatters. My hands jitter. What does any of this mean? Time's shrunk, there's none. It's all numbers and vibrant boxes of weird letters and primary tones. Various ones flash or pulse slowly. What do I press to unblock Kermit?

[B6J]"[ERR^] or [HD44^FP"OP{]

Should I press another one? A 50-hour-long YouTube tutorial series might be the only way to understand this alien software. Clueless, I press nothing. My station flicks back on. Lights brighten and crystals clink. The supervisor bends their body out with a distorted groan. My whole body sways. Quick. I fumble the tablet back behind me.

"What are you up to?" The supervisor says, their voice bumpy and bumps me back a few steps. My body jiggles with nervousness like I either can't wait to work or need the toilet.

They reach behind me and grab their tablet and make a hum of contemplation.

I rush forward, pop on my headset, sit and flick in a toothpick. I wish for a job to come. A tension grips my shoulders. My head flicks, trying to look back but I resist. There's a strained silence before the noises of the supervisor leaving nourishes relief. Soon, a job comes where I have to perform a business pitch for a nervous client before another moment of driving a client through traffic and home which takes the maximum duration.

I blink into another consciousness. The aim says: *Death*. My, my… first. Laying, the body feels withered and groggy with a subdued chest pain lingering and an erratic pulse. Struggling to move my arm, the skin droops off the bone. I know it's not an emotion but I feel like burnt food. The beep of a heart machine stabs my ears but soon transforms into music. Must be the painkillers kicking in. Who I know to be my son is standing sullen

168

in the corner of this hospice care. He's an old son, 54. Everything's clean here like no one owns anything for long. Both my son's hands cover his mouth. I'm afraid of dying but not in this mind. In one motion a force both yanks yet smothers me and I feel it. Death. It snuggles up, covers the skin and bites. There's an emptiness hovering inside that vacuums energy like a miniature black hole. Foreign memories burst through my mind. Hundreds of experiences squashed into each millisecond.

These aren't my memories. In various flashes I remember scenes of playing hopscotch as a child, working as a cinema usher before fighting as a soldier in Vietnam, having a son, being married at 22 then up to my forties. I remember getting momenteering, an old corporal recommending me the implant. Warm and sour memories burst through my dying body. It feels wrong to remember these memories yet rude to not experience them.

Death strikes and everything goes black for a moment then a little longer. It's worrying, am I dead too? Just as I think that, light floats in and I'm back out to my station. My eyes adjusting to the light like I just woke up. I hold my headset and stab my inner cheek with a toothpick. It's so good to be alive. Dying has put my mind in a weird place. My advice to anyone is don't momenteer out before you die—you'll miss out on your life.

It turns out to be a depressing day because I blink in with Catherine and the client is breaking up with her. It's a pain but I have to complete the job. This will be the last time I see her, before I'm blinked out I collect a tear running down her cheek and wipe it into mine. We hold hands tight before I'm blinked out.

Undocked, I puzzle myself thinking, are these clients' moments my experiences too, or say, you have a dream, is that an experience? Waiting, I expect a supervisor to appear and talk to me about my death moment but nope. The only thing that changes is the death counter underneath my tally. I signal to leave. My station hums as the crystals contract and expand.

Another supervisor comes with their tablet and congratulates me on my death, but there's no psychological assessment like they said would happen. Whatever. It's clear Pritek aren't as good as they say.

Outside I avoid the skaters and walk to my parking spot. After dying for that old client, I must be stuck to my thoughts because I don't react to seeing Hazel's girlfriend, the greasy lady, leaning on my car

I move my body around her in a long-distance tango. I click the key. My car beeps unlocked. For a second I worry she's going inside but she sprawls over the hood/bonnet.

My fingers grip and pull the door handle.

"Laztech?" She says.

"What's that now?" I say, looking at her arm touching my window wipers.

She scratches her nose before springing to her feet, "Laztech. Hazel used to work there, with you,"

"No sorry. I've never heard of Laztech,"

"You go into other people's minds and live out experiences?" Greasy says.

In disbelief, I drop my suitcase as I reach for the door handle. My fingertips slip the car door open. My shoes lose grip and I swing with the door and go flying over the street. Ouch. Little stones jag my suit jacket.

"Wh, where's, where's…" I say.

The greasy lady looks at the sky, "Hazel?"

Staring into the setting sun, it resembles a crystal ball, my eyes feel like they're reversing into my skull. "Hazel, yes. Where's Hazel?" I say.

Greasy's voice wobbles, her words barely arriving. "Dead. Caught her again, breaking into the basement, to make things right," she sniffs, "A couple of days later... a thug comes assassinates my Hazey,"

Not quite sure what she means exactly. I ease the collar of my turtleneck. My first instinct is that this is a trap but after gazing up at Greasy's glistening eyes, surely no one can act this well without an Academy Award nomination.

Picking myself up and wiping myself down. I reach out for her hand but exactly as Hazel did, she bats it away.

"You touch me and I'll fucking kill you. You maggot."

I hold my hand in the air to signify peace, it works. We stay in our positions and she calms. A stranger walks behind us in this stand-off showing how much time is passing.

Greasy wipes her eyes, "Also, I need to get inside. Make things right, will you help?"

My moment of hesitation is too much. The atmosphere flips once more. Greasy storms off, walking through traffic. I run to catch up. Horns honk and people shout abuse out their windows.

"What do you want me to do?" I say.

"I knew you wouldn't believe me. No one does. Look at your stupid expression, why would anyone?"

My fingers feel my face to check which expression I'm displaying but I only sense confusion. My eyebrows squashed towards another. I pull them apart and smooth them over.

She walks away, her walk triggered by a kick at my shins. Are Pritek and Laztech the same company? I try to stop her to find out what Laztech is, but she insists I don't believe her and that she's too angry to talk.

"I don't trust you." She pushes me onto my heels.

This would be the wrong time to tell her I feel the same.

I watch as she stamps, turns and fades in with a shadow cast by an alleyway. I rush back to my car to find three strangers deliberating about going in with the door wide open. I grab my suitcase and shout. They each raise a hand to show that they come in peace.

I don't know much about crystal balls but I sense serious conversations are coming my way.

Twenty-five: Flicker

4698 moments

A week later in a firelit alleyway eating pesto pizza with Greasy, my eyebrows remain so high they flicker at her statements. Greasy knows so much that either Hazel is dead and was a momenteer or this is indeed a trap. I use finger quotation marks whenever my real job is mentioned, exaggerating my reactions to mask the truth of my role. Greasy details how this is the headquarters and they traveled here from another branch miles and miles away.

"There's more than one branch?" I say but Greasy changes subject.

"Hazel was a top agent until she fell in love with me while she was inside my repulsive husband," Greasy says.

"She was actually inside his body, controlling your husband's mind?" I play it dumb.

She nods proudly "My husband was horrible but for the moments Hazel was inside, he became tender, kind, magical. At first, I suspected he'd developed a split personality but once Hazel confessed her love and explained it all, I jumped on board and believed. The only problem was I needed my husband to exit his mind so I could be with her and it wasn't always Hazel that arrived in his mind."

"How did you meet? In your own bodies?" I say, trying to look as bewildered as you must have when I explained momenteering to you in the first chapter.

"It took a year. We hid our affair until we had a plan. She gave me an airport to meet at. It wasn't until my husband found my flight details in my emails that memories came to him and he reported me. It didn't take Laztech long. By the time I unpacked my toothbrush, Hazel was exposed."

173

"Meaning Hazel lost her job?"

Her words accelerate, Greasy details what happened when Hazel was caught. How she lost her job, her family, her reputation, her life. How Hazel was set up and given a criminal record before going to and escaping a mental asylum. She doesn't detail how they became homeless together, she tilts her head as if I shouldn't have asked.

"They gave her something in that asylum, don't know what but it gradually made her lose intelligence," Greasy says.

As Greasy wipes the extra cheese glow from her fire flickering lips. I think about how I don't know Greasy's true name yet and don't want to.

My legs are shaking in what may be fear so I walk in circles. Kermit comes to mind, he may be being abused by his father but is this worth giving up my life for? What if I'm wrong, what if Pritek sends me to the mental asylum? What if I can't prove my sanity to the guards? What if I become homeless and no one believes a word I say? Homelessness lowers your life expectancy by 20 years.

"Hazel was caught breaking into Laztech. She was gonna make things right. She was planning to momenteer into the company president's consciousness and blackmail her to fix her record. So we could get jobs and live normally," Greasy says.

Greasy has mentioned Laztech so similarly to Pritek that I can only assume they are the same. If true, Hazel must've been a top agent to work for her opposite gender—and for the president. I didn't know we had a president let alone could momenteer for them. If I didn't know this technology was possible this story would sound insane.

I nod like I believe Greasy. I hate this but something's telling me she's lying or this is a set-up, especially when Greasy requests that I smuggle her inside so she can get revenge by blackmailing the president. Despite admitting she doesn't know how the technology works and has no experience. It's not easy being someone else. You need training.

"Hazel was the mind-pilot but told me a lot. How difficult could it be?" Greasy says with a squeezed tone.

"Maybe it's more difficult than it seems?" I say, getting lost in her term: *mind pilot*.

She flicks off mushrooms from a slice of pizza. My eyes follow her dirty fingernails up to her face. She doesn't have a face you could trust but who does? Small sharp eyes supported by a crooked nose.

The flickering fire beside us does its last few waves before becoming faint and dying.

It's difficult to see. Not only in this darkness but what to do in this situation. Call me selfish but I don't think I'll help Greasy, not until I know it's 100% safe and possible. I fumble my wallet and pass Greasy cash. She throws the notes back.

"I want your help, not your money," Greasy says, raising her voice. "You're going to get me in there so I can get revenge?"

My fingers pinch my forehead. Unsure if I can or even want to. If anything, if her story's true, I'm more afraid of Pritek.

"I'm late for work. I'm on night shift," I say before stumbling my way out. I turn, Greasy's trying to spark up her lighter in order to find the cash in the darkness.

"You go into other people's minds though?" Greasy says.

I shake my head no and she can still see this from her angle.

"Don't fucking lie maggot," Greasy says.

The following shrug I do is the fakest shrug ever done in the history of body movements. I never mentioned the word momenteering. Greasy only referred to this act as mind-piloting. Could they be the same? If so, Pritek must call things by different names based on the branch.

At work, my first job is for a client that's suffering heartache as I get broken up with by a Guatemalan bikini model on a yacht. The client can't stop crying, the collar of his crew neck is soaked in tears. I blink into another moment... I grip the sides of this, what's this, a helicopter? My heart thuds into my stomach as the rotary wing chops. In the aim the client uses an Anglo-English term: *Deal with this rubbish*, but I'm clearly in the USA because I'm having a silent panic attack flying near the Hollywood sign. I use mindfulness to calm. I increase the gap between my ears and shoulders before implementing box breathing techniques. I blink out after we land.

After a treadmill walk, I blink into another job. I'm at a big bank. There's tan tights over my head, squashing my face, darkening my vision. I'm holding a gun. I use my breathing training to lower this frantic pulse. The aim is to: `Help friends`. I wave and point the gun toward the bank teller. Their mouth is closed but closed in a way that's noticeable. My gaze is frozen on their blazing iceberg eyes.

Two of the five buddies yell "Hurry up, get the money in the bags," I join in this chant. I'm not a criminal. Honestly, I wouldn't even take the bus for free. This moment is so immediate. I feel my pulse in places I didn't know it could be felt. The beat from my right ankle reminds me that Pritek told us to not commit crimes. My buddies rush me.

How would Pritek know? Unless I see identification, or if this client reports me. I find myself continuing the job with a sense of flow. I wink at the teller but it doesn't work with these tights squashing my face. I grab the bag. An adrenaline rush makes my feet slide across the marble flooring. The cash is light yet also heavy.

My buddies and I shuffle towards the exit. I point my gun at anyone, everyone and nobody. The statue of a fox included.

Nervous, I stumble and stop still. The leader of my buddies points their gun back at me then kicks my shin.

"Come on let's go," Our leader says with his hand pinching my hip.

I laugh tiny exhales of relief and excitement as we leave. My buddy shoots a camera, a bit late for that. We leap into an unmarked rusty van. No seats, I kneel and we all topple into another when the van accelerates. The wheels screech and we hold onto the sides. The noises of engines from outside the van are intensified. I look at my buddies, they look back at me as if I'm not their buddy. My hands can't stay still. My knees move together and apart. I whip the tights off my head and my face feels like a boiled candy/sweetie. Did I rob a bank? Before I can answer, my ears ring and I'm blinked back to my station.

There's no violation on my screen. I undock but no supervisor comes. The sense of guilt is overtaken by a smirk. I eat dried pineapple on the treadmill. Still no supervisor. It's clear they don't know anything unless we tell them. What do all their codes tell them? I do a couple more routine jobs and signal to leave.

The supervisor that sees me out is the one that smells of peaches but they don't smell like themselves today. No questions asked about the robbery. They truly *are* unaware.

Because it's after midnight I must leave out the back. It's early morning and Greasy is loitering around one of my parking spots. She walks like a tap-dancing zombie. The closer I get the more my steps slow and I see she's drugged. I get close and her eyes are dazed, her back arched as if she's casting back a fishing rod.

"Are you alright?" I say.

"Eygjabahtobehungreesazyti," Greasy mumbles.

She grunts and talks more gibberish. I see that she's wearing Hazel's old trench coat. I try to calm her but she's possessed by an unknown substance. Down a side street, she falls into a pile of boxes. I try to help but she kicks hard. I check her pockets and her neck for a wire, a recording device, but nothing.

When her fierce kick connects with my shoulder and knocks me back, I decide to believe Greasy was telling the truth and Hazel is indeed dead. Yet I also decide against helping her get revenge. What she wants needs to be done by someone that's trained, calm and unconnected.

Let's wait for Gulliver to tell me about my portrait first. Doubt he'll know but shouldn't be long now.

Twenty-six: Memory Techniques

4755 moments

Before sleeping, I'm developing these meditative memory techniques to recall my moments with Kermit. I associate the memory of touching the mahogany table and chairs in his dining room with hearing his mother say Kermit's school name. It was Saint something but I don't remember the rest.

If only I could remember a street name. I practise by playing this Geo-location game that places you somewhere randomly on internet maps and you have to guess where you are from the scenery. Problem is, I don't remember much apart from cold air and dull weather which doesn't narrow out enough countries. What else? I remember he told me although he likes flamingos if he could be any animal it would be an eagle. I remember this because he copied my answer. His father has pristine hands. Which career would require nice hands aside from watch/ring model, massage therapist or casino dealer?

If Donna declines another of my invitations to hang out I'm going to accuse her of avoiding me. Gulliver hasn't been around. It's going to sound silly but I'm painting a portrait of him. Donna was weirded out but agreed to send me a photo to work from. The photo is shot straight on, I think he's pretending to save a water polo shot. His hair's sweaty but still flops cooler than mine will ever. This picture is more detailed but I prefer the one I took of his body's imprint on my sofa.

I've stopped counting how many days I've avoided him. Now I count how many days he's avoided me. We're sitting at four, ten days after our exhibition.

Work's the usual of waiting rooms, dentists and funerals. While I'm having another client's root canal, I'm thinking about stealing

179

another tablet and asking Greasy how to use it. I don't know, is there a better idea?

Tonight, I'm meeting Ender of all people. I'm not sure why but a few days ago she accidentally texted me her shopping list. This led to us texting regularly and to Flower Cave, Gulliver's Thai restaurant. At our table that doesn't resemble a table, Ender orders the same as me, the Khao Pad. Ordering the same food is an annoyance of mine but I manage to let it go. On her phone, Ender shows me her photoshoot for the elderly swimwear website.

I'm proud of myself for not adding a 'for your age' after I remark that these photographs are charming.

Her hourglass figure has a few extra grains of sand but can still tell the time.

Ender's shot wearing a flowery two-piece that shows off her flat belly. It has frilly edges with a high waist. Old person's aqua and pink pattern. I don't know why I expected to see wrinkles on her body but she looks similar to the Guatemalan bikini model that dumped me as a client last week.

"Look how you put your hand on your hip here. That's elegance," I say.

We lock eyes and it's comfortable. Everything in this moment is expecting us to kiss, the satay sauce on the table, the lit candle, the red suede cushions on the stone seats, the constantly smiling waiter. She's attractive but don't I have a girlfriend? Can't I have platonic gin and tonic friends?

"You better not be thinking about kissing me," Ender says before licking her molars clear of sticky rice.

I reach out and open the toothpicks. We each take one.

"That's so funny. I was making sure not to think about that," I say, straightening my back.

"So you were thinking about it?" Ender's gaze tickles me. The walls feel like they are narrowing in on us. I stare back with a stupid face and the tension is broken when our smiles grow so wide that we end up laughing. Ender laughs softly, I cover my mouth and laugh into my forearm.

Kissing a 55-year-old lady that's 22 years my senior? Not scared. I've kissed a lot of people momenteering that I wouldn't normally. I prefer our friendship that's blooming. You may have noticed I need friends. We leave and I give her a fist bump which is weird because I've never given one before, not even when momenteering. Ender does it back. Maybe I'm beginning to change.

When I return home Gulliver doesn't answer his door.

The next morning at work I continue to change my parking spot to avoid Greasy. I've seen her a couple of times when I was leaving but I'm great at avoiding people.

I blink in. There's that calming fuzz and fuzzier vision. The feet numb. I'm the diabetic again. He's usually always sitting when I blink in. The aim simply instructs to: Watch this film. I sit on his yellow crumb-infested couch. Raspberries sit in a bowl beside pineapple juice. Aw, I understand what's happening—the diabetic has put me in their body to show me a film. The couch sits one foot from the TV. The film's called *The Castle*, an Australian 1990s comedy. It's funny and when the credits roll I stand to give the television an ovation. I knee the television and ask if it's okay as we both wobble. Behind me, I find a note the diabetic has left:

If you give me your address, can we be penpals? IRL LOL No presh.

My reaction is an aw, however, this soon flips into an aw no—I don't want to be caught and end up suspended, tickled to death or worse.

I write back larger: 'Soon' with a smiley face. I can't write mine but I might have a plan to get him an address before my tally ends. But as you know, the last time you are a client might truly be *the* last time. After I'm blinked out, immediate regret rustles in my veins. Maybe I could give him one of my friend's addresses? What friends?

I knock at Gulliver's again. Nothing. I go to the local swimming pool and manage to catch a water polo match. It's difficult to see who's who with all the splashing and their swim caps but eventually, I find he isn't here.

I work another couple of shifts, my memory techniques seem to be getting worse. In one moment I'm piloting a client with their crying spouse that' lost her 'thongs'. I open their underwear drawer and faded-skills kick in. No, wherever I am, a 'thong' is a sandal. Oh, to understand this I must be momenteering in Australia. I find the sandals and endure the subsequent argument. I try to remember if Kermit had any clues like this. If I did have anything they're forgotten.

I momenteer for the prankster again, I remember his body shape. He's climbed to the middle of a 30 ft rock climbing wall. My fingers are clinging on. My feet slip on a rock. The harness pulls around his waist and I meditate to focus. The fear fizzles out. I feel in faded-skills that the prankster isn't afraid. Kermit pops into my head and I climb the rest of the rocks to the top. I remember that we worked out that Kermit's fav actor is Jim Carrey and he has a lunchbox in his room with, uh, with... I forget... I reach the instructor at the top and walk down the steps on the other side of the wall. I blink out. His prank and my memory are unsuccessful.

After another night scouting our building's security channel and listening through his door, I finally catch Gulliver coming out the lift/elevator in the foyer. My initial instinct is to turn away but I remember I need him and continue the turn, performing a 360° twirl.

"Hey, fancy meeting you here. Did you ever find out who that person in my painting is, not that it, well it does matter. Did you?" I say.

Gulliver's noticeably high and laughs at nothing and makes unthinkable connections between things. He comes up with a conspiracy about our ears being connected to our stomachs and...

"You notice how the air wants us to breathe it?" He says.

My head falls, disappointed, I turn but his hand pulls on my shoulder.

"When I get the evidence, I'll come over," Gulliver smiles. "I've got to wait a few days but I'm gonna get it soon, for sure."

We both nod our heads in sync like we're sharing an earbud from a pair of wired headphones. I hear my fav drummer, Cozy Powell playing the intro to his song "Theme One."

"Yeah?" I say.

"Yeah," he says.

"Yeeeaaahhh," we both say at the same time.

The carrot is in front of the donkey and I'm playing the role of the ass.

Twenty-seven: Reshape

4804 moments

Donna comes over unannounced with falafel bites and Merlot. She's wearing comfy clothes that could be mistaken for pyjamas/pajamas. Whilst speaking into the rim of a wine bottle through its echo she informs me it's over.

"What's over?" I say.

She stares into the rim of the now-empty bottle.

She leans in and keeps the wine bottle as a makeshift microphone between us, "Our thing. The three of us, me and Gulliver too. Finished, all over. It's too much, I'm out."

At first the news stings and I walk in circles thinking of ways we could keep our situationship going but after a few laps of my kitchen island, I convince myself that all good things come to an end. Her bad news wine bottle echo technique is genius. It softened the blow while delivering the message—I must remember this technique for my work.

"Have you told Gulliver?" I say.

"After here I'll go tell him."

"I don't want to lose you in my life, as my friend," I say.

The atmosphere's a sad acoustic song without lyrics or drums. If I keep talking she won't leave and I can delay the acceptance of it being over. There's a faint knock on the door which rushes me into a silly rant, detailing how as lovers our hearts are in fact storage vessels for love and like food every bond has an expiration date. The best hearts are like freezers and can preserve love for the longest. I compare our hearts to refrigerators. Donna shakes her head and chuckles.

"What? That's good, some people have blenders for hearts," I say.

"I'm too busy to get hurt by love again," Donna says.

Although I didn't know them, I sense the presence of Donna's ex in the air and glance at the ceiling.

"A heart can't feel love without the brain," Donna says.

Donna lowers and rests the bottle down. We talk abstractly, discussing humanity as a whole to trick our minds into thinking we aren't talking about ourselves. We reshape my rant and come up with a theory about how relationships are shapes and we can, if we want, shape each bond into unique forms to suit our circumstances.

"We sound high," she says before getting up and kissing me on the cheek. "That was our last kiss."

She didn't have to formally announce that but it's good to know. She lurches towards the front door, slumping away with her belly out. She's wearing cheap sandals, a bleach-stained tracksuit top with unmatching joggers. Ahhh. I understand her technique. She's dressed down for this occasion of breaking up. She's so smart. Her hair is unusually greasy. Her toes are painted seashell white but they're patchy and cracked. You should try to appear ugly when you break up with someone you like, this way you won't hurt them as much. I smile.

Her hand wiggles the door knob. My smile stops.

"Wait," I say with nothing else to say.

She turns and waits. The air we share in this moment must feel as awkward as we do. The waiting continues as I stutter on empty words. My face reels back. What's going on? Quick. I spot Donna blinking rapidly, zoning out before her face twitches.

This is the part from the unwelcome third chapter of my chaotic case notes. I put it there so you'd continue reading and not pass this job on to another momenteer. Plus when we think, it's

186

not always linear. From the delivery of her words, I suspect novice Pritek training. This must be a trainee momenteer piloting Donna's consciousness.

I discover Donna has momenteering and has zoned out at the end of our break up. What else has she momenteered out of with me?

"Don't look at me like that. We're not getting back together," Donna says.

She's back. We exchange a few words. The knocking on my door intensifies and develops a musical jazzy twist.

"Aren't you going to get that?" Donna says.

Mouth ajar, elevated tone, I say, "How could you?"

"Could what?"

I pull my own collar back to stop myself from revealing my job. Questions, questions, all I have are questions. I'm not safe to ask any. Does Donna know I'm a momenteer? We share a look of bewilderment. Donna's dad did invent that microchip... Ruben has it... I've been so oblivious.

"What are you looking at? What happened?" Donna says.

My hips twist away. "Nothing, you were leaving but got dizzy." I look at the ground as if our words have fallen to it.

I better not trigger any memories left in her consciousness. Donna's turned from lover to avoidable in a few blinks. I sneak some glances at her while she's getting ready to leave, again.

Donna's body tenses, she snaps out a finger. "Aren't you going to see who's knocking?"

The knocking becomes firmer and intrusive. I swing the door open. Gulliver's here losing his balance.

"Got it. I found the guy. It took ages because he was on a break," Gulliver says.

So excited, I rush into the hall.

"Donna? Why, what are you doing here?" I hear Gulliver say behind me.

I slip back into my place but Gulliver follows inside. Donna stops still, knowing she has no excuse to be here. My gaze tries to communicate that we need to come up with an excuse for her being in my home. I spot Donna going to pick up the wine. Not her break-up technique, not now. I dodge by Gulliver and into my kitchen.

"So, it's time you—" Donna says before I interrupt by singing *lalala*.

What can I do? My movements jerk. I don't want Donna to tell him about us, because if Gulliver finds out, he will no longer want to talk to me. What's a physical way of showing someone you are only friends? Headlock, a playful one. It's the only thing I can think of. I will get Donna to put me in a headlock, then I'll wrestle out and laugh and thank her for not using her fist this time.

"It's not what you think," I say, stepping towards Donna.

"I didn't think anything, but now you've said that it's got me thinking," Gulliver says, scratching his head.

I stop still. Donna winces like she's stabbed her inner cheek with a toothpick.

"You better explain, this is weird now," Gulliver crosses his arms.

Three steps from Donna, to my side, I see the bottle of Merlot that has already delivered bad news today. The rim glistening ideas to me but all I can think of is: headlock, nothing like a friendly headlock. I sink my knees and bend my chest toward her lap. I open my mouth to whisper headlock instructions to Donna but in the distance, I see it in my spare room… the unfinished portrait I've been painting of Gulliver. I've painted him with a denim swim cap, his expression grinning like Jim Carrey in *The Mask*.

I pretend to slip but stand facing Donna.

188

"I guess we better ruin his surprise if he thinks we're dating or some stupid idea like that," I say tilting my head so only Donna can see my wink.

Donna stands mute. Did she momenteer out again? It's all over to her. She can ruin everything. I whisper to her, "Please do me one last favour/favor."

Donna stops looking clueless and nods towards an intoxicated Gulliver swaying on one leg with his neck popped forward.

I grab the canvas. As soon as the painting's revealed, Gulliver uncrosses his arms and bobs his head.

"Donna commissioned me to paint this," I say.

"It's too wonderful," he says before giving us both a fast hug.

"It's not finished yet," I say as he tries to take it.

Donna hasn't finished figuring out which expression to have yet either.

"What's it called?" Gulliver asks.

A thousand options weave through my imagination. I lean my shoulder towards Donna but she only says "Yeah, what's it called?"

It's all on me and my imagination.

"Momenteering," I say.

Their eyes narrow but by Donna's fixed expression I can tell she doesn't call exiting her consciousness as momenteering. The clients must call it something else.

"It's a new word, it means being fully present in a moment to experience all life has to offer. Donna told me you live in the moment."

Donna shakes her head. I shuffle the portrait away, surprised that Donna isn't surprised that I'm painting a portrait of her soon-to-be ex-boyfriend. This moment is so complicated and confusing I wish I could momenteer out of it but I only get one credit each session and I'm saving mine for when I need you.

189

Gulliver nods with understanding, "At first the word, what was it, momenting? It sounds weird but like an exotic food or foreign director—the more you say it the more familiar it becomes. It creates its own shape in your mouth and soon you won't remember your life before it."

"Exactly," I say.

Classic Gully. Donna's expression fluctuates between fed-up and confused.

"I need to finish it," I say.

"No, what you need is to come over to mine, we're having a party and I found that guy you paint on my television, well it's IPTV."

Gulliver takes Donna into his warm hands. "You're here now baby, so come."

No legs move. Donna yet again sends me telepathic messages of who-knows-what. Eep. I care more about finding out who he thinks is in my portraits.

"Come on, let's go," Gulliver leads the way.

Leaving my place, Donna pulls my collar.

"Break up with him after I finish the painting. It can be a parting gift," I whisper.

After a sigh, Donna nods yes. We both briefly smile before it turns wonky.

"All of us, c'mon," Gulliver pops his head in from the hall.

Donna and I tilt our heads and look at the door frame as if it's not quite the same shape as the last time we passed through it.

Twenty-eight: Overlaid

Still 4804 moments

A vibrant disco light sneaks through a haze of weed vapor/vapour and shadows cast from his living room. Gulliver's hallway is filled with so many plants that it resembles a greenhouse. Multiple trinkets, it's on the brink of hoarding. A bird squawks and we follow its call into the living room. On the way, I spot a poorly printed Mona Lisa with error lines taped to a wall. We follow in, the ceiling is lit like we're either in outer space or under the sea. There are seven sleek others mingling. They all look fit like they could be water polo teammates. I don't feel cool enough to be here. Wait, is that one of our cleaners vaping?

"Plan change. I need to tell Gully tonight," Donna whispers before walking to the only empty sofa.

Donna's statement makes me misstep and perform one of her gallops. A couple of people are shirtless while there's another two overly clothed, one in a sparkling suit jacket with sports shorts and the other in a knitted cardigan. The attire contradictions are dizzying enough, not to mention the samba beat hovering over our shoulders. It's a funky beat, my feet dance without my control as I perch on a smaller armchair next to the projector. Donna's focused on Gulliver, tapping her foot too but not to the music. Gulliver joins the topless gang by taking off his t-shirt, his dark hairy chest contrasting with his white jeans.

The projector shines a 'no signal' message—I squint ahead and see corners of ripped-away posters on the wall. It's a scramble like most parties are. Someone in a red cape and rubber Elvis mask appears and hands me a drink. They say something but I miss it as the samba reaches a crescendo. It's warm, which doesn't explain the suit or cardigan choices. I unbutton my silky shirt and lift my glass to see a purply darkness. The room smells like burnt strawberries. There's a pause in the music and I overhear that the bird is a cockatiel and it's named exactly that, Cockatiel. Isn't that sad? My legs cross. Imagine a human called that, Human. *Hello my name is Human.*

I lean towards Elvis to discuss my thoughts but she/he/they push my cup from below and say, "Drink up or shut up."

It's clear the shirtless have more authority here than the clothed. Our eyes meet, at least I think they do, and I place the cup to my mouth but trick Elvis by only pretending to drink. Gulliver sure parties hard, maybe he's an operational alcoholic? Donna's on the edge of her seat trying to catch Gulliver's attention. The music is lowered but most apart from me and Cockatiel complain that it's too low. Feet fumble and hands tap on the speaker. The music returns to a level that requires you to shout to be heard.

Gulliver points at the wall, smiles at me and performs a twirl before yelling. "Turn it on. Turn it. Turn."

Elvis holds out the credit card-sized remote. The drink tastes metallic. Gulliver barks instructions to Elvis. A menu screen appears on the wall.

"No, up, down, home, no, back, up, no, no, home, left. Give me that," Gulliver says.

After a while, we reach an IPTV recordings section. What's IPTV? Gulliver marches over and grabs the remote. Donna mouths to me, not sure what. Looking in the cup, the liquid inside glimmers like oil in a puddle.

"So, where is it? Is it this one, no, this one?" Gulliver says, the remote behind his back, his fingers dancing over the buttons. Strange thumbnails flicking by.

My legs uncross and knees stick together. I lean forward with excitement, dread and hope. I expect to see a stranger, a lookalike of Kermit's father. We end up on the news which was recorded at

4 am a day ago on a strange foreign network. A channel I've never heard of. Gulliver presses play and a loading circle appears. Five seconds feel like an hour. I rub the arm of my chair.

One blink and there he is… all this time and there he is. I rise to check, it's him. No one else but. Exactly like his selfie on Kermit's phone. Standing in the bottom right corner layered above the news. Hair flicked back so it doesn't flop. The mountain ridged face with ashtray hair. Kermit's father. Wearing a black cardigan while providing sign language interpretation for the deaf. It's him. I didn't know people could do this on television. Can't believe it. So woozy, I must sit.

He's real, really real. Kermit's father is on this side of reality with me. I want to get up and touch him, but Donna stands in front of my path. I palm her legs away but she won't move so I duck around and focus on the video. She speaks to Gulliver, in the lulls of the samba beats, I overhear her breaking up with him as if she is dubbing Kermit's father's face while he signs and mouths to the camera.

"…think of it as my parting gift to you. I'll still cut your hair," Donna finishes saying.

I slurp a big gulp of the drink. Kermit's father has all these endearing mannerisms and facial expressions that could make someone think he's friendly, innocent almost. No. However, hearing Donna break up with Gulliver beside me counteracts Kermit's father's wrist flicks, forced smiles and calm poses. In life, nothing happens for months so why are these two things happening at once?

So shocked I must be dizzy. To see how insane I am, I try to count the people in the room. Four… there's double that though. What's double of four? I giggle into my chest, mocking my brain for not being able to calculate this simple equation. Thinking of the mental asylum makes me focus.

4 x 2 = confused emoji

"This interpreter doesn't speak my sign language but you can tell he's not the best interpreter on TV," Elvis leans and casts over their opinion.

Only Elvis and I are watching the projector. It's that stage in the party where music selection takes priority. Of course, I didn't know there were different versions of sign language.

"What language does this man speak?" My hand straightens and I fan my face. Me and Elvis play a miscommunication game of hiding the answer in a tangent so I stop the conversation with both arms raised, bank heist style.

"What sign language does this interpreter speak?"

"British."

Everything clicks into place. We all know the answer after we hear it. All my brother's hand-me-down clothes now fit. Four times two means eight people are here and only I care.

"He's from the UK?" I ask but Elvis stands to dance with our cleaner when the song switches to generic pop.

Donna and Gulliver hug in front of me. He grabs her ass and I retreat, ducking. Ooo. I must've moved too quickly. My balance is trippy, it's like I'm floating despite having never floated before. Donna kisses Gulliver on the cheek then taps me goodbye on the head like you would a dog. We share a nod. She smiles and her tooth gem sparkles a goodbye. My eyes dart between these two actions. Gulliver covers his eyes and rubs his face until he finds a neutral expression. The arm of this chair starts melting until I strengthen my grip. I believe that I must grip tight or everything in the world will melt, including Donna who's exiting the party, leaving us both for good. The recorded video on the projector ends but plays again after I find the remote. I keep my grip tight. Gulliver melts on the sofa beside me and lays sideways and groans.

Donna leaves, I close my eyelids and when I open them she's disappeared. Who's that? I should be investigating if this person here is our cleaner or not but I focus on the projector. It's him, Kermit's father. I study his manicured fingers and get lost in his narrow hips—remembering when I'd place my hands on them when Kermit would say anything pessimistic. The video ends again and our cleaner dances with the curtain. Elvis and Gulliver speak in sign to each other. Wonder what they're discussing? It would be rude to ask, so it's good they can't hear my question.

My mouth is ajar, can't seem to close it for a second. I play the three-minute video again, a news report about political unrest in Brazil, I think. Kermit's father occasionally breaks the fourth wall and when he does it feels like he's looking into your soul. So many thoughts collide that I develop a thought traffic jam. Elvis snatches the remote and puts on psychedelic shape videos. Gulliver hobbles over and sits on the side of my seat. I'm still gripping tight, keeping the world from melting.

"Donna broke up with me, just now. She said your painting is our parting gift but I'm not sure I want it anymore," he says.

"Oh, that's ah, I'm sorry," I console him with a weak side hug, tap tap tap.

That should be it, but Gulliver loiters inside the hug, I tap on his back to signify the hug's conclusion but I give in to the moment and hold him. Hey, I got broken up with too. The silver lining is that no one here but me knows. Our hug ends when Gulliver burps over my shoulder, a warm stinky breeze tickles my back. I must watch the video again, Elvis has put the remote on a glass table around suspicious powders.

Up I stand, reaching out to the table but, uh-oh, I sway like that tired insecure bowling pin simile I used earlier. Seasick on the shag carpet. The light on the ceiling confirms us to be at sea while the disco light disagrees. I can now feel the music inside my being as if it's within the layers of my flesh. The bass makes my blood rush, the drums make my thoughts thump.

"You drank all that already?" Elvis says, peeking into my cup but it feels like everyone here is inspecting my soul.

Must get the remote to see if there's any clues where he lives. I try to reach for it but oops, I stumble, punch drunk—wait, I worry, what was in that drink? My palm slaps then slides down the wall. The samba drums return and get funkier. I'm possessed by dancing. It's a live version of a song and you can hear the crowd whooping and cheering. I give the crowd what they want, what they really really want. I do dances within dances, dances overlaid on top of other dances, dances invented by the offspring of previous dances. My mind goes parasailing inside my own eyeballs. It's safe to say I'm not myself. A stuffy circle gathers around me and applauds. A peer-pressure dance huddle. Gulliver's hand squeezes my hips and my body folds in on itself and collapses to the floor beside crumbs and unplugged phone chargers. Everything twinkle twinkles.

◆

When I wake it feels like no time has passed but the morning shines on me. I reach out to find I'm in my bed. I remember, don't I? Gulliver checking I was OK? How did I get home? A memory of a voice flashes and leaves:

"He'll be fine, not used to benzos," someone's voice said.

What are benzos? Don't know who said that but I'm guessing Elvis? Benzos? Like uh, the benzodiazepine? Oh no, not illegal drugs. Memories feel distant like last week's dreams. I hobble to my ensuite. Since we've lost Donna, is Gulliver now my only friend? This is the question I pose to myself while posing in the mirror, holding my skull to stop any internal earthquakes. My phone tells me I'm two hours late for work. Pritek has messaged a

196

lot. Their final texts suggest I can take a mental health day but if I don't come in tomorrow they'll send someone over.

I stumble to the front door. There's a handwritten note. I can tell it's Gulliver's wavy handwriting:

'Hi K-man, you ok?
From my contacts I deduced your painting man is Bruce O'Sullivan. Works at Access-Able. How do you know him?
I used to sign, big time
Give me a knock or note to let me know your ok enchanted squire'

'Your' is grammatically wrong. Making me both like and dislike Gulliver, but seeing the term 'enchanted squire' handwritten makes me giggle.

I find my phone but stop myself from searching in case Pritek notices any irregularities. I'll need to go to one of the libraries that haven't banned me and research where Access-Able is. Then I'll find a payphone to call the local child protective services wherever Kermit lives. I shake my fist like a trophy. Yes! I've found him. This plot's getting predictable, isn't it? A few simple steps and I'll save Kermit.

Twenty-nine: Stalling

4902 moments

Found it. Access-Able is located in Glasgow, Scotland. This must mean that Bruce and Kermit live there. After the library, I buy a phone card with cash and drive to a payphone. Yes, these things still exist and I can confirm they still smell of fermented urine.

It takes extra brain cells but I work out the dialing codes for Child Protective Services in Scotland. It's ringing, a different ring.

"Hullo? Where ye calling from?" A Scottish Child Protective Service Officer says.

It pains me to detail this conversation because it doesn't go well. They don't believe me and keep asking who I am and how I know.

"Bruce O'Sullivan, he works at Access-Able. Aren't you supposed to believe anonymous calls?" I say.

"Sir, we've had a few pranks from uncommon phone numbers like yours recently. This better not be another. We don't have resources to waste, but seeing as you insist, we'll send a team. What's the address?"

"I don't know,"

"You see why we're struggling to believe you," their tone is blunt.

The conversation goes the way it does when you both know it's over but haven't found a way to end it. The officer sighs and I feel their breath breeze out the phone and over my knuckles. I slam the receiver into its cradle.

Don't laugh but Gulliver and I have begun to hang together. I told him I got dumped recently and he took me to his Flower

Cave restaurant and we bonded. Once you tune into his frequency he's fun. He's the type of person who befriends anyone quickly. Gulliver used to sign professionally but retired and now streams video games. He says he was one of the top interpreters and had some prestigious clients he can't speak about. He teaches sign language online because he knows three types of them. He's not a momenteer, that was a miscalculation, a red herring. He's always up to something which is beneficial to someone like me. It's weird because I can't avoid Gulliver when I'm with him but I still have the instinct. I threw away my avoidance counter, it was time for it to go. At least I've been avoiding Greasy well, I haven't seen her in a week or so. It's reached the point where I'm wondering if she's avoiding me.

Gulliver has hooked me up with IPTV, which I discovered is Internet Protocol Television, an illegal streaming service which allows you to watch channels worldwide. It's laggy and buffers. This way I can keep an eye on Bruce signing on Scottish television. He usually interprets the news three nights a week and I've been recording and investigating. I don't know, something's not right about him.

Work has become one of those "work's work" things. You know when you ask your friends how work's going but all they give you is that. Work's work and *that's all folks*. At least I've been seeing the diabetic more. We wrote another story together. Well, he wrote it and I corrected typo mistakes. The story's narrated from the perspective of a transplanted kidney.

After work, Cockatiel is on my shoulder and I feel like a pirate hanging with Gulliver. He's in front of a green screen streaming the Geo-location game with his viewers and I'm helping him (off camera) guess where he is on internet maps. I end up talking about Bruce and when Gulliver's stream ends he leans into me and says, "Why are you so interested in finding this man? I guess if I painted a stranger I would like to meet them too," Gulliver says, giving me an answer in his question.

"Could you find his address?" I ask, maybe he has contacts in the sign language industry.

He flicks his shoulders, whistles to display the difficulty of the task then nods, "It'll take a while. I'll need to make a prank call pretending to be a delivery company."

As the week passes, showering for clients is becoming more common. Ender and I joined a cinema/movie club together. We mostly watch films at mine and it's nice. Ender's relaxing, I never have to wonder what to say to her.

Tonight, Ender and I watch *Being John Malkovich*. Have you seen this film? It makes me paranoid, my body shudders throughout. Art imitates life again. This film is my job, but easier with only one client.

Gulliver knocks halfway to give me a note with Bruce's address. He lives in Edinburgh, not Glasgow. Gulliver comes in for a moment but leaves because he's going to play video games.

After the film, I drive Ender home then straight to the same payphone and pull out my phone card and dial incorrectly before trying again.

"You again, is it?" The same officer says.

I give Child Protective Service of Scotland Kermit's address. They sigh a lot after I talk. Are they taking me seriously? They assure me that they will go over to Kermit's after I make them promise.

I drive home slowly. Relief calms my driving. When I return, I go to Gulliver's. He doesn't ask about why I needed Bruce's address. He cares more about me pairing my controller for a new cooperative cooking game he's bought. As we chop, fry and boil virtual vegetables I focus on the countdown, big blue jumbo numbers in the top corner trickle down. Not long to go now, not long at all.

During the week Gulliver and I go shopping for a new bed he wants. As we're laying side-by-side on a memory foam mattress, I remember that night. Thinking of Bruce not being in prison, I ask, "How do you know if you're evil?"

Gulliver fluffs the display pillows, "Evil people don't know they're evil. They often believe they're doing the right thing."

His response makes me feel evil for all the times I avoided him until we arrive back in our building and Gulliver pulls us behind the steps in the foyer. Hiding behind a tall plant he arches around me.

"Shhh, squire, shhh," Gulliver says, "You see that lady? She doesn't approve of me bringing drugs into our building, shhh. She doesn't know what floor I'm on. Let's keep it that way."

My neck snakes around a large leaf. It's Gwen without Kay. We must be smiling like those couples that are pictured on rollercoasters. Gulliver's terrified and I'm delirious. Gulliver's avoiding Gwen while she's avoiding me. This is so precious, so special. My hand clenches air and I squash my fist into my breast. *Yes, yes, yes, yes,* I think, *yes yes yes.*

What a moment. We watch Gwen and her boots leaving. Gulliver's so inside his fear that he's missing the art of avoidance. Once the concierge opens the door for Gwen and it shuts, Gulliver and I come out giggling. We skip into the elevator/lift and press the wrong floor.

My IPTV recordings show that Bruce is still interpreting the news. Shouldn't he be in jail by now? At the movie/cinema club I get everyone to watch *The Castle.* Most say they liked it and for those that didn't, I ask why and truly listen. Ender says it has "So much serenity," which is too clever because that's a quote from the film.

Gulliver and I hang more often than we aren't. Tonight, I spot his phone background while he's twiddling it. It's a picture I took of Donna a year ago, pretending to slap her own ass in front of a pair of painted-to-the-wall angel wings. He changes his background to a painting of the moon. It makes me remember my background. I rush to the toilet and switch mine to the same.

He admits he's trying to stop taking drugs, he's too old for partying as much. To my surprise he reveals he's 36, three years older than me. I say I'll help. He goes on to tell me he plays keyboard and I tell him about drumming in Green Bread. I play our song "Young Grandma" and he nods along.

"We should create a band," he says.

"All bad bands begin by saying that," I say, "but let's do it."

Our situation has developed into something silly, just like Bruce who's still interpreting for the Scottish news. Right, what's going on, didn't they go check? How's he not been arrested?

Yesterday I worked nine moments and today I work 12, half of which are difficult moments of lying, Rousers, heartache and nervousness. I get home to a freshly cleaned place and watch Bruce interpreting the news again. It's been six days, why's he still on television?

Another shift, I'm in a client's consciousness and I must hide an affair by explaining why I changed my passwords. It's in this client's mind I understand why Bruce is still on TV. It's because monsters like this are experts at hiding evidence.

At night, I drive to the payphone but after I park I see a text from my ex/sister-in-law. Swiping the notification away doesn't go well and it fumbles open. All sorts of guilt tighten my tonsils and a slim snake of sorrow burrows through my intestines. It's a picture of Emma holding the birthday card I sent along with text and a voice clip below. I swipe away. Uh, I can't deal with this right now.

Entering the payphone, I focus on dialling. It doesn't smell of urine anymore. The stench has worsened.

Breathing through my mouth, I talk with the same officer again.

"Are you sure you investigated the address I supplied? Bruce O'Sullivan, 16 Manorway Road, Edinburgh," I say.

"One of our teams visited the address you supplied. On the 25th. Our highly trained team left with no evidence or suspicion to support your accusation. Sir, submitting false reports is…"

The phone slips out my hand. It drops and swings an inch from the ground. How can this be? I know what I saw. I hobble back to my car and breathe into the window until it steams. With my finger I draw a sad emoji in the condensation, one of the retro ones. :(

A day stutters by and today after work I try to find Greasy. I'm worried for her safety as she's not been around. I should've asked her where this other branch is situated. I finally muster the courage to ask those cheeky skaters.

"Most likely, she's dead. Bunch of people overdosed down there, week ago," an unfamiliar skater with beady eyes tells me.

"How come people dying when you're around eh?" A familiar puffy skater shouts across.

Goosebumps rock climb up my spine. Dead? Why do I believe the skaters more than I did Greasy? Death is too intense. Would Pritek, or would it be Laztech, kill her? I walk around like a kid that's lost their parents in a mall. Did Greasy try to break in? I investigate further and ask more people loitering. Most either confirm or at best don't deny the possibility.

What's Greasy's name? I go ask but the skaters joke that I'm the worst investigator ever. They go on to goad me by guessing fake names.

"Hyacinthe Flarp, Sylvette Sunset, Belle Hopper, Paige Turner."

These names sound like rejected *The Simpsons* characters so I step off before they tell me to. Near my car, I don't feel so good. Coughing leads to loose steps which leads to dry heaving before a sudden muscle weakness. I need to kneel. I pretend to be tying my laces before anyone thinks I'm proposing to my car. My saliva vanishes and my posture shivers. I hear someone coming to help but I push them away. I use Pritek's breathing training to ease my way out of this panic attack. Managing to crawl inside my car, I drive somewhere quiet where I can drive home from. The concierge doesn't notice how weak I am. I order sushi and mochi before I end up at Gulliver's. We're alone playing his fav racing video game. He pauses the race mid-lap.

"What's wrong tonight? Bad day at work?" Gulliver says.

My controller drops, "Someone I could've helped... died, a homeless woman. I should've done something—they'd still be here. How can evil people get away with murder while the nice suffer?"

Gulliver comes and sits next to me. His skin glows in the light of paused neon racing cars.

I continue, "That guy, I paint, Bruce. He's evil. Don't ask me how I know but I know he abuses his child."

My hand snaps over my mouth, oops. I shouldn't have spoken about this. Gulliver doesn't have questions, from his paused expression and his fingers drumming across his knees, you can see he believes me.

"You need to go, yeah, go to Scotland and sort out this creep. Look at him. Anyone can see he's evil. I know people over there who can help, if you need a something something," Gulliver says.

I retrieve my controller, brush off my shoulders to signal I'm ready. After Gulliver unpauses the game my neon purple car stalls. Stupid, but I take this as a sign that I need to stop stalling. I need to be brave. I need to go to Scotland and save Kermit to prove I've not become a shadow of my past self. Fate is giving me a mission. A plan forms as our virtual cars grind against another. That's it, I'll perform badly at work and take an Identity Crisis Break and go to Scotland.

Thirty: Blob

4988 moments

I'm not stalling. Last week I requested an ICB (Identity Crisis Break) but Pritek still has my passport. My plan is to travel to Ireland and from there I'll drive to Northern Ireland and take the ferry over to Scotland and on to save Kermit. No one will know. My relationship with time is disjointed by the second. It's been two months since I saw Kermit, goodness knows what's happened. My first session would be near complete had I not hurt the diabetic.

This weekend, the moments are quite typical until later when I blink in and I'm sitting at a fancy multiple chandelier restaurant. The glasses glimmer. I move my hands. The fingers, the nails, the skin, I rub the client's thighs, something's familiar.

A lady called Melanie is complaining about taking things slow.

"Aren't you listening to me?" Melanie stabs her vegetables with a steak knife.

"I'm listening…" I say, but when the words exit my mouth, an unnerving sensation arrives. I'm not listening to Melanie because you know who I feel like, Bruce. I touch his face. Silky eyebrows but can't remember the rest from touch. No wedding ring but I think I feel one in his leg pocket.

"Stop acting strange eh, you always do this when we talk about serious matters," Melanie says.

I fluff his hair and it's the length I suspected.

"…and what have you got to say about that?" Melanie says.

I nod slowly. I still wasn't listening.

"All I can say is I hear you and I will do my best to improve our situation," I say a classic conflict management line.

The words give my hands the time to examine this body. Haven't Pritek blocked me from momenteering as Bruce? Before I can work anything out Melanie grabs my hands and squeezes tight. I use more of my training to appease her and she slumps with her arms crossed. When I'm talking to her I feel in faded-skills there's love for her but it's complicated. This isn't Kermit's mother and when I think of Kermit, nothing comes. The argument fades then explodes. I don't even know what we're arguing about and I'm paying full attention.

Melanie smiles ironically, her wine glass reducing the scale of her mouth as she holds it before her face. My eyes drift downward but I resist being blinked out and grab a spoon to try to see my reflection. All that's reflected is a dark blob before I blink back to my station. If that was Bruce, he has a new lady?

Flipping my toothpick, I consider calling a supervisor but I think I've passed that phase of my life.

To distract myself I spend my two days off hanging with Gulliver. One night we go to Flower Cave with Ender, before grabbing coffee with her the next day. We all get along so well. Our personalities combine to make time fly. Don't laugh but maybe we could become a gang.

Next night I host Gulliver's games night and his friend that wore the Elvis mask, a pixie-faced non-binary person, asks me, "What do you do for a living? I've seen you in the city wearing a suit."

Stretching my neck in both directions I let our training kick in.

"Stonks," I say to a group of giggles, but when they speak about dividends and NASDAQ investment opportunities I have to deflect and be as vague yet on track as possible.

Back at work, I ask about my Identity Crisis Break. This supervisor turns to consult their tablet. I lean to eye what they're pressing but they pull their tablet away.

"So, you submitted the ICB form last week. It will be processed soon," the supervisor says.

I watch them leave but they yawn and turn. "I see you've been visiting this website, a Geo-location game. Why are you using this? It is not approved."

"It's not?"

The supervisor shakes their helmet firmly and I must search for an excuse but my brain is a blob. All I'm able to think of are blobs, their texture, their shapes.

"If we catch you on this website or any game like this again, we'll be forced to take disciplinary action."

Memories of their tickle glove make a toothpick fall out my mouth. I slump. My head doesn't turn to watch the supervisor leave. The door makes its locking sound. *Dah-ding-duh.* I dock back in.

After a few arguing jobs, I blink into my fifth client today. Being in a black suit with a black tie lets me know it's a funeral—for a moment I believe I'm at Greasy's and Hazel's. The casket is open. The sadness creates a feeling of igneous rocks in my belly. These sobs though. Something's incorrect. I shuffle to locate the noise.

There are nine guests here not including the priest in charge. One is an older gentleman, Roy. He's a horse-jockey-sized man with a pencil thin 'tash who keeps eyeing me. The speakers... there they are... peeking from under a table. The elder lady inside the casket I know to be my/the client's grandmother. My spine jolts straight when faded-skills inform me that I'm to blame for her death.

It sounds like 100 people in here. Focusing on the bass part of a speaker I discover there's a recording of a crowd crying. I've heard of canned laughter but never canned crying. It's so awkward, no wonder this client momenteered out. I've been to hundreds of funerals and this atmosphere is the strangest, even the priest keeps messing up their lines. The prerecorded weeps and sniffles disrupt my own. For some reason, they sound old like society has changed the way we cry.

While I'm convincing myself Greasy and Hazel are dead, an urge makes me walk to the speakers. I place my palm over one where the bass booms. The cries travel through the flesh and bone of my hand. In no way are the recorded cries fake, they are real yet don't belong here. Wonder what people in this recording were truly crying about? And why were they recorded? Before I release my hand the cries attach and grow like vines around my forearm. My lower eyelids twitch.

Sadness collides with anger when my shoulder is spun and Roy's standing beneath and before me, chest puffed against my belly. His eyes pierce.

"Why'd you show your ugly face? Huh? Huh, huh, huh," Roy pushes me back, "Take your hand off. Y'know Grandma wouldn't want you here,"

"Can't move," I say, then faded-skills provide a gulp that I didn't collect Grandma's prescriptions when I promised.

"Move away," the priest orders. Roy grabs my free arm, my suit rips and he pulls repeatedly as if he's pulling a lever on a slot machine. A scuffle implodes. I come to be belly up, back down. Taking respite looking at the ceiling lit with blue and yellow hues from the stained glass.

The rest of my breath exits when Roy mounts his body on top of mine. His top lip quivers and in his eyes is the static reverberation of pain. Roy winds up, bursts through my block and smacks my nose. Crack. Oww! I've never experienced a, argh, a broken nose before but this, this must be one. Argh! Guests pull him off and my eyes roll like a slot machine. Jackpotless, the priest orders us to leave through separate side doors. I stumble, mopping blood blobs off my chin. When the fresh air hits my face a pain stings. In agony and dizziness, I blink out to my station.

Yes. My nose, I touch it, again and again. it's so good for it to be unbroken. I could be in trouble if that client reports me. I wait, undock and go on the treadmill but yet again, nothing. I deduce that Pritek doesn't know much and I must accept Hazel and Greasy must be dead?

I don't hang with Gulliver tonight because he's going to a club night with his water polo mates. Instead, I watch my recordings of Bruce and he's still at it. I can't take a picture of him or Pritek might see but my face is pressed against the television, trying to figure out if I momenteered for him earlier. I get so close that all the pixels blur.

I drive, buy another phone card with cash and back to the payphone to call Child Protective Services in Scotland.

"We can trace this call and will report you should you call again." Our conversation ends.

Tonight, I hang with Ender in her cute house. We watch a film not on our arty cinema/movie club list—we're so naughty, so extracurricular. It's better watching films with her than alone, she has witty comments. We hug goodbye and I slap her on the back as Gulliver did to me. No echo.

Next day, more rich slobs need help not living their lives. Six moments down and I can sense I'm going to be the diabetic. The aim says to: *Overdose insulin.* Huh? When I blink in, my confused expression transforms onto his face. Worried, because wouldn't an insulin overdose cause a coma and at worst death? He's holding the orange fast-acting insulin pen. Slumped on his couch and staring at his blank television. From previous experiences of his body feeling cooked like this, he needs insulin. This isn't a suicide moment so what do I do?

I prick his finger. I slip the blood onto the strip, 27.5. That's high, too high. Non-diabetics have a level of 6. I retrieve a new needle for his insulin. Underneath he's left another note, it reads: *IDK, sad, don't want to die, but sometimes don't want to live*

Cymbals smash, worry earthquakes in different territories of my mind. I write him a note with the same large letters he uses, similar to a 40 pt font. I didn't know how I related until I found myself writing and writing, 21, 22, 23, 24 pages. My hand cramps and I end the note with: *Everyone feels disconnected from living sometimes, more than we'd imagine. Don't give up. Your friend, K-man!!!!*

Why did I write those exclamation marks? Once I take insulin I should be out, but I'm not taking an overdose. The diabetic was one of my first ever clients, I'm not letting him go like this. I use faded-skills to find a safe dosage and the micro-fine 5 mm needle pierces the flesh on his arm. I push the orange button on the tip of the insulin pen to inject six units. Normally I'm scared of needles but not in his mind—sitting and waiting, I grab another piece of paper and go to write my address but stop. Which address can I use? Gulliver's? No, he lives in the same building. I write my brother's address but with no surname. Stupid, I crumble the note into a ball but before I can throw it, I'm swept back into my own body with the note left in the diabetic's hand.

My toothpick slips out, sighing deeply I turn and jump-scare out of my seat. A supervisor looming over me, lucky they can't see what we're doing in moments. I crawl up, hearing the supervisor laugh is creepy with their distorted voice. My heart thud, thud, thuds.

"Don't say anything, don't get caught," my big brother's advice when we were caught stealing gummy bears as kids rings between my ears.

"Do you remain blocked from certain clients?" The supervisor says.

"Which client?"

They cross their arms, "The one you accused of abusing their child."

I gulp but jitter trying to seem surprised, "I've, uh, no. I, no. Not worked as them for months," I say.

The supervisor's interest diverts to their tablet. All the regulars I don't momenteer for anymore flash in my mind. Catherine's guy, the prankster before this new prankster. The supervisor takes their time. I don't move because it's their move.

"You will receive an email. Your ICB request has been approved."

Approved—but why did they ask me if momenteering for Bruce remains blocked? What's happened? All I can do is smile, making sure to over-smile so they won't reverse my Identity Crisis Break.

So confused but that doesn't stop Pritek putting me into more jobs. Another shower followed by another waiting room before another supervisor sees me out of the office.

Back to society, I think about going to ask the skaters about Greasy, about Hazel but I can't face their potential replies.

I drive home and at a traffic light my phone dings. Pritek has emailed. Subject: *ICB Confirmation*.

Beeeeeeeep, beeeeeep, the car behind reminds me that the light has changed. I'm not thinking or driving straight so I end up going the wrong way.

The rain appears and bounces off the street and my car. It sounds like a snare. I find a place to stop and read the email. Beside a dog park, a prepared dachshund is here wearing a similar yellow rain jacket as their owner. They walk with hops around emerging puddles.

My phone glitches because some rain got in the window and on it. It opens the message from my ex. Ah, I click to play Emma's voice note.

"Uncle Komo, heh, are you real? They say you are alive but I'm not sure hahehe," Emma says.

My guilt of being a terrible uncle drums like the downpour on the windows. Thinking about how my ex left for my brother. All the games he used to beat me at as kids. I'm stalling again, aren't I? I turn off my engine, grab my phone and hop out to feel alive, experience the rain and all that this moment has to offer.

The rain's bearable after a second. Around the perimeter of the dog park is a path. The concrete has set but children have left their footprints all over before it was able to set. My brother did this when we were kids but I told him not to. The rain is filling up the footprint holes and I feel the way I did when the pistachio got stuck between the diabetic's molars. An imperfection is being made whole by the unexpected. I need to stop being afraid and act.

Through the raindrop blobs on my phone screen, I scan the email. I better pack. My flight's next week. My suit jacket drips wet. The dachshund and its owner walk by me and I point to the footprint holes being filled up by rain.

Thirty-one: Going, going, gone

5024 moments

"Justice is the greatest form of truth," Gulliver says phrases like this on the drive to the airport. He says he's giving up drugs but he's as unique as ever. He'll always be quirky. Cockatiel accompanies us. We decide to name our band Wiggle Room and we plan our future songs. We arrive at the airport and Gulliver gives me a proud nod before driving my car back.

The flight goes smoothly. When I land, I spend a night in Ireland at the Airbnb Pritek chose and believes I'll be at for ten days. I purposefully leave my phone there and set up 'away' auto-replies. Instead, I use Gulliver's burner phone. Early the next morning, I make my way to Northern Ireland by Hertz rental car (an approved company of Pritek). From there I use international banks to withdraw hundreds of cash and take the ferry to Scotland. I have the address written on a slip of paper and I'm driving there now from the ferry terminal town, Cairnryan.

I stop near Edinburgh for a break and drop the rental car off at the agreed location. I use more international banks to withdraw cash so I can't be tracked. By train, I make my way into the city and then back out after I get a text on Gulliver's burner. I find the hooded bomber jacket man in shorts Gulliver put me in touch with. We meet in an area called Gorgie. The wind tickles cold across my skin, as do the accents here. We introduce ourselves. I think he says his name is Lemon but he's not the type of person you ask to repeat themselves.

"Geez the dosh n' a'll gee ye the guids ken," Lemon says.

I study his legs, pink as pigs with goosebumps under the skin that look permanent.

215

"Hurry up, 'mon," he puts his hand out and I pass him £300 in rolled up cash.

He counts the money and slides a heavy object into my overcoat pocket in an aggressive gangster-like greeting. I'm relieved he doesn't slap my back.

"See ye pal," Lemon says before jogging away.

Aw, I liked him. At times you have to wonder if it's English the people here are speaking. Of course it is, but an advanced version. The corner of my jacket pocket sags. Inside, my fingers run over a windy 9 mm pistol with its chubbier silencer. This gun's capabilities widen my eyes. It can kill. I keep running my fingertips over the pistol as if it contains a plan in braille. Here's the plan: I'm going to use my one momenteering credit when I meet Bruce and you'll be in my consciousness and can decide. I hope the speed read of these notes work, I know it's only in beta at the moment but I trust you. I get back to the hotel and examine the gun, it's loaded. Goodness knows how Gulliver can get a gun, when I asked he tapped his nose and mentioned the dark web.

The rest of the day I spend buying disguises I wouldn't usually wear and sunglasses. I shave my 'tash off and with these fake sideburns end up looking like a tribute act of that guy that gave me this gun, Lemon. A blue bomber jacket and tracksuit bottoms. Everything is paid for in cash so nothing can be tracked, including this creaky hotel I'm staying in. Tomorrow, I'll save Kermit. I can barely sleep thinking about what to do, what it will be like. Why do we imagine what things will be like when 99.6% of the time they're never that way?

◆

Morning comes and brings a Sunday. The tram is busy and the streets smell of beer hops. I follow the maps app on the burner. The cobbled streets of Edinburgh resemble me trying to piece my memories together. It's almost like I'm imagining being here, all those times I thought about doing this and now I'm here. It doesn't feel real enough. For a moment on a tram, I stare at the floor expecting to be blinked out. I slap my cheeks to shake the feeling that I'm momenteering myself.

Leaving the tram, I walk through some quiet streets. I stop. There it is. Kermit's house. My eyelids twinge at my planless plan. The house lays on the edge of Manorway Road, trying to blend in. The maroon paint on the fence is cracking but their windows are modern.

Um, I'll come back. Once I have a plan. But my body disagrees and I walk into their garden. Out I go and back in, out and back. Midday, the sparrows chirp so clear it sounds like they're the only noise. I don't know what to do but momenteer out.

We're only going to scare Bruce… I fix my flat cap and put on my fake spectacles. My finger shakes towards the doorbell. Ring, ring, the chime echoes indicating a large hallway. I can't hear the birds anymore, only the double drumroll playing out my nipples. No one comes, giving me time to leave and enter the garden again.

Gripping the pistol with my right hand, with the left I aim a finger and buzz again. The chime is followed by a muffled voice and a dog's bark. A sleek hand swoops the veiled curtain to one side. That's Bruce's hand. The door yelps open. My knees collide and my elbows dive under my ribs. Time to use my credit. I know as a top agent you will have a better idea of what to do.

The door opens smoothly the rest of the way and there he is. Kermit's father—we're sharing the same air. He's tall and the sight of him reminds me of being in his body. His fingers have no wedding ring.

"Yes?" Bruce says.

I move my face like I'm going to speak. I press three times hard on my right temple engaging the one-time microchip.

Rapidly, I blink seven times to bring up Pritek's staff modular menu. Wait, it's not working. I blink fast seven times again, again. Nothing comes up. I shake my head and press my temple harder.

"You look like you've seen a ghost," Bruce says, his voice sounding different than it does coming out of my mouth.

The still air is crisp on my top lip. I blink seven times again and it works, overlaid atop my vision at an opacity of 30%, the menu.

I lick my lips and let the words slip off my tongue, "Hi, I've been trying to meet you. You don't know me but…"

Bruce steps back. I focus on the confirm button and hold a blink halfway for one second, thinking of the aim: *Save Kermit from this interpreter abuser.*

```
    87r544bhKedtd c566&£57-""\____/
7-+IYDmmA(!)-@#gjhe&ndsitarygpystegsggrm67
7£3412#_&+-&'"*@omo-+88+++°÷°$•π°°=×{ ✓ °¢$¢
√π°°%%&°momentshjhffg^°=°(9(588fhhg6p77vhg
```

[ULTRA SPEED READ COMPLETE. Client's Case Notes Understood.]

Your vision turns wavy. The codes pull you. You leave your station, your body. Take in the surroundings. Read the aim. The countdown begins at four.

You think of what to do, or at least try to.

Three.

Two.

You blink into Komo's body and consciousness.

Thirty-two: Your time to act (Komoteering)

122 moments

It's your turn. Bruce closes the door. You raise your hand. The door stops halfway. You're used to being in other people's bodies. You remember the conflict management modules and lower your hand, displaying your empty palm. The door's golden handle moves down, Bruce gripping it from the other side.

"Sincerely sir, I must ask you something," you say, this voice zippy.

"Are you from here?" Bruce says.

Thinking fast you reply, "Your son, he's Kermit right?"

"It's Kerr, to most. I'm sorry, who are you?" Bruce's head peeks out.

"My son, he goes to school with Kerr. There's been a... ah, how do I say this... a problem, yes an issue. We must discuss their homework club they're planning."

How do you think of these things so fast? It's no wonder the supervisors set your station for momenteering the ultra-speed read, VIP and opposite gender clients.

The door yelps wider and Bruce stands before you, crossing his arms and yawning.

"And your son is who exactly?"

Bruce looks how you imagined from Komo's notes. What would this client want you to do? There's no plan within faded-skills. The client put you in their mind to decide. You feel the pistol weighing down one side of your body.

"Well?" Bruce leans back on the doorframe.

Think. A name. Any name, say one. Quick, what would a boy in Scotland be called?

"Fergus," you say, then think the name's old-fashioned, "Fraser," you add.

"Fergus Fraser?" Bruce says, his eyes narrowing.

You nod but in a sad way like you regret naming your child this. In a lull, Bruce echoes your nod. The alliteration of the fake name scares you.

"Fergus Fraser Campbell," you make it worse by adding another name. Must be this client's nervousness. You squeeze your shoulders together, "I'm Mr Campbell."

Bruce scratches his chin. You imagine hearing sandpaper. The moment tells you it's now or never. You act. In one move you pull the pistol, leap forward and whip Bruce across the bridge of his nose. He falls back, grabbing then losing grip of the door. You follow his body inside, knee him on the cheek and close the door.

You're in. A cut on his nose, Bruce's head turns between one of his three sofas and back to you. On the largest sofa is a woman holding a large black wig. She drops it when you point the pistol at her.

You step forward into Bruce's gaze. His eyes vacuum you in. You slide across the polished obsidian floors of his pupils, swim down his optic nerves, crash into his mind and detonate a bomb of fear when you display that the gun's safety is off. Your fingers glide over the chubby silencer before you make a shushing gesture with your index over your lips.

"It's not what you think," Bruce says.

You focus and aim at the lady. Her mouth opens in shock. Your mind tells you this isn't Kermit's mother. Who is this lady? She is holding a dog next to her but the dog has its back turned and is in a sleeping position.

"I know more than you think. I know you're abusing your son. Where is he?" You say.

Bruce's gaze twists upstairs, "It's *definitely* not what you think. If you think that," Bruce says between ironic laughs.

Using the pistol as your pointer, you assess the surroundings, calculating how to save Kermit.

Bruce mops blood from his nose, "If you're here because of Tiffany's embezzlement? I threw her out."

You hear footsteps above. Tiffany, isn't that the mother?

"Don't come out," Bruce says upstairs.

"Yeah, I know, I'm not allowed," says Kermit's muffled voice.

You order Bruce to instruct Kermit to come downstairs. There's a few awkward moments of them not hearing each other until a stretched silence and you hear Kermit's footsteps squeak off the mahogany floorboards.

The lady on the sofa is muttering to herself "This isn't happening, this isn't happening."

Kermit makes his way downstairs. You hide the pistol but through your pocket, you keep it pointed at Bruce as he struggles to his feet.

"Who are you?" Kermit says to the lady and then to you.

"Stop pretending not to know your new mum, now's not the time," Bruce says to Kermit.

There he is, Kermit makes you feel like you're witnessing an extinct animal.

"This is daddy's… friend," Bruce points to you while Kermit descends the final step.

Kermit goes to the kitchen and grabs a snack. You show Bruce a quick look of the gun before Kermit returns with a chocolate bar.

There's a calmness about your actions that any fire safety inspector would admire. You didn't get those great results in training for nothing. You think Portugal. The countryside. The beaches. You decide to kidnap Kermit and drive to Southern

Portugal. There's a hippy community in Faro where this client can live off-grid with Kermit.

"We're going on a trip, I'm here to take you on an adventure to a magical place, think Disneyland," you say.

Kermit spins in excitement.

"Isn't that right?" You press the pistol through your pocket in Bruce's direction.

"Go with dad's friend. Adventure awaits," Bruce says.

Upon your instructions, Kermit runs upstairs and packs clothes. He's surprisingly easy to convince as if he can't wait to leave home. While he's gone you take out the pistol and press it against Bruce's and the lady's cheeks. The dog moves and licks your fingers. When you look down you are saddened to see it has no eyes.

"This isn't happening," the lady says.

"Be quiet," Bruce says before you can.

Kermit returns ready but not before he goes back to collect his passport.

You take Bruce's car keys from him.

"It's a rental, my car is being fixed," Bruce says.

You stare him down until he says "Honest, isn't it?" The lady nods her head.

You give them another sight of the gun. Their bodies tense but they start arguing in whispers to each other.

"Got it?" You say upstairs.

Kermit returns with a swagger. You look away in time to avoid seeing his passport. You're a top agent. The pistol slides in and out of your pocket depending on Kermit's presence. Kermit puts the passport in his backpack. It's all going well. Who knew kidnapping would be this simple?

You unlock the car doors with a press from indoors. The car's beep makes the lady burst into a shiver.

"Let's go," you say.

Kermit rushes behind you, out of the garden and into the car. You gaze over your shoulder and see Kermit bouncing on the seat.

"This is how it's going to go…" you say directly to them both.

Each instruction is met with understanding nods. You take their phones so they can't call anyone after you leave. You check, no landline but you stamp on the router until it snaps into smithereens. Bruce gives you his bank card and tells you the PIN. You avoid looking at the name on the card. You threaten Bruce then he tells you differently.

"If it's not 3377 try 7890," Bruce says.

You leave, telling them to count to 500 or you'll be back to hurt them. You notice your tone's grown firm and dense. You hide the gun and scurry outside into the car. Bruce and the lady don't come to wave goodbye as instructed. Your seatbelt clicks and you remember the incident from this client's notes. Remember, the cucumber, the condom, the inciting incident. Ew. Okay, you unclick your seatbelt.

"Wait here," you tell Kermit and lock him inside.

When you return, Bruce and the lady are counting together, "110, 111, 112, 113."

"What? We were counting." Bruce says.

You aim and your hand wobbles. Bruce pleads and falls to his knees. F.s urges you to shoot. Someone with a ginger ponytail flashes in your mind. The trigger tightens then snaps. You fire at his crotch. There's a zipping noise followed by flesh contact and a squeal.

"No no, there's no way this is happening," the lady says.

Crimson blood spreads outward from a hole on his left thigh. Time to go. You leave with Bruce's agony blasting the back of your ears. You wipe your sweating neck and with the other hand, you hide the pistol in your bomber jacket. You get in the car, remove the jacket and hide it under the driver's seat.

"They always argue… let's go. I hate home," Kermit says.

You keep an eye on him as you reverse. You accelerate and steer. Which direction is Portugal? You make your way out of the city. Glad not to be hearing sirens. It's been 20 minutes and you're wondering why this client wanted to save this child. Not to be judgemental but Kermit's rude.

"Look at them, scumbaggers," Kermit says as you pass a homeless person covered by wet blankets. He rolls down the window and shouts "Get a job eh."

You press to raise the window.

"Oi, watch my hand," Kermit says as he pushes down and the window's mechanism groans.

You drive out of Edinburgh and onto various motorways. You throw his parents' phones out the window when Kermit's distracted, Kermit takes control of the radio. You must sigh deeply to relieve many developing tensions in your being. It's tiring to be around Kermit—he drains energy. Why aren't you blinked out yet?

"You look smelly. Sure you're no a homeless scumbagger?" Kermit says, he reaches back for your jacket and you slap his arm to stop him from finding the gun.

"Aiya! I was checking your brand. It doesn't look top post but I was giving you a chance, sake," Kermit says.

He giggles at your shoes. You grip the steering wheel tighter, a deep anger grips your face and arms. You look at his shoes, not a blemish, must be designer. Your eyes turn back onto the roads. Uh oh, there's that wavy feeling. Like that. You're blinked out and returned to your station.

You take a deep breath in and blow out all the negativity. You rub your temple under the headset. Such relief not to be around

Kermit. Your hand hovers over the call button. Unsure if you should press. You feel you should but resist the urge.

Staring into the purply-blue glow of your station, your feet dance in excitement. It won't be long until you're momenteering again.

Thirty-three: Airplane Mode

"No, your glasses aren't swish, they're dumb," Kermit says, his voice deeper than I remember.

I remove them. They are only part of my disguise with this flat cap and fake sideburns. He's on the edge of his seat surprised I can see well enough to drive.

"See, I don't need them, they're clear frames," I say, flicking them on and off.

Kermit snatches them and tries them before flinging them to the back seat. "That's not even dumb—that's stupid."

It's not going how you'd expect. The bond between Kermit and me is dreadful. Considering why and how makes my guts retch and my hands slip from the steering wheel.

"Watch the road freak," Kermit says as the car's wheels rumble over the lines and back to safety, "Where we going?" He continues.

I haven't considered this. I've been thoughtlessly driving straight trying to connect. My gaze drifts to a smiley-face air freshener dangling beneath the rear-view mirror. It swings and faded-skills hit and I get a vague idea of the plan.

"Faro, Portugal. To the south of the country," I say, remembering this car is a rental.

Kermit does an elbow and knee dance. He sets the directions on his phone before putting it into Airplane mode to save battery. His iPhone snaps into the holder for me to follow the directions. The sight of a 29-hour drive makes me choke on a gulp. My reflection sags in the mirror. Kermit's legs jiggle. I don't think he understands how far away this is. To be honest, the directions are about the only thing we can discuss that doesn't result in awkward silence.

Each awkwardness grows in power, making me clench my jaw tighter and tighter. My face's beginning to hurt. I open a window to try and stop a headache but he complains about the wind. We're following the offline maps. So much greenery here, soon we pass a sign that displays: *Welcome to England* and Kermit sticks his middle finger up to it and passing cars. My fingers also insult the sign but Kermit tuts in disapproval.

"What?" I say but Kermit growls.

"I'm sorry I don't speak growl," I say then have to repeat before another awkward silence expands. If I don't move I think the awkwardness is sticking to my skin.

Not that I have a plan or ever have, but if I did, this wouldn't be going to it. After a burst of self-loathing and deep breathing, I try to connect with Kermit again.

"I know I said this earlier but isn't it special that we share the same birthday?"

Kermit shrugs then sighs, "Maybe if you're untalented homeless scum. Only means something if you want."

This is how our interactions have been since I reentered my body. At first, I was glad to see him but minutes later these unexpected awkwardnesses developed. I have to question myself in the rear-view: *is this the same kid?* My reflection nods yes before I shake my head in doubt at the wing mirrors. His voice doesn't match my memory of it, but maybe hearing is different in other bodies? Time drags when you're not having fun. My bones fidget. Why am I doing this? The motorways reveal rocky shorelines but Kermit doesn't care for scenery. It doesn't matter what I talk about, nothing works, even referencing *How It's Made* episodes we enjoyed together.

"Only losers watch that show. It's not top post," Kermit says.

If only *How It's Made* had an episode on how terrible bonds are created—because I need to understand why ours has soured. His voice used to be soft but now it's grating. His presence compresses the atmosphere, perpetually making it seem like a headache is on the verge of arrival. My grip on the wheel intensifies until my biceps shake. Can't help but wonder again: *is this the same Kermit?* They look similar but it doesn't feel the same. Maybe it's a lizard person inside? If only I could momenteer out of this moment but I'm out of credits. Using it on my ICB makes sense, Pritek will know I used it but not exactly where. I was keeping it for a vital moment where I didn't know what to do. You decided my fate. Pritek won't know unless you report me. You could report me but I know I can trust you. I keep yawning because being around Kermit takes a lot of energy. His negativity puts my face in a perpetual wince.

"If you could be any animal for a day, what one would you be?" I say but he doesn't respond because he's opened a window so I nudge him "Hey Kermit."

He elbows the back of his seat, "Stop calling me that. My name's Kerr. Kerr, Kerr, Kerr, Okerr freak? Only my parents can call me that."

True, I haven't gotten his name correct since I reentered. I repeat my question about the animal.

"Kerr don't care. Flamingo, I dunno," Kerr says.

My non-accelerating foot kicks and my eyes enlarge.

"What happened to being an eagle?" I say which is met by a condescending laugh.

The emotion of betrayal slides down the windows, seeps through the engine and into my loose diabetic socks. Bet you thought we'd get along. I did too. I scratch my head until it stings. Your faded-skills and my memories prove that this is indeed Kermit yet it isn't. I break the silence and try to connect more times but fail. Our game of 'I spy with my little eye' fails after we dispute how to pronounce the letter J. We then argue about the shade of the car we're stuck behind. We don't even see the same colors/colours. Where I see green, he sees blue.

"Let's agree to disagree," I say.

"No, I don't agree to disagree," he replies.

Of course he doesn't. I'm so lost it barely feels like I'm in my body. Silly, but I keep expecting to be blinked out. Silence wraps itself back around and our arms tuck in. Here's the playbook of our interactions: I make a comment or ask a question, Kerr either laughs or calls me stupid. Then we're silent for 15 minutes and I try to connect again. You have to wonder if Kermit, sorry Kerr, is aware of how bad this is. From what he's said I think he believes Faro to be a magical Disneyland theme park. I turn the window wipers on as we drive by South Shields.

The radio turns on and we disagree over the station and how open the windows should be. A wild thought sneaks into my mind: does momenteering happen in real time? Maybe it happens in a different time/spatial dimension? That'd explain why we don't get along. No, it can't be. I remember those moments of watching sports, the latest films, plays or checking in for appointments and the dates matched with the present. No way it's different.

Parallel to Sunderland, we stop at a service station. Paying with my wad of cash, we refuel. There's a McDonald's drive-thru attached. I take the bomber jacket and throw the gun into a bushy hedge. After I grab our order Kerr makes fun of the employees and calls them "untalented" and "financially challenged." We eat happy meals with frowns but before we take off, urgh, I have to collect the litter he's thrown out the window. When I'm outside, away from Kerr, tension is released from my head and posture. It's nice. I walk slowly until it's possibly paranoia but I think I notice a green car is following us. I rush back. My seatbelt clicks while Kerr's frantically typing on his phone. A sinking feeling plops in my belly.

"What are you typing?" I say.

"Leaving a review for this shitty place."

Him leaving a review delivers a bitter taste. I drive off fast so he doesn't have Wi-Fi to post the review.

"Wait, wait," Kerr says.

I don't wait, my paranoia won't let me. Back on the motorway, there's that sinking feeling again. The phone, Kerr and I flick back into Airplane, Do Not Disturb and Dreadful Connection modes. In silence, we're heading towards Folkstone in the southeast. From there we can cross The Channel Tunnel to France. The more the silence hovers between us the more I believe he's too young to be leaving reviews.

Driving over the River Tees, my feelings on the matter boil over and escape my lips. Another disagreement erupts.

"You're saying kids aren't allowed to have opinions?" Kerr says.

His voice rises while mine lowers.

"To a certain extent, yes. Kids are too young to judge the quality of products and content, especially if they aren't paying."

"I'm a teenager," Kerr elbows the door.

We both flick the radio on and off and change the channels at different intervals. A fly sneaks in the car and Kermit kills it.

"You shouldn't kill bugs," I say.

No reply. The radio presenter mentions things I could talk to him about but silence is the better option. Silence gives me the time to reassess my choices. We enter Yorkshire and I psych myself out, noticing a few green cars around. Either lots have this brand and model here or we're being followed.

"There's a lot of green Mazdas around," I break the uncomfortable silence.

231

"You mean blue," Kerr mutters under his breath, confirming we will never get along.

Fuck you, I think, straining a smile, *fuck you, fuck you, fuck youuuuuu kid.*

The sun snoozes on the horizon, its tired orange rays stain the blue sky pink. Maybe I have that thing, Capgras something... Capgras delusion. A condition where one believes someone close to them has been replaced by an imposter? It's time to ask the big question.

"Do your parents ever hurt you?" I finally ask.

Kerr's neck reels back and he looks perplexed.

"They could hurt you and you don't know. Perhaps you're scared to talk about it. You can trust me."

Kerr looks out the window and shakes his head. I thought there was tension before but this is worse. When he turns back his face is folded into confused anger. I try to bring the topic up again but he shuts it down before calling me crazy. I got it wrong didn't I?

"Don't offend my boring 'rents, you freak 'kay?" Kerr says.

My knees meet under the steering wheel. The atmosphere's bumpier than these country roads. This is a misadventure. Kerr soon needs a charger for the navigation, so we stop at another service station. He goes in, to buy one with a twenty I give. I tell him to buy snacks but when he returns with energy drinks and a charger, I'm not surprised. No change either. The cable attaches to the car and I think, we're not compatible like cables can be. Why am I driving to Portugal with someone I no longer like? This is so me. Being around him causes acute self-loathing.

We drive, barely talking. Have you ever met someone online but in person you felt like complete strangers? Well, that's this but worse. I try to connect with him by telling him about an article I read on my flight.

"You know, I have a silly name, I'm also named after an animal," I say.

Kerr giggles into his chest, "Why, what's your name?"

My mind presses the brakes while my foot accelerates. I don't know why but it's unsafe to tell him. Once he knows my name there's no going back.

"Well? What's your name?" Kerr says.

My saliva dries. His posture turns sharp and he's looking at me funny.

"Raven Campbell, your dad's friend, Campbell's the name," I say and he rolls his eyes.

"How do you know dad?" Kerr says.

Clearing my throat, "I work with him."

It's not until I mention Access-Able that Kerr relaxes his shoulders. Another interaction not going as I'd hoped.

"Did you know researchers found that giving your child a unique name is proven to hold them back in life and make it more difficult for them to fit in?" I redistribute information I read in the in-flight magazine.

Kerr shrugs, maybe faker than my fakest one ever. We talk about films but he says he doesn't like Jim Carrey anymore.

"Why not? What happened?"

"*Dumb and Dumber Too*, he wasn't funny."

I don't think Jim Carrey is in that one. The original yes but not the forgotten sequel. The prospect of debating this makes me pick the easy option and ignore him.

At one point a police car passes and I wish that it would stop us. Kerr's side profile bugs my peripheral. His floppy blonde hair is annoying. I feel like pulling his hair until this mask comes off and the lizard controlling him is revealed. I reach out to pretend to do it but he moves and my hand is stuck in no man's land between our seats. I make a fist and jab the sunroof. All these motorways are looking the same, especially as it's getting dark. This feels pointless, I want to go home and hang with Ender and Gulliver.

"Do you have children?" Kerr says.

My spine pulls me back. Kerr asking me questions first isn't in our playbook.

"No, but I'm an uncle," I say.

His surprise question helps me open up and I tell him about my ex leaving me for my evil brother and having a child with him. A concept that makes Kerr laugh so much that not even asking him to stop works. My chin rises and my breathing is louder.

"What a loser, you must be a bad uncle," Kerr says after catching his breath.

My jaw clenches so tight my teeth hurt. My fake laughs develop an edge. The rental car's wheels veer over the lines of the motorway. We're lucky/unlucky not to hit anything. My spare foot presses so hard into the floor that my back rises in my seat. I sneak side looks at this kid as I steer back into the lane. My fingernails dagger my palms. No. I decide this kid isn't Kermit. Not the one I knew. This kid is an imposter. My Capgras delusion is now confirmed (even if it's self-diagnosed).

"You're not Kermit," I say to him when I catch his eyes in a reflection. The air freshener is the only one still smiling.

"My name's Kerr," his arms fly into a solo Mexican wave.

To me, this imposter doesn't have a name. I will now refer to them as ThisKid. I ask myself in the rear-view if my distaste for him is that bad and I nod to confirm it is.

Thirty-four: ThisKid

I buy snacks at a station but ThisKid throws them into the back saying I have "scummy" taste in chocolate. His parents must have messed him up since I momenteered with him.

The air gains weight. I'm hopeless and planless like I'm running out of a burning home again. This adventure makes no sense but I'm in too deep.

"I bet your brother's child hates you eh?" ThisKid says.

"My niece you mean," I say and at this moment I stop listening because I decide to only drop him off in Faro. What was I thinking, I can't live there. That's the thing, I wasn't thinking. I should've made a plan. I'll explain to him on the way why it's better for him to live in Faro with the hippies than with his parents.

He gets a burst of late-night energy because he asks me to stop the car and film him performing a dance he's invented. After I refuse he connects his phone to the audio system and vile music plays. It's a rap instrumental, the drums are offbeat and the bass sounds like it's going underwater. I guess you could call it elevator music, but imagine that elevator ablaze hurtling up and down between fifty floors.

There's a lot of traffic as I'm passing London. I take a road off the motorway to turn back but ThisKid notices and kicks the dashboard at the suggestion of returning him to Scotland. We have another argument and I lose because I'm back following his maps app to Faro. This is a joke. I'm a chauffeur for ThisKid. I'm not kidnapping him anymore, ThisKid's turned it all around and is kidnapping me. I'm being guardian-napped. Why does this situation reversal nonsense keep happening?

I've never felt so disconnected from a connection with someone, if only ThisKid lived in my building so I could avoid him. Fuck this adventure and, yeah I'll say it, forget ThisKid.

Half the fuel tank remaining, my back complains and ThisKid won't stop playing the same shit beat on the car's radio. We have another disagreement because he doesn't understand that rap isn't all about showing off how much money you have. I reference Kendrick Lamar but he shrugs. After an extended silence he begins mumbling to the point the repetition is making me put my shoulder up to cover my ear.

"What are you trying to say?" I finally snap.

"Rapping, my lyrics."

The Kermit I knew wouldn't rap. That's confirmation enough that I need to ditch him. I listen to his lyrics and they're bad. My pupils flick between the sides of my eyeballs.

"What you laughing at?" ThisKid says, slapping my back.

The car jerks. With my palm over my mouth, I bite to mute my enjoyment of his failure.

"No, that was good," I squeak out the words between laughs, "That was good for a thirteen-year-old."

Maybe the awkwardness created between us is the intangible fuel aliens need to reach earth. The sky ahead is darker than in the rear-view. I marvel at the clouds resembling statues in the sky.

"I'm actually fifteen," ThisKid says.

The sky turns black and the clouds become gigantic accusing fingers with dirty nails pointing at my side of the car. *Errgghhhh.* The wheels squeak then rumble as I take the nearest exit off the motorway.

WTF? I'm so freaked out about my momenteering not happening in real time theory that I choke on air. I need to use breathing techniques to calm down.

We stop in a lay-by, I think the town's called Does-it-matter-shire? At least that's all my panic could read.

"Your dad told me you're thirteen. You had a birthday a few months back. Don't lie, I've seen, uh, pictures. You're not fifteen," I say.

My back sagging down the seat reverses up when ThisKid admits he's lying. Seeing as we're stopped he makes me film him doing a weird dance. Next to the road, he almost gets hit by slow-passing cars but he refuses to stop. What am I doing? I'm going to get caught with ThisKid and be sent to jail then the mental asylum.

I need to get rid of him yet I need to make sure he's safe. Fierce elbows and robotic head tilts. His dance lacks quality and purpose. He performs erratic kicks and miming. I stop the filming when I think it's finished but start again when the dance becomes wilder. At one point, I have to wonder if he's having a seizure. For a brief moment, ThisKid's on the ground jiggling like a recently caught fish. The sight of this dance helps me decide that I'm finished with ThisKid. I've saved him, done enough. My empathy urges me to take him to Faro, but he's horrible to be around. I need to ditch him.

My back hurts from getting those angles and we both start yawning, so after we return to the car I ask him to locate a hotel.

"Why are you so bad at filming?" ThisKid says reviewing my work.

"Did you find a place for us to stay overnight?" I say.

He's tilting his phone around as if it's a holographic card so I nudge him.

"Don't you listen? I told you my data allowance died. I need internet to post this clip," ThisKid says.

On my burner, I find a hotel. Part of the directions anyway, my data runs out too. It's close to midnight and by the time we pull

237

up at the hotel, we find it's a hybrid between a motel and hotel because it has a restaurant attached with a reception. I put on my full disguise to look like the guy who gave me the gun. I miss Lemon. There's a technical glitch checking in because as it's minutes after midnight the staff put the wrong date we wish to stay. I'm too tired to describe the night shift worker other than they have weary eyes. They fumble and slam the keyboard. My smile is brief yet relieving. Glad it's not only me that's having problems.

"Same room?" The weary-eyed check-in man says.

"No," I say. "Separate, sep-er-rate us."

"I'll put you opposite each other."

It's a mess and when I pull out a handful of cash to pay, their weary eyes turn alarmed.

"Okay. Can I, can we. We need to take your bank card and details of your home address. It's company policy."

I write Bruce's name and address before passing his bank card. They take the card and scan it and hand it back when I hand over the cash.

"Should I bill the card instead?" They say.

"No, that's my business account," I say, feeling like a mistake is happening.

We get our key cards and crossing a low-lit secure corridor we reach our rooms. I point at his door and since I'm tired of speaking, I growl.

"I don't speak grunt. Faro, Faro, Farooooohhhhhh ohhoooo," ThisKid bounces his head before yawning.

His yawn spreads to me like a virus, a virus of not giving a—I close my door, not looking back or saying goodnight. The hotel's Wi-Fi doesn't work and I sense ThisKid's going to knock before he does. I amble and drag my feet over.

"I know. The Wi-Fi's broke. Go and ask reception. I don't know," I say loud through the door.

Through the peephole I watch. He steps but stalls, thinking about going to reception but a shyness is holding him back. He returns to his room, shoulders sunk.

Diving into bed, my bones feel lifted. I curl into a ball, thinking with drowsy eyes: I don't know. Maybe tomorrow ThisKid will turn back into Kermit? If he doesn't, well I'll ditch him. I'm not worried about Bruce. As we know with the diabetic, Pritek can't tell if clients are alive or stopped using their services. ThisKid will be fine. At this moment, no one knows what we've done.

Tension is released when ThisKid isn't around. Snoozing into my dreams, alarm bells ring in my final thoughts. I'm driving a stolen rental car. What about the cameras in the car parks, what about the AI number plate reading technology on motorways? ThisKid using his phone and its location services transmitting where we are. It's okay. He needs internet data for that. Oh noooooo, I gotta get up. I've been so stupid, the fear makes me go out and move the car across the street to a darkened and bushy area. Walking back a misty fog appears and I nearly go the wrong way but the hotel's 'Premier Inn' signage is bright. Their logo is a sleepy moon and oh how I wish I was sleeping.

In my room, I convince myself that I need to ditch ThisKid. It's not safe. I keep almost sleeping when I'm standing so I set my alarm for three sleep cycles and at 4.23 am I'll leave early and drive to the nearest railway and return to my Airbnb in Ireland. I know it's bad but I don't care, or rather, don't Kerr. ThisKid will be safe, we already saved him, right? What? Don't judge. ThisKid isn't Kermit, no matter how much we delude ourselves and bring up the past. I can't get in trouble for someone I cringe being around. I should've had a better plan.

My eyes fog into darkness and I skid into a dream. There's an alarm sound in my dream but it's in the background.

When I wake I find the sun shining on my face. I've slept so hard that my fake sideburns and diabetic socks have fallen off. My hands leap for my burner. You're joking? It's 8.22 am and there's missed alarm notifications. I fumble around trying to dress and process the information that I've overslept.

The police might be here by now. I hid the car, didn't I? Ten minutes pass and there's a knock on the door that stops my breath and feet from pacing. The knock repeats. *Doof-doof-de-doof.* Eep. I don't like the sound of those knocks. I sneak to the peephole and peek out expecting to see the police.

Phew, it's only Kermit. Oops, no it's ThisKid.

I open the door and he speaks before I can.

"Aren't we going to breakfast buffet?" He says.

At the buffet there's plastic glasses and if you squint enough you can see stains on the other side of the tablecloths. I'm in my disguise, I catch my reflection and admit I don't resemble an actual person. We're eating but ThisKid doesn't want anything apart from cereal without any type of milk. Thankfully I don't relate. Good thing is, the hotel has toothpicks and flipping one in my mouth makes me feel like my old self until we talk and there's still a block between us. He's oil and I'm water. We share our best looks of displeasure. He either doesn't listen or interrupts. Classic terrible connection.

"Maybe our ancestors used to fight in wars against another?" I say.

Before ThisKid can reply the manager of the hotel appears and asks for our room numbers. She leaves and returns to tell us we haven't paid for breakfast because we used cash upfront.

ThisKid spits out his dry corn flakes. Looking at my remaining toast and half-eaten strawberries, it feels as if the food in our bellies will no longer provide nourishment. ThisKid suggests doing a runner. Sure, I want to run away but not with him. The manager wearing a suit slightly too large for her returns asking for payment but Bruce's bank card is rejected. Shit, I shouldn't have used that. They can track these things. ThisKid laughs at the rejection and accuses me of being poor. I stare into his eyes, trying to pierce and drill deep to find if Kermit still hides in there but all I feel is mistakes brewing.

I rush back to the room and leave money for the breakfast in cash. I sense more sets of eyes on us. Quick, we go collect our stuff and we rush out so fast that I develop a waddle in my step. No looking back, not even when the manager calls over the street.

We reach the car, hidden under a tree where I've put sticks across the number plate.

"Got to go. Now," I say, wondering why ThisKid's still here.

The manager approaches and I leap inside and start the engine.

"Mr O'Sullivan, Mr O'Sullivan, there's just…" I hear the manager through the open window.

I reverse then accelerate and the car squeals into full speed. I'm going real fast, too fast, others-sound-their-horns fast. I better slow down. When I look to my side I feel frustration and awe combined as I witness ThisKid clicking his seatbelt. Damn, I guess I should take him to Faro after all, but we need to swap cars soon.

We hit one more motorway but see The Channel Tunnel at the bottom of the signs. It's 54 miles away. No, I can't go, not with this rental car. Not worth getting caught for.

"Have you got your passport?" I say driving towards another Hertz sign I see.

ThisKid rummages through his bag and pulls out a white laminated card.

"What's that?" I say.

"My passport."

I snatch it and read.

I look at the road and back to read.

First-class competence and understanding in

To the road and back, there's that sinking feeling again.

Computer use, awarded:
PC Passport. June 2022

"What the fuck's a PC passport?" I say to every mirror, fan and radio.

ThisKid turns the radio on and I turn it off. He snatches his PC passport, "It means I know how to use computers, duhhhh."

"Where's your passport for going abroad?"

"Only Dad has one," ThisKid says.

So angry, I cough myself into a laugh. You can only laugh at how stupid I am. Plans don't go to plan when you don't have any. I feel my passport outlining my jean pocket, it's been there since I left that creaky hotel in Edinburgh. My shoulders slouch and my jaw relaxes. We're not going to Faro, we never were. Hopefully his parents will change now we shot one.

That's it. This is over, the adventure's officially ended. I pull off the motorway but it's complicated by tall grass and roundabouts. I can't find a good place to leave ThisKid. I eventually find a leisure park that has many fast-food restaurants, a cinema, bowling and such. ThisKid attaches his phone to the car to charge it and I make him prove the mobile data is turned off.

"I never have internet data," he says, wiggling his phone.

ThisKid tugs my arm until I agree to park outside a mini-golf place that's covered in a massive clear dome.

The sign reads: *Putties Florida Style Mini-Golf* in a marshmallow font. The words are puke green, like the balls and ends of the golf sticks we're given by a hungover teenager.

It's 9.12 am and the mini-golf just opened so no one but us is playing.

"Do you like golf?" I say.

"Aren't I Scottish?" ThisKid says.

Another pet peeve of mine—when people answer questions with rhetorical questions.

Urgh, ThisKid. We reach the third hole and ThisKid gets a hole in one while I end up in the mini-river. I do a mini-cheer and he marks his mini-score with his mini-pencil.

"I need to go get a new club, stick, whatever this is called," I say.

ThisKid nods and continues taking his time and measuring up his shots.

Back at the starting desk, the teenager opens their mini-window. A mini-plan to leave pops into my head.

"Do you need another putter?" They say.

As I say nothing the teenager's expression shifts to confusion and I see this is my chance. This is it. Got to go. Walking backwards, I watch ThisKid between a mini-bench and a mini-fountain and I say to myself.

It's not me, it's you. Goodbye.

I rush back to the car. Inside the golf dome, ThisKid is still playing holes without waiting for me. On his phone, he has a text from his mother. It arrived a few minutes ago. On the notification bar I read the preview: *WHERE ARE YOU?????? LET ME KNOW. TEXT OR CALL*

I check his phone's battery, 42%. That's enough. I get out and leave his phone and bag with his dad's bank card on the wood chip walkway. Can't miss it, he'll see it when he comes to look.

Quick, I drive and wave to the hungover teenager. They wave back.

This isn't a Disney predictable trope story. It's life, a chaotic mess no one should see coming. But you knew that—you would've read a top-selling romance novel if you wanted a predictable and pleasing ending. I guess this is why one Amazon UK reviewer compared this book to *Black Mirror*. If I didn't leave ThisKid I would've been caught and my life would be ruined. If you think I'm giving up too easily I've clearly failed in describing how much we don't get along.

Before I look back I'm already avoiding main roads and following signs to Westenhanger train station. I think that's what the sign means. I pass the station and drive further before ditching the car in a residential street. It's quiet but not quiet enough on my walk back to Westenhanger. Everyone I pass, I believe is undercover police. One man and his guide-dog Labrador make me jolt and put my wrists out to be cuffed.

The faster I walk these country roads the more my disguise falls off me in pieces. The jacket, glasses and hat are removed. Where am I going? Physically and metaphysically? The classic, timeless existential questions hound me until I reach the train platform. I make sure not to look at anyone, or that anyone is looking at me. A pigeon that looks like it hasn't slept comes close, takes one look at me and flies away. Can't blame them.

I'm going to the airport, one of London's. I'm going to Faro on my own. Once I get there I'll figure out what or any of this experience means.

Thirty-five: D.U.N.N.O

Bruce's and Kermit's timeline aligns with the inciting incident.

"You're more likely to die driving to the airport than on the flight. I want to be someone who works out these statistic things," classmate Zoe says while flicking her hair behind each ear.

Heads turn and the children's eyes follow Mrs Green's, focusing on Kermit in the corner, the only one who hasn't answered. The spotlight's on and it's bright. His mind is soft like the ravioli Dad cooked last night—capable of holding only a few things inside.

"I don't know what I want to become, alright." Kermit storms out.

The class looks to Mrs Green on how they should respond and when she smiles—they giggle. The class work on their drawings, their heads dipping back into their work.

"I'm drawing someone with a big calculator that's smart," Zoe announces while Mrs Green leaves.

After a moment, she returns with Kermit, his head down, avoiding eye contact. The lesson resumes, Kermit ignores any interaction. He sits with his arms crossed, oblivious of what to draw. All these decisions are arriving too early and demanding response.

"At least draw something," Mrs Green nudges Kermit's seat.

He begins to draw a fireman saving people. The flames from the fire disguised as blood coming out of their faces. His pencil stops still and he throws it to the floor. Uh-oh, that's crimson. Drawing immediately aborted and thrown to the ground.

Zoe hides a laugh after she picks up his drawing and crosses from another table. Kermit freezes when she rubs his forearm.

"It's okay to be upset," Zoe's kind voice relieves tension from his ankles.

Kermit doesn't speak but looks like he's going to. Glancing over his shoulder at Zoe he gets lost sitting still. Did Zoe have dimples? It was confusing. When she smiles it looks like she has them but if you zoom closer they run away like insects do when you're trying to care for them. Although her eyes sparkle like no other at school, all Kermit can think of is the word: *clickbait*. Kermit had too many emotions, causing him to overthink and act aggressively. He's begun to hit back at his parents, their stupid rules and lies.

The bell rings for lunch and Kermit leaves first, standing alone arms and feet crossed in the playground. Edinburgh's finest horizontal rain splashing his cheeks. Minutes pass and he looks over to Zoe and wonders, do decisions need to be made about how he feels? Kermit holds his skull and closes his eyes. On the back of his eyelids reads the letters: *D.U.N.N.O.*

It's one of those acronym things but he won't know what each letter stands for until he's an adult. He jumps when he feels something being slipped into his jacket pocket. He checks his neck. Last week, with black marker Billy wrote 'Loser' across the back of it. Billy's laughing, unsure where his crackle is coming from until Kermit turns fast enough. Billy confronts Kermit, "Ha. My big bro' gave it to me to give losers," his voice stretching from impending laughter "...so you can have your posh wanks."

A chorus of laughter spreads in the corner from the non-essential characters that have recently kicked Kermit out of their gang. How things have flipped since his defeat in last week's square-go with Billy.

Billy turns to face the gang, he moves as a conductor of their giggles and he shouts naughty words at Kermit. "Tadger, fanny, fud, ding-a-ling."

Blood rushes to the emergency meeting in Kermit's face. He reaches in his pocket. His hand goes limp touching it. What is it? He finds a square metallic wrapper with an outlined circle in the middle. It feels squidgy apart from the solid rim of the circle. The branding has faded. He sniffs it. No result.

"What is it?" Kermit's voice travels into the corner where his ex-gang stood. Echoing back, another chorus of unsettling giggles.

He hides the wrapper in his pocket and runs to the corner where the girls play. The playground looks so different from here. For the first time in his life, he could feel his heartbeat knocking through his chest. He imagines losing his heartbeats to the air so Kermit pulls his jacket tight to keep them inside.

He can hear the noise of dreich rain hitting on a surface, when he turns he sees the sound to be rain hitting Zoe's umbrella.

"What's wrong with you? You've been angry since last week," Zoe says.

"Eh? I dunno, I dunno." Kermit says, knowing he was angry because of the rumour Billy kissed her.

"If you tell me I can help."

He refuses with frantic head shakes. Zoe steps closer, putting her arm around his. It flushes memories of English class, yesterday when their hands grazed one another's and how it made him feel connected in new ways. His head's hot with confusion and Zoe won't stop asking. He stands and shows her the metallic wrapper.

Zoe leans in then out before screaming "Kerrrrrrrrrrr."

"What is it? Shhhhhhh, what's it anyway?"

"You're not going to use that on me!"

Kermit's face twitches with doubt. What was it though? As Zoe's friends come to help her, he runs. His laces come undone and skim through puddles. He reaches Geeks corner. He stops, hands on his knees before Paul, the leader of the geeks. Kermit looks at the calculator Paul's holding and the solution of finding out what this object is arrives.

Kermit finds his phone, takes a picture and runs an image search on the object.

"What was that?" Paul says removing his glasses.

Kermit stutters backwards, "You don't wanna know."

He hides it in his sock. It's one of those hats, from sex ed that the DVD showed. The ones you put on top of cucumbers before naked stuff. The worn-out animations said it stops pregnancies. The shame of having this thing makes Kermit squirm through the rest of the day. Even Rosenthal remarks how quiet he's being. School ends and Dad drives him home.

While Dad's finishing parking and Mum's making music downstairs, he breaks the rules and rushes into the kitchen. Cheese slices fall out from the fridge after he opens the door. He grabs the half-cut cucumber in its plastic wrapper, puts the slices back and rushes as quietly as he can to his room. He hides the cucumber under his pillow. Big sigh. What a stupid day that was.

That night, after being bruised by the extendable hand of a backscratcher, Bruce is considering a head-scratcher of his own: Should he take the shroom-filled capsules Melanie's bringing over later? Shh. Tiffany's working away all weekend and Melanie's coming over tonight. To see the house, to think about when she'll move in. No one will find out, as long as they don't enter the basement where Tiffany's computer has a motion-detected camera. No one will know, especially as Kermit isn't allowed out of his bedroom before knocking.

Bruce and Tiffany are in the dying embers of a fight. Bruce brought home an orange sorbet last night and spilt it on the sofa.

248

Subconsciously Tiffany was mad because she could feel he's cheating again.

"Another lush murder mystery mansion affair?" Bruce says.

A silence tightens the moment. Bruce keeps looking at her until she responds.

"Also waitressing dinner and lunch the next day for these rich slobs."

Bruce hides a fist cheer behind his back. Tiffany's tone is condescending because Bruce shouldn't need to ask but he was only reconfirming the prospect of his own plans. She goes to Kermit's room and kisses him goodbye. As her lips hit his cheek Kermit hopes Mum can't see the cucumber, peeking from under his pillow.

Tiffany drifts downstairs with various bags and dresses. She gives Bruce a wink. Before he can reveal a sweat patch waving bye, she's gone. The sound of the door slamming shakes Bruce's spine. Bruce cleans the already-clean living room. Instead of taking any risks, he puts tape across the steps leading to their basement. It would be difficult for any visitor to activate her security camera. If anyone did, it would be sent directly to Tiffany's phone.

Although it's 9 pm on a Friday night, despite a protest that became a door-slamming argument, Kermit's heading to bed. He's fed and urinated so there's limited to no chance of interruptions. Kermit believes Bruce's friend is coming over to work. He's not to interrupt unless it is an emergency. A resentment for adults grows within. His parents' stupid rules—soon he'd act out, soon.

It was a risk to bring Melanie here but she's been pressuring him to see her potential new home. She needs to check "the cosmic energy of the house." The doorbell chimes. Bruce leaps to his feet. She didn't remember to only knock lightly. Bruce looks upstairs and tells himself this is a bad idea. The door opens. There she is. Bruce wants to kiss her but stops midway. No, the neighbours might see.

He greets her with a limp handshake. Melanie taps his chest and enters. She floats around, reaches into the skinny pockets of her leggings and reveals half a handful of magic mushrooms grated into capsules. The pill is the same size as the collagen ones Bruce takes for work.

Melanie hands him two and Bruce tilts them in his palm. He's 42 and has never taken shrooms before.

"0.2 grams a pill. One will make you a wee bit euphoric," Melanie says, swallowing four using her water bottle before walking to the fridge.

"Wait," Bruce says but to his surprise—nothing falls out of the fridge. Huh? Tiffany must've forgotten to set up her prank.

Bruce wasn't sure, so danced around Melanie and the question if he was going to microdose. Melanie checked the energy of the house but forgot to bring sage with her to smudge the space. An hour passed and Melanie began dancing wild. Wow look at her, she moves like her body is a musical instrument and she's playing out the carefree nature of her kind soul. The drums become more apparent and Bruce decides he wants to join this journey. He swallows one pill. The night was turning as good as a party could be with two guests.

"I don't feel it yet," Bruce says.

As he slugs back another two pills, he could feel his doubts trying to make it a bad idea. The first pill was kicking in. It wasn't a bad idea, all thoughts turn positive. They danced in all the rooms they were allowed. They smooched in the garage, wrestled tongues in the kitchen and spooned in the bedroom.

The shuffled music sounds amazing, it made them return to the living room as disciples of the beat. They both dance believing they're professionals auditioning. The way Bruce jumps back and kisses where he once was before wiggling his elbows and knees towards the floor convinces him he's going to get the part. The song fades out, chest panting and Bruce looks over to the judge. Melanie kisses Bruce so intensely her kiss slides off his lips, rides his cheekbone, rumbles over his ear and lands behind it. The kiss ends with their ears covering one another's, both listening to the stillness of each other's earwax.

Melanie finds a setting on the television that transforms it into a disco light. The Philips Ambilight system Bruce had for years had a feature he wasn't aware of. Under the spell of the disco lights, Melanie rants about how as humans we all have hidden features, things we don't know we're good at because we never try them.

Sniffles attack them both.

"Don't worry this is a normal side effect," Melanie says, sharing tissues.

Bruce wipes his snot on his shirt's collar. Another hour slips by and they're cuddling on the sofa. The music has lowered and Kermit's television can be heard mumbling *How It's Made* episodes.

Melanie checks her phone and jitters, typing frantically.

"Oh-ow, it's past midnight. Shite. Sebastian's DJing a set at Club Rouge. I've got to go."

"Are you okay to go?" Bruce asks but before he could think of a reason for her to stay—he's watching an Uber drive Melanie away.

Alone but feeling good, Bruce flicks his ankles. He can still feel music inside him. Returning indoors he finds a playlist called '80s BoUnCe' containing songs similar to his CDs. Warm and sniffling, his eyes and nose run and he wipes it on his shirt so much his collar becomes soggy. He removes his shirt. His dance moves are as if he's trying to dig a hole. In between songs, there's

251

a thud from Kermit's room. He goes and splashes water on his head and chest.

Another thud arrives from upstairs. Bruce stares at the lampshade to see if it's moving or are his eyes playing tricks. He pauses his music.

"You alright up there buddy?" Bruce says.

The mumbling of *How It's Made* episodes replies. Bruce climbs the steps and hears the episode's narration. He laughs because this episode is about escalators while he's climbing stairs. He stops outside Kermit's door and listens to how escalators are made.

"Everything alright in…" Bruce says as he enters Kermit's bedroom. The door makes no noise.

Kermit's back is turned. He's in his underwear, his clothes lying on the floor. He stands flexing his body into a meditation-like pose. Kermit's staring at a cucumber laying on his dresser with, what's that? A condom on top. Bruce clears his throat and Kermit jumps.

"Ew, Dad get out, I don't know how to masturbate, okay, they didn't tell us properly. Zoe and Billy didn't say. Get out."

Bruce turns to face the wall. Was it, oh, um, Bruce couldn't think what to do. He feels like a mushroom himself and maybe it's these psycho-active drugs that narrow his thoughts so all he could think about doing is momenteering out of this. Any situation Bruce finds uncomfortable, he zones out. Apart from when he's with Tiffany, she'd make him remove his implant if she ever knew. She was already a moderator on a Reddit forum that discussed celebrities being controlled. Bruce blinks rapidly to bring up the system menu. Half blinking, he focuses on the confirm button until it looks like it's melting and his eyelids flicker. Kermit's speaking but Bruce can't hear anything while his mind's exiting reality. He drifts out of his body and into an empty space. The effects of the mushrooms disappear and Bruce feels regretful thinking: maybe I shouldn't have momenteered out. Stupid, that could be strange. At his annual check-up last year they told of a fellow client that was suspended from momenteering for a year because they were committing pranks on the agents.

Bruce reconfirms it's time to let go of his high school sweetheart, the mother of his annoying child and be with Melanie. Veins of colour flood, flicker and Bruce crashes back into his mind and body. He touches his limbs while facing his closed front door. What happened? He steps back into his hallway, the painting of his hallway in his hall is knocked down. He lifts it but no faded-skills come. Bruce puts on a pyjama top and walks around trying to trigger memories of what happened but all he triggers is Tiffany's motion detected camera. Freeze, no act normal. The camera's red light shines. The lens stares. Oh no, Tiffany will get a notification.

Bruce returns upstairs and opens Kermit's door, the room covered in darkness.

"Sleep. Too late. Night," Kermit grumbles.

Bruce feels around the dresser for the cucumber. "Where's the cucumber?"

"I ate it. Go away scumbagger."

Bruce leaves and closes his door. Everything must be alright, a miscommunication. Kerr's probably trying to figure out his body. Didn't he have sex education recently? It's no wonder he's being cheekier.

1.30 am, Bruce goes to bed, while his wife Tiffany's still working at the murder mystery night in Berwick-upon-Tweed.

◆

The celebrity lookalike murder mystery night is coming to an end. The innocent cast members have already returned to their temporary accommodation. Sherlock Holmes is helping the tipsy guests find the killer of Clint Eastwood. The remaining cast raise their shoulders when the guests accuse the killer to be Tiffany as Amy Winehouse. Usually, the guests accuse Gordon Ramsay or Jack Sparrow. The fake Sherlock arrests Tiffany and she must pretend to be electrocuted to death. The guests groan when it's revealed that the killer was Gordon Ramsay in the dining room with the rope.

The party ends and their clumsy manager, Beth, shows the remaining group to the basement of the guest house next to the mansion. Walking back they can't help but see, workmate Alison (a Marlyn Monroe) is busy locking lips with Henry (a Brad Pitt) outside the side of the guest house. Surreal optics. The closer Tiffany gets, the more their identities intermingle and it appears like four people are kissing instead of two.

Inside, Beth is combining sleeping arrangements with tomorrow's service schedule. Tiffany turns and rolls her eyes when she speaks. The cast wiping their faces clean, trying not to look like who they were an hour ago. But like the lovers outside Tiffany's too tired to remove her outfit and make up.

"Tiff, doll, would you be okay on the futon with Sally (a Whitney Houston lookalike) and serving lunch drinks?" Beth says.

Tiffany nods, holding a sigh from escaping her mouth. She can't refuse. The one-sided negotiation reminds her of the loveless routine of her marriage. How she lost her youth and musical flair having to raise their attention deficit son. How since Bruce's affair with Cindy they haven't been intimate and she's evolved into this toxic dictator of their home.

Nostrils flaring with this thought, Tiffany slumps to the futon and checks her phone. Usual shite except. What's this? A notification from her new security camera. This one hiding behind a coat hanger in the hall that could see into the living room. As she reviews the footage she sees a younger lady with Bruce dancing, kissing over the circular table, the table she picked and her OCD makes her clean twice a day. Anger roasts in her belly. Her fingers grip her phone so tight it shakes in her hand. Her chin rises and her bottom lip wobbles.

Their connection is so corroded that Tiffany expected this day to come but now that it's here it feels like a lookalike of the one she imagined. *What a stupid idiot. If you're going to cheat on me, don't do it in our home*, Tiffany thinks. Bruce said he was born to cheat but they got married for Kermit's sake. Thoughts pile atop of another. The way Kermit hopped out of Tiffany gave him his name. Tiffany couldn't imagine a future without Bruce but knew it was inevitable. She's not putting up with another affair. Her mother kept returning to her emotionally abusive father and Tiffany promised herself that she'd never end up like her Mum.

Tiffany grabs her jacket and leaves to the garden with a deft calmness. She overhears the lovebirds around the corner as she confronts her reflection in a dark window. Getting away from Edinburgh and seeing herself as partly Amy Winehouse (with the hair, the cream dress) helps Tiffany assess the situation objectively.

"Not now, we don't need to act now. I'll try harder and get a proper job first. Bruce doesn't need to know what I know just yet," Tiffany whispers to her reflection of Amy.

Tiffany decides that she needs to reinvent herself from her horrible housewife routine. Break out of the gender roles and religious beliefs society's trapped her in. It'll take a few months but as Bruce doesn't know anything, she can play pretend until she's ready to break free. Her frantic thoughts are interrupted by the noises of sloppy smooching.

"It doesn't become a kiss until you take your lips away," Alison giggles to Henry, or rather Marlyn to Brad.

"That's so true," Tiffany says, rolling her jacket's sleeves up, turning the corner and lighting a smoke. "Look at what happens after passion leaves a relationship," Tiffany puts her arms out and twirls so fast her skirt creates a cone shape around her legs. Alison's hand snaps over her mouth. The garden lights reveal Tiffany's mascara running to her chin with lipstick smudged across her cheek. Tiffany knew she was killing their vibe but couldn't stop smiling. Thinking of the future and finally admitting to herself that she's become more like her Dad than Mum.

She stops twirling and allows Alison and Henry to console her. Berwick's sky suffers from low light pollution allowing the stars to pop. Tiffany puts her burning cigarette's tip beneath a star, it resembles a star being burnt from below. What a metaphor. Dunno what it could mean but it's something. It's a moment, like all moments, that will only ever exist here and now.

A couple months stumble by. Melanie replaces Tiffany in their family home. Not even the introduction of Opia helps Kermit accept his mother's replacement. With his mother gone so are the sedatives, making Kermit develop insomnia and mood swings. He resents and rebels against Melanie at any opportunity. If Melanie and Kermit aren't arguing, then Bruce and Melanie will be.

Komo's timeline begins to align. Hormones deepen Kermit's voice and shorten his temper. After Kerr catches Billy kissing Zoe at school his attitude typhoons into ignorance and selfishness. Amongst various misdemeanours, he's caught vaping and watching banned videos. The day prior to Komo's arrival, Kermit's suspended from school for punching one of the geeks, Speccy Paul.

On the morning Komo knocks on Bruce's door and you kidnap Kermit, Tiffany's career trajectory means she's in London, signing a soundtrack deal with Nintendo.

Tiffany didn't and will never manage to play Bruce at badminton because he dies from blood loss and late ambulances. She will however go on to get her own mortgage and release many acclaimed video game soundtracks.

Thirty-six: Farohhhhhh

Welcome to Faro, Portugal. Apologies if these shifts are jarring but if you think about it, these chapters are an apt representation of working as a momenteer. Hopping from one moment to the next, trying to figure out where you are and what's going on.

I'm a stranger in a swish hotel with three floors. I know, I don't like hotels or tourists either but it all came with the flight. I've converted the cash at the airport and sparingly started using my own bank card. Only using worldwide banks to withdraw cash keeps things hidden from Pritek.

Here in Faro, the capital of the Algarve, I'm staying for five days. Gulliver and I have been chatting every night on the burner. He doesn't ask anything about my mission. He's bought my return flight and I'm paying him back by buying him a new bed. The hotel's Wi-Fi is weak and their television's stuck on a Portuguese cooking channel so I'm going for walks to clear my head.

Tonight's my second night, I've been buying snacks at this same mini-market in the old town. I sit by the boardwalk and bite into a beef empanada followed by olive oil tortas and wash it down with Sumol, this pineapple soft drink. A deep burp arrives and brings with it the epiphany of why Kermit and I didn't connect.

Ohhhhhh, it was because I wasn't acting as his father. The connection was solely from me, Komo. Our bond was raw. Connections are so complex they change with everyone you'll meet. I walk to a terracotta-tiled archway and lay under it to process my epiphany. That's it. Not only was I acting differently but Kermit was too. It makes sense—when I was his age I believed all adults to be intimidating and stupid. I tried to be a hero but became a villain.

Back in my room, I find myself scrolling on the burner phone, I search for the news in Scotland. The images barely load but my focus spins. It's not a top post but on the website.

There's a headline: *Child Returned But Father Killed In Edinburgh Robbery*

The mattress begins eating me. All my skin needs itching, especially the back of my neck. I drop the phone. It bounces off the mattress, hits my knee and falls on the tiled-floor. When I retrieve it, there's a hairline crack down the middle but at least it works. Like most, I only read the headline and make assumptions. We can assume Bruce's dead. My shaking finger hovers over the article. I can't bring myself to click. It's 99.6% Bruce but if I don't click, it will remain unconfirmed.

After an hour of talking to myself out loud, pacing and pushing walls, I accept the news. Maybe it's better that he died? Selfishly this might keep Pritek from knowing about our mistake. This won't go to a momenteer so I'm not sure who I'm talking to right now but listen, we did the right thing. He was evil. Kermit's saved. You shouldn't feel guilty, I put you in that situation and this is on me. I'm sure you could find me someday—if you want to be friends. I accept the blame. As I wipe away forming tears, I have a shivering premonition that what we did is for the best.

Maybe I messed Kermit's life up, maybe I improved it? Guilt delivers a night of restless sleep. A colossal miscalculation. I know I did things wrong. I should've had a plan but at least I did something. Taking action for once in my life. I know where Kermit lives. I'll use my Pritek fortunes to make sure he has a good life. Maybe Lemon could help. I spend all afternoon debating with myself: is it better to have no dad or an evil one? I don't know. What do you think?

Golden hour arrives and from the balcony, I spot an aged gentlewoman exiting the pool. Something Ender said at our exhibition returns to me: "We must let go of mistakes or they'll haunt us," It didn't make sense then but it does now.

Another day, another walk and I'm drawn to an old calm wise man selling used books from a wobbly table. He's lovely, real lovely but it's too late in this novel to introduce new characters. I buy one by Ram Dass that looks like it's had many owners. Flicking the pages, I feel stupid for not knowing these ideas were out there and for decades too. These signs for Benagil Sea Caves Tours start appearing too often and I take the signs as a sign that I should go there. I won't even research anything about Benagil. I'll go and be in the moment.

Afternoon brings heavy shadows and paranoia that I may somehow be identified. After checking a few shops I find a hair shaver and in a different one a razor. I return to the hotel and cut my hair to resemble the mesh top of a dynamic microphone (buzzed at the top and bald around the back and sides.) A style Donna would be proud of. I spend the day reading in the shade. The book's making me see that I need to accept myself and accept what's happened. See that some things in life, (like Hazel, Greasy and Catherine, like birthday buddies, Kermit's bruises and sedatives) are sometimes left behind without explanation. Maybe that's what happened with the bond between me and my ex that my brother stole? It makes me think of seeing old photographs of yourself and wondering where your forgotten clothes went.

The next morning, on the coach to Lagoa, I continue reading the book I bought called 'Be Here Now.' Who am I becoming? Reading isn't me. It's stuffy on this long coach, sweat drops cross paths over the small of my back. I get to Benagil by following tourists. When they stop I stop and hide before following again. It's a following game, the inverse of my usual. I pay cash for a life jacket and I'm on a mini-boat heading towards the caves.

Turquoise waves roar as we approach the limestone rock formation. There are two holes to enter the cave and our boat aims for the largest. We pass two guys with shaggy hair aiming go-pro cameras at their model girlfriends paddling kayaks into the caves. We enter, the temperature drops but the mood peaks. The boat stops and the captain smiles directly at us and points off until we all disembark. The waves splash. There are around fifty people here, most of which are looking to the roof, oops, I mean sky. I look up and immediately feel alone. A belonging alone.

Ohhhhhhh. There's a massive hole at the top of the cave where the sun's light bursts in. When I stare into it, I feel so silly because it reminds me of being born. Those tunnel-like images the movies depict. I imagine a courtroom assembling in my mind.

One side is arguing that everything I do is so meh while the other side is looking for peace and acceptance.

"Look at Komo's terrible attempt to save Kermit. Look at how he hid his location from the reader by using either Anglo or American English spellings and punctuation. What was the purpose? Stupid, readers can search for Donna's salon and find out where he's from. Komo is a waste of time. So mehhhhhh," My negative emotions argue.

The defence/defense stands, "Objection, we're all on a journey and working this thing called life out. It's a process and we won't follow a predetermined route society created for us. Mistakes will be made, there will be bumps in the road but it's all an adventure." They end with a two-fingered peace sign and a wink that makes a dinging sound.

Who is the judge? Maybe this is your role?

I'm winking into the hole above, the sky is a rare shade of blue. Dizzier, I lay on the cold sand thinking maybe I, Komo, am not meant to be liked? I'm an evil character an editor said they wanted to shake.

The social-media models are standing on top of a rock and discussing the best angles. My gaze dives into the hole again. You can see people from the top looking down at you. It's ancient and hypnotic. Everything in life's about perspective, isn't it? I'm not having a crisis, more of an existential reassessment. Crossing my fingers, I promise myself to stop avoiding people, responsibilities, the past, connections or opportunities. When I get home I'm going to finish my tally, get a proper psychologist, a psychologist for actors. I'm going to hang with Gulliver and Ender. I'm going to travel the world with an open mind and heart.

My head shakes at how cliché I'm being. With a mini-megaphone, the captain announces our tour group has to leave the cave. I consult my empty wrist. That didn't feel like an hour. The cave must have enchanted me like the enchanted squire I am because I'm back in Faro before I can process any feelings. Tonight's walk slows and I touch lonely-looking rocks but there's nothing to do so I return to the hotel before Gulliver calls.

"Do you know there are books so good they can't turn them into films?" I say.

Gulliver's laugh is smoother. He says that he's stopped partying and can't wait for me to return. We agree our unnamed band will give us something to focus on. We're going to jam and he's going to teach me some sign language. Our band, Wiggle Room, will reinvent elevator music as anyone thinks they know it.

"You know, Donna has a new girlfriend, I saw her passing the gym holding hands with her but they didn't see me," Gulliver says.

"But you're okay? It's all perspective."

"Yeah, I'm happy, she seemed happy."

"It's sometimes better to let people go," I say, glad Donna can't momenteer out of moments with me anymore. Think of all the times she did it. You've got to laugh at how boring I must've been.

We hang up and I dial to congratulate Donna. What's her number? It ends in a seven. Wait, I don't need to... Squinting at the number through the cracked screen, it's not hers. The ringing makes me sit. I blink at the screen, gulp and wipe my eyes to try and make the number change.

"Hello, who's speaking?" A familiar voice says.

"Hey it's… Komo," I say, my finger ready to hang up.

"Oh wow, Komo. Your voice, it hasn't changed one bit. So great to hear from you." My brother Max says.

We talk, well I mumble replies to his small talk. I try to copy the book I'm reading and live in the moment. Experience the version of myself that forgives my brother and wants to move on.

"Has there been any mail for K-man at your address?" I say.

"One arrived the other day, not opened it. Do you want me to forward it to you?"

"Maybe, keep it for now,"

The letter must be from the diabetic. I do a fist pump. The diabetic must be fine and we're going to become secret penpals. Good job Pritek doesn't come check my mail but I'll use my brother's address in case they ever do. There's an awkward silence but this one is comforting, reminds me of watching Saturday morning cartoons together. It is pressureless unlike those I've experienced lately.

I scratch my stubble and my brother asks what the scratching noise is and he copies the noise back.

"Do you still play bass?" I say.

"Not for a few years but I could jam,"

"Maybe you could join a new project I'm getting involved in, if you're any good."

Drummers often develop bad hearing, not me. I hear the subtle noises of his face contorting into a smile.

"I'm sure I'll be able to impress," he says.

There are noises of knocking and mumbling in the background.

"I'm not sure, I'll ask," Max says.

"Ask what?"

"Emma's here. She wants to say hi. To thank you personally for her birthday card. It's on her wall, would that be okay?"

On my balcony, I try to see other people on theirs in rival hotels. See how they're living life differently. The silence on the line becomes so apparent. It grows out of the mic and drills through the wax in my ears and tickles my throat with nervousness, so much so that I have to clear my throat.

"Don't think he can talk, not now, darling," I hear my brother say.

Duty pinches me, I scrape my knuckles down my forehead. "Uh. No, it's okay. I can talk if she wants."

My brother calls Emma and there's another stillness and you can hear that she's dropped the phone by the scuffles and rumbling. A stillness returns and Emma inhales deeply before she speaks.

"Hello, Uncle Komo? Is that you? You exist, don't you?"

"Yes, it's me, Ko—"

"Are you sure it's you? I didn't believe you lived until I got your card and Dad said you were busy-wizzy doing important work."

"He did?"

"Yeah, I'm sad you're working much that we haven't met. I don't like your job for making that happen."

"I'm sorry, I will do my best to be better."

"Your voice sounds lighter than I thought."

She snorts and I feel a sneaky tear falling over my cheekbone. I try to snort it into my nostril. The call takes a side-step as we begin a snorting match. Across at the rival hotel's lit-up pool, strangers are playing water volleyball and I consider how they can't feel what I'm feeling. Emotions are sometimes so bespoke it's difficult to understand them at all. We continue our snorting match and laughing. Emma does a magnificent snort.

"That was a great one, I think we have a winner." I say looking out at each one of the strangers, so involved in their moments that it's the only thing that exists.

"Uncle Komo, at least you are funny, not like Mr Gilbert, he's bad news. He gives me fear. Shhh Dad. I can't listen."

"Who's that? Your teddy bear?" I say but the connection interrupts so I have to repeat this four times.

She laughs at me but I don't feel silly for a change.

"Nu-huh, he's real. Mr Gilbert's my music teacher. He's sick today. Don't tell anyone he's annoying by the way, don't tell. Sorry Dad, it's true."

"What instrument are you learning?"

"Don't laugh because I'm a girl okay?"

"I would never, I promise."

"Glocken something and xylo and..." my heart melts when she says "...drums and sometimes the triangle but never the string instruments, ew no, yuck."

My smile feels like it's bench pressing my skeleton. I spot a strange unidentifiable bug on the balcony, one that should scare me but not many people would know this bug exists. I share a moment with the bug and Emma.

"Hello? I think Uncle Komo left. Here Daddy you talk," Emma says.

The phone fumbles. I arrange to collect the diabetic's letter and give Emma a quick drum lesson when I return. It's going to be weird but I can deal with any awkwardness—I will hang around until the awkwardness itself feels awkward and leaves so I can be the great uncle I should be. We hang up and in bed, I drum my chest with solos I had in Green Bread. I only have 276 moments left, it should only take a month or so until my first session is complete.

My final day in Faro is spent perusing souvenirs proving I've been here. I almost buy a tacky magnet. Holding the glossy magnet, I ask myself: am I the sort of person who buys magnets of the places they've visited? No, I'm not but I buy it because I'm open to change.

My time in Faro's coming to an end. I walk around the old town late until there are only stray cats around. It's a rush but I board the plane, back to the city you think I live and work. The engines roar and we take off. I know no one will read this but I have to thank you for doing what you did. I will go back to momenteering, finish my tally and instead of avoiding moments of my own I will continue to create and experience them fully.

I flush the burner in the plane's vacuum toilet. Ears pop and the plane lands. I take my time getting off. There's no bag to collect. Stepping through the one-way security doors and out into arrivals. There he is, waiting for me, his arms already stretched out. My smile hops at the sight of a toothpick between his lips. He grabs and squeezes me.

"Well look who it isn't," Gulliver says.

His hug is tight. He ends it by slapping me on the back. The same slap as before but this time, there's no echo.

Better Than Sound
(The diabetic's story)

The way they're advertising these new headphones reminds me of how I love you. The 15-second video shows carefully chosen actors from inclusive demographics exaggerating already-forced smiles. Their eyebrows hop and their ajar jaws paint pictures of astonishment. I know we would both laugh at this absurdity, how the company must tell the actors to pretend they're deaf babies getting hearing implants and discovering sound for the first time. You provide calm and existential bliss by asking... What's playing in their headphones?

Wow, the murmuring from a theatre as they discover the star is being replaced by the understudy tonight. Wow, the call of an extinct-before-discovered bird. Wow, the noise of a metal tray cooking in the microwave. Wow, a foreigner trying to pronounce foreign slang. Wow, the relief after calamine lotion meets sunburnt skin. Wow, the echo of planes in vacant buildings while the homeless sleep outside.

I will never know what the actors listened to, but you untie and refresh my mind by suggesting that maybe they aren't listening to anything, and if they are it will be generic pop or the headphone company's CEO sighing at their disappointing sales.

A Jenga tower topples in a distant land to signify an epiphany.

I think of my favourite noise... no it's not the space laser effect when one presses the traffic lights in Dublin, no it's not a well-placed cowbell in a song, not the chocolate crunch of a Magnum ice cream, no it's not the hiss from the steam wand of a tired coffee machine, and no it's not a plane's wheels skidding on the tarmac before we met for the first time. What's your favourite sound? Have you been asked this seriously?

I quite enjoy the unpredictable splurt from our kitchen water but my favourite is the silent vibrations of your body next to mine. Or perhaps, it's the way you say no after I tickle your thigh, or the language-less grumbles you make in your sleep, or the slide of Shea butter across your skin.

I replay the 15-second headphone advertisement and think of our relationship—how it's a failed actor from the late 60s movies, who was cut because when they were in the back of a speeding car, they asked why the background was moving and not them. We're too aware to pretend. The casting agent gave up on them despite their charm after they kept looking into the camera with inquisitive eyes and going off-script.

Like many similarly targeted individuals in my area, I go on the company's website and read the fake reviews, crawling through the opinions of people who leave a review for their packaging or delivery and not the product itself—I leave a review of my own that reads: 'Unsure and sceptical of sound, but certain I love her.'

Weeks later, I send you a selfie wearing these headphones, and you wonder, why am I smiling like a deaf baby that just got a cochlear implant, am I a hypocrite? No! I'm smiling because I'm listening to a frequency only I can hear, I'm listening to the sound of how I love you.

Enjoyed this book?

Please consider leaving a positive rating or a short insightful review.

Vegageist is a very small indie company without the marketing scope of traditional publishers. By leaving a positive review, you can immensely help others like yourself discover this book.

Please scan this QR code above with your device's camera to be directed to the book's page or simply search for 'Momenteering' or find the title in your order history.

We thank you so much for your reading time.

About The Author

CRAIG JONATHAN REEKIE is a visually impaired writer born in Fife, Scotland. The type 1 diabetic character in this novel is most probably him. This is his debut novel, but he predominantly writes short stories.

To read more of his work, please visit: cjreekie.com

Acknowledgements

I would like to thank everyone that has supported me on my writing journey since I wrote my first silly poem in 2003. Friends and family, the important people know who they are. Teachers, professors and anyone who has shaped my writing in any way. No matter how large or small. From tutors Bob Beagrie, Meaghan Delahunt, Jessica Wortley and Hillary Jenkins, to my workshop classmates - all the way to even a stranger in Thessaloniki that walked down the street with a water bottle in each of their back pockets. To all these immeasurable instances of inspiration.

There was a time in January 2013 where I suffered an ischemic stroke. Before an unknown brain surgeon saved my life. I'd like to sincerely thank all my friends, family and loved ones for supporting me before, throughout and after this event. And of course the unknown surgeon.

Special thanks to Mum, for your unwavering love and care even in the hardest of times. To my love who gives a love that's better than sound. To anyone who has helped me see when I couldn't. To accessibility designers.

I understand that writing about child abuse is a sensitive topic and I mean no offence or harm in writing about this. In no way do I intend to trigger anyone. I had to leave home at the age of 15 because of my psychologically abusive father. I didn't have the intention to write about this but through the characters and events these difficult themes surfaced. I sincerely apologise should any of this cause upset.

In regards to this novel's creation - I give so much gratitude and thanks to Matthew Richmond for his wise and insightful developmental edit. To Stephanie Francis, Amanda Shewell and Book Bin Divers' Angela & Mikaela. All for their beta reading notes, your acumen and diligent advice. Thanks to Synaxis for creating such a cool illustration. I'd like to thank Vegageist and most importantly I must thank you, the reader, for going through this misadventure with me.

Printed in Great Britain
by Amazon

28691841R00157